HINGES
MEREDITH MCCLAREN

BOOK 1
CLOCKWORK CITY

"MANY THANKS TO ALL THE IMPS AND ODDS, WHO PUSHED, POKED, AND PRODDED ME ALONG."

- MEREDITH MCCLAREN

IMAGE COMICS, INC.
ROBERT KIRKMAN - CHIEF OPERATING OFFICER
ERIK LARSEN - CHIEF FINANCIAL OFFICER
TODD MCFARLANE - PRESIDENT
MARC SILVESTRI - CHIEF EXECUTIVE OFFICER
JIM VALENTINO - VICE-PRESIDENT

ERIC STEPHENSON - PUBLISHER
RON RICHARDS - DIRECTOR OF BUSINESS DEVELOPMENT
JENNIFER DE GUZMAN - DIRECTOR OF TRADE BOOK SALES
KAT SALAZAR - DIRECTOR OF PR & MARKETING
COREY MURPHY - DIRECTOR OF RETAIL SALES
JEREMY SULLIVAN - DIRECTOR OF DIGITAL SALES
EMILIO BAUTISTA - SALES ASSISTANT
BRANWYN BIGGLESTONE - SENIOR ACCOUNTS MANAGER
EMILY MILLER - ACCOUNTS MANAGER
JESSICA AMBRIZ - ADMINISTRATIVE ASSISTANT
TYLER SHAINLINE - EVENTS COORDINATOR
DAVID BROTHERS - CONTENT MANAGER
JONATHAN CHAN - PRODUCTION MANAGER
DREW GILL - ART DIRECTOR
MEREDITH WALLACE - PRINT MANAGER
ADDISON DUKE - PRODUCTION ARTIST
VINCENT KUKUA - PRODUCTION ARTIST
TRICIA RAMOS - PRODUCTION ASSISTANT
IMAGECOMICS.COM

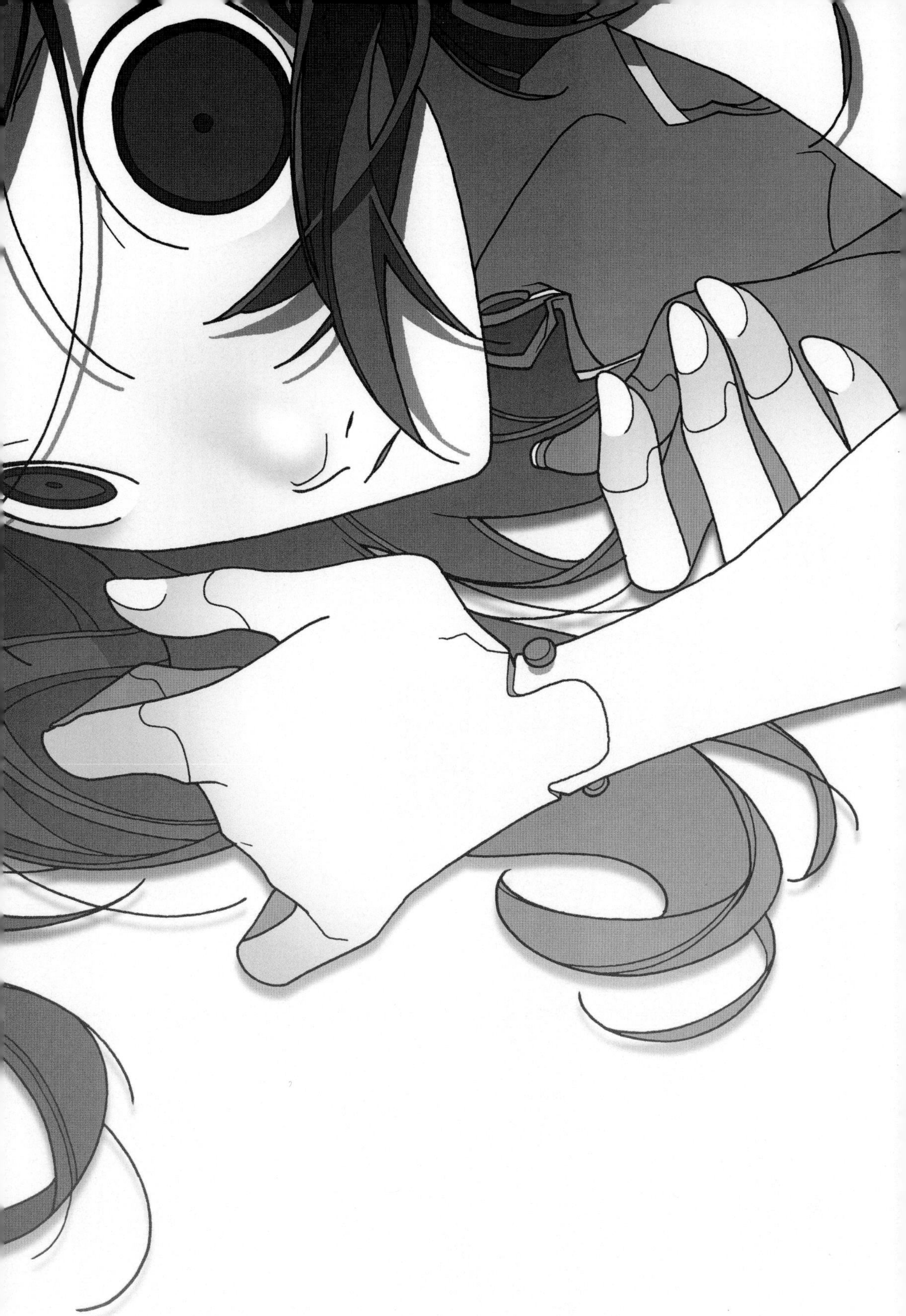

HINGES
CHAPTER 1

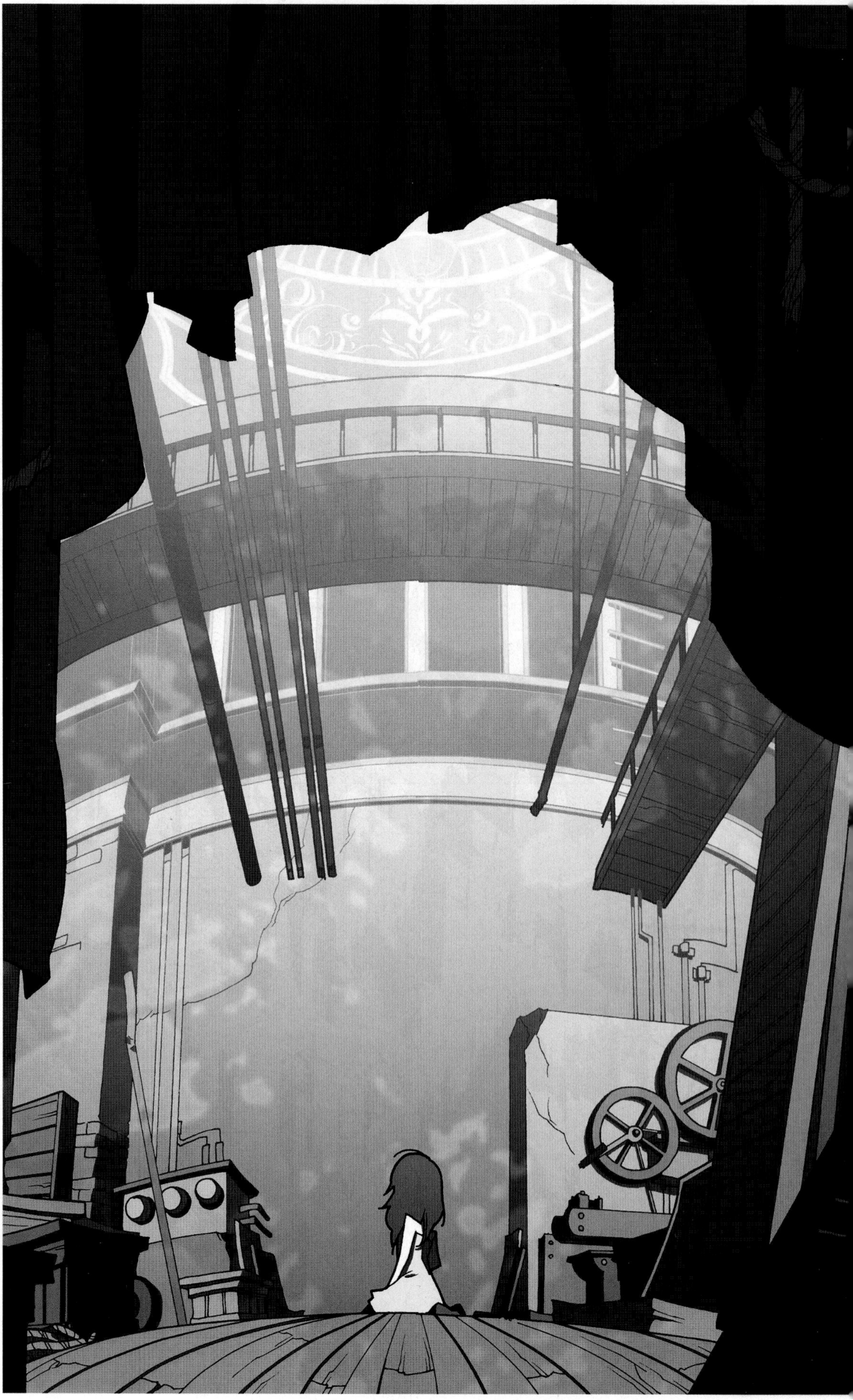

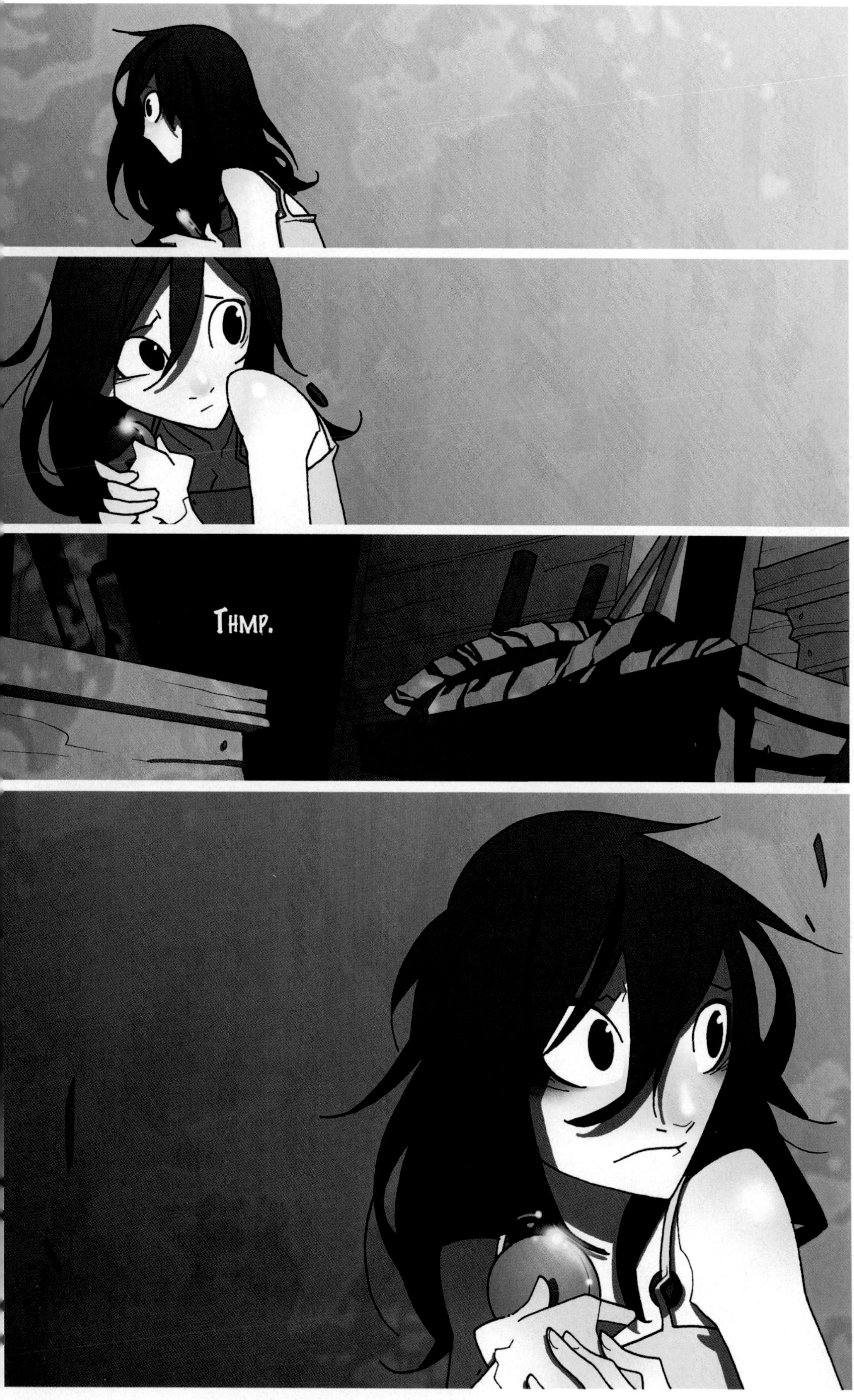
THMP.

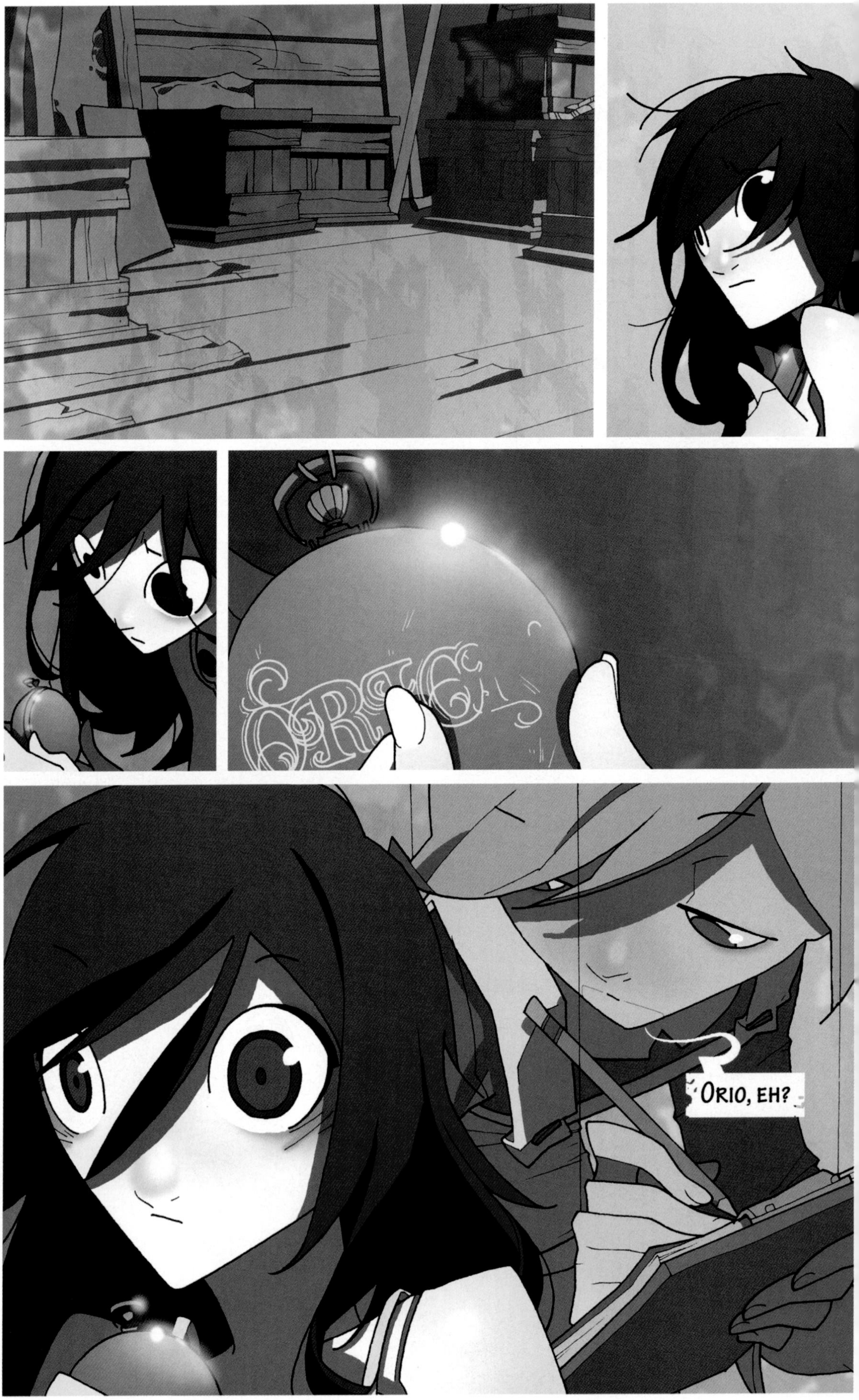
ORIO, EH?

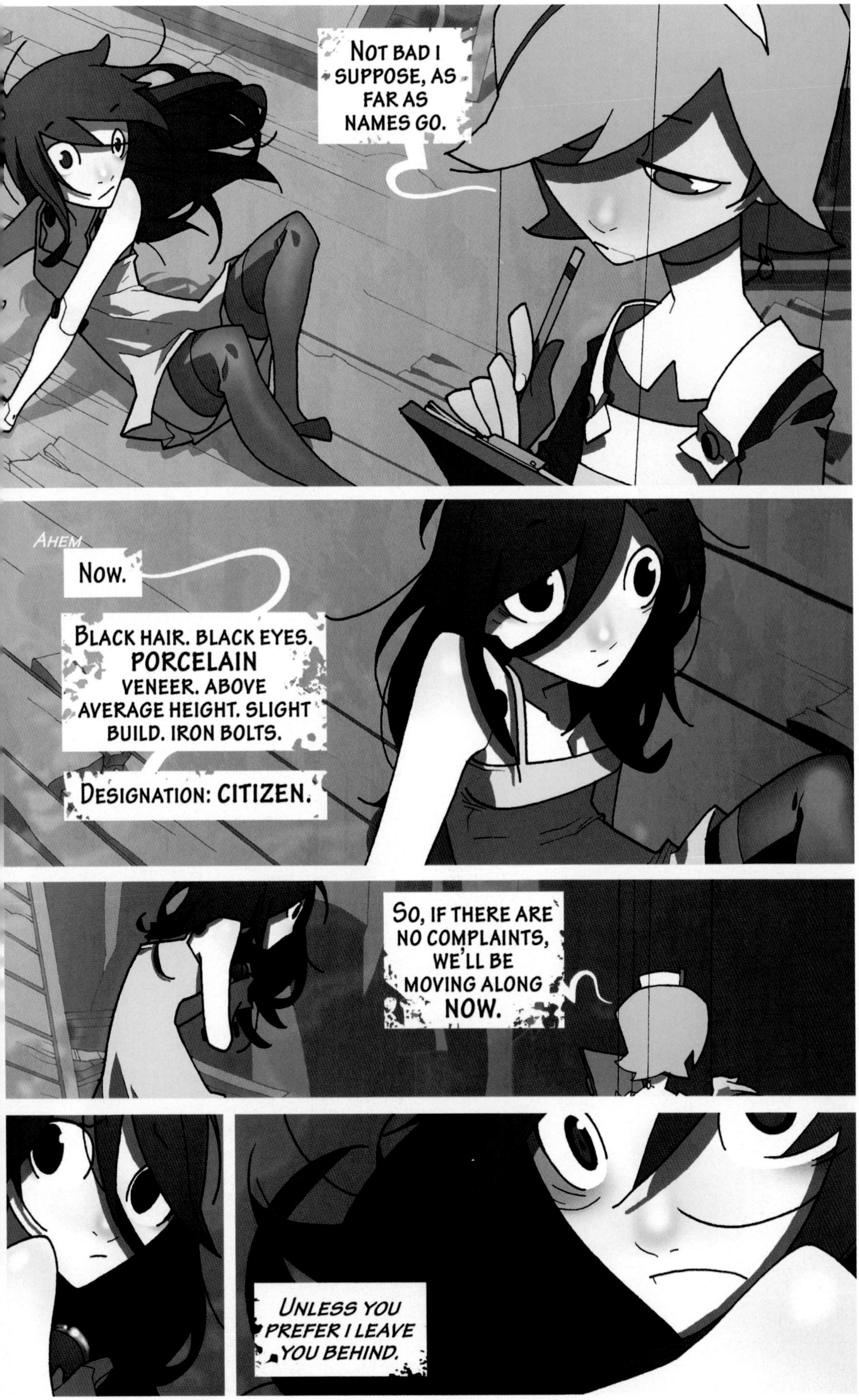
Not bad I suppose, as far as names go.
Ahem
Now.
Black hair. Black eyes. PORCELAIN veneer. Above average height. Slight build. Iron bolts.
Designation: CITIZEN.
So, if there are no complaints, we'll be moving along NOW.
Unless you prefer I leave you behind.

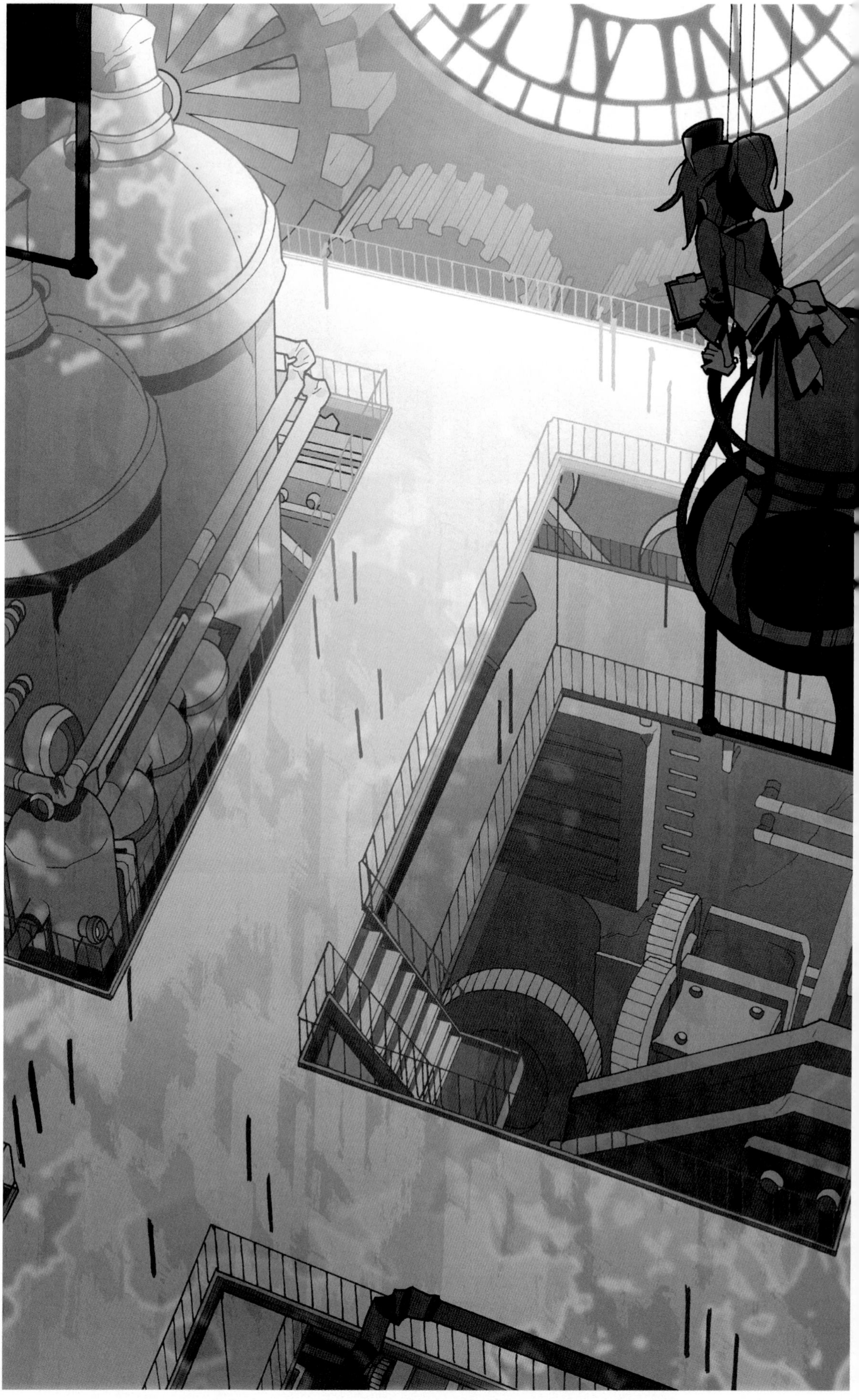

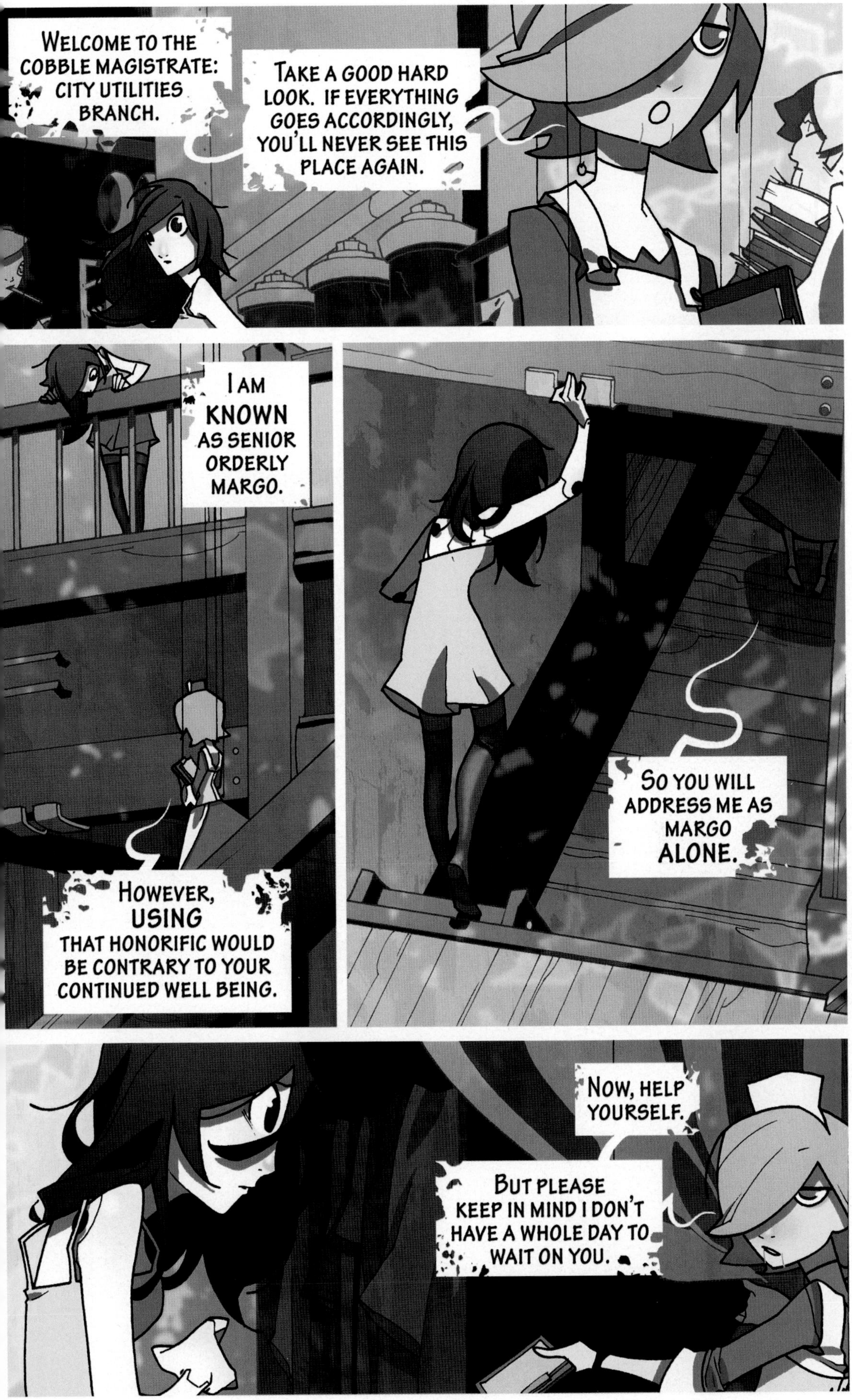
Welcome to the cobble magistrate: city utilities branch.
Take a good hard look. If everything goes accordingly, you'll never see this place again.
I am KNOWN as senior orderly Margo.
However, USING that honorific would be contrary to your continued well being.
So you will address me as Margo ALONE.
Now, help yourself.
But please keep in mind I don't have a whole day to wait on you.

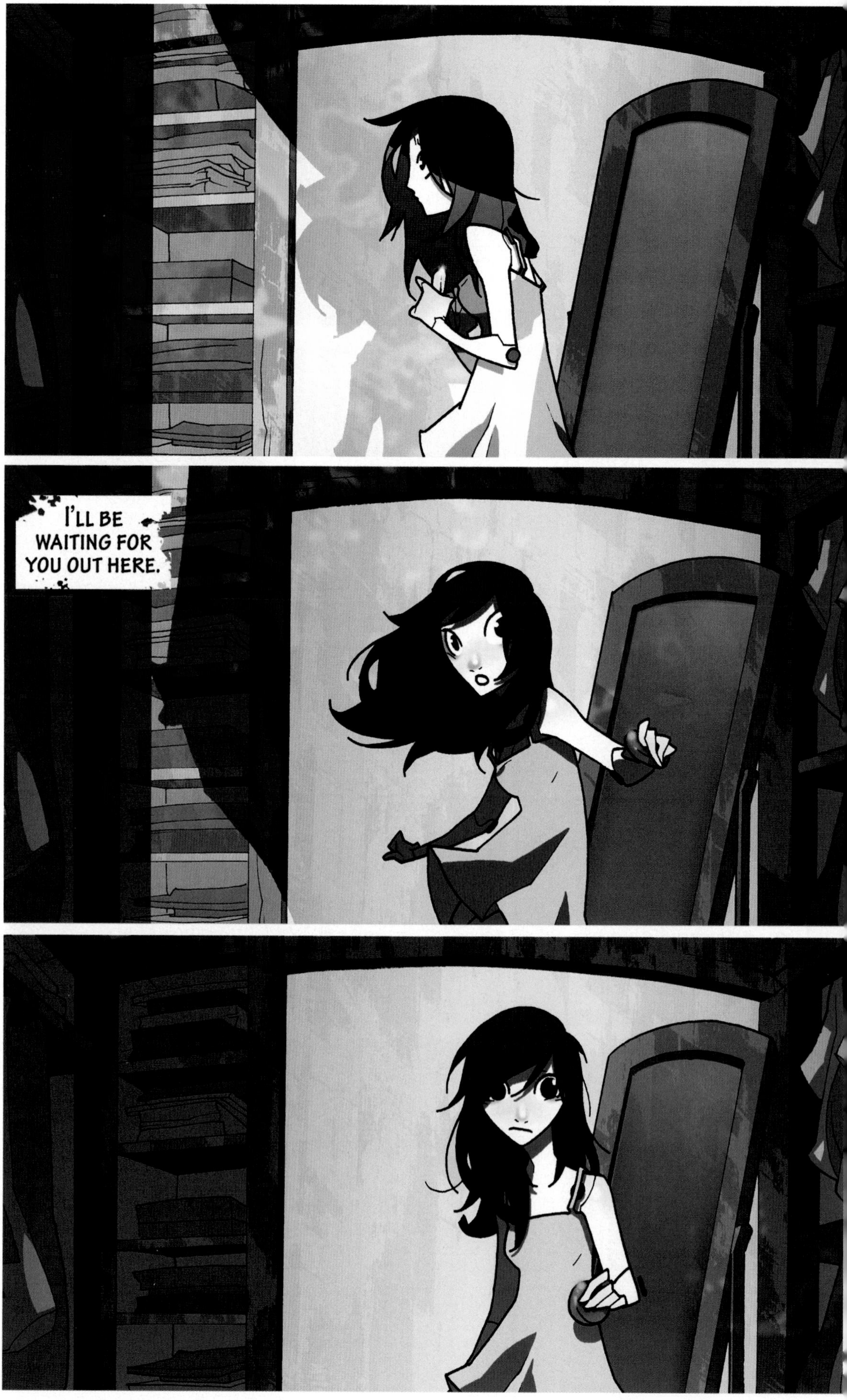
I'LL BE WAITING FOR YOU OUT HERE.

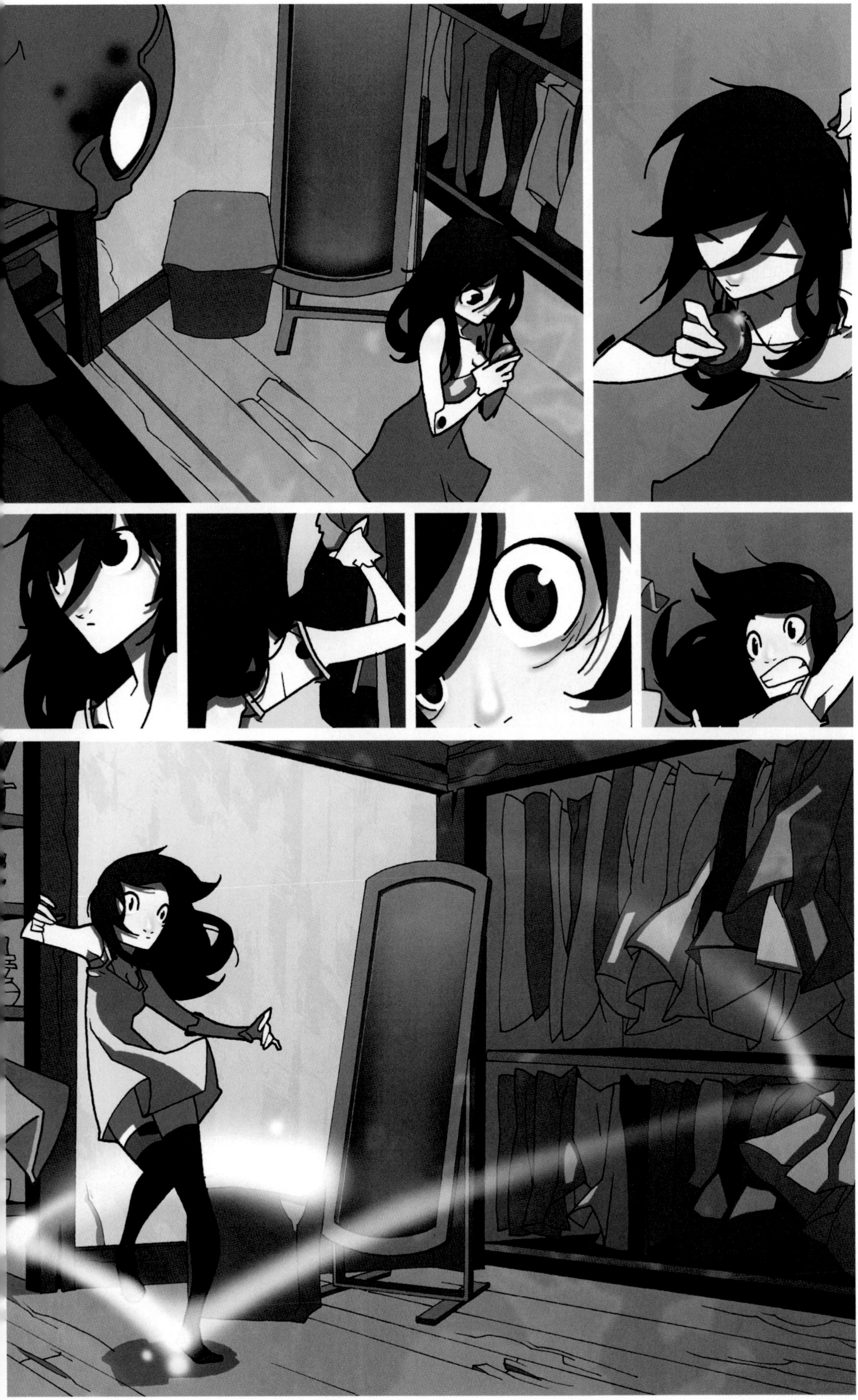

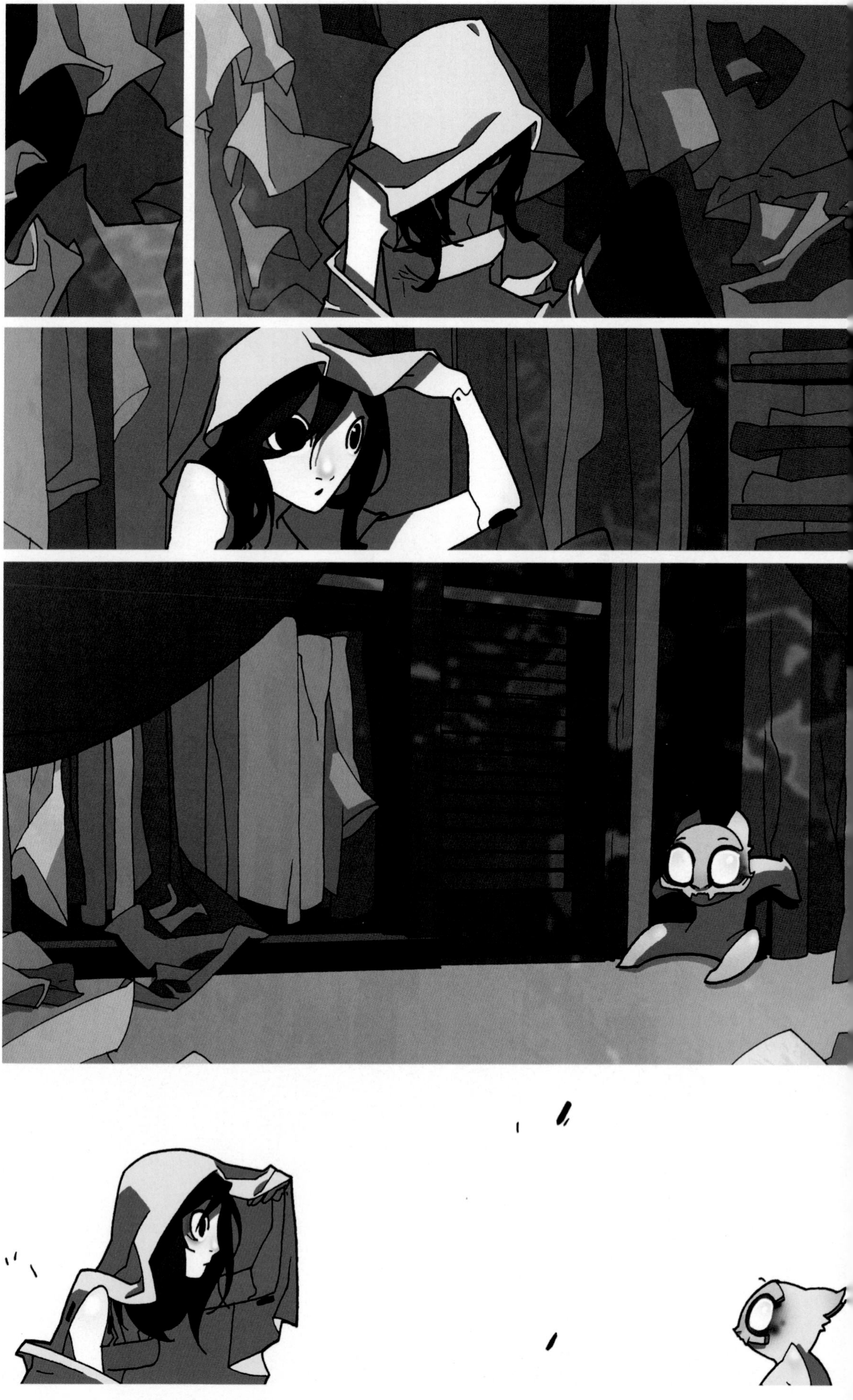

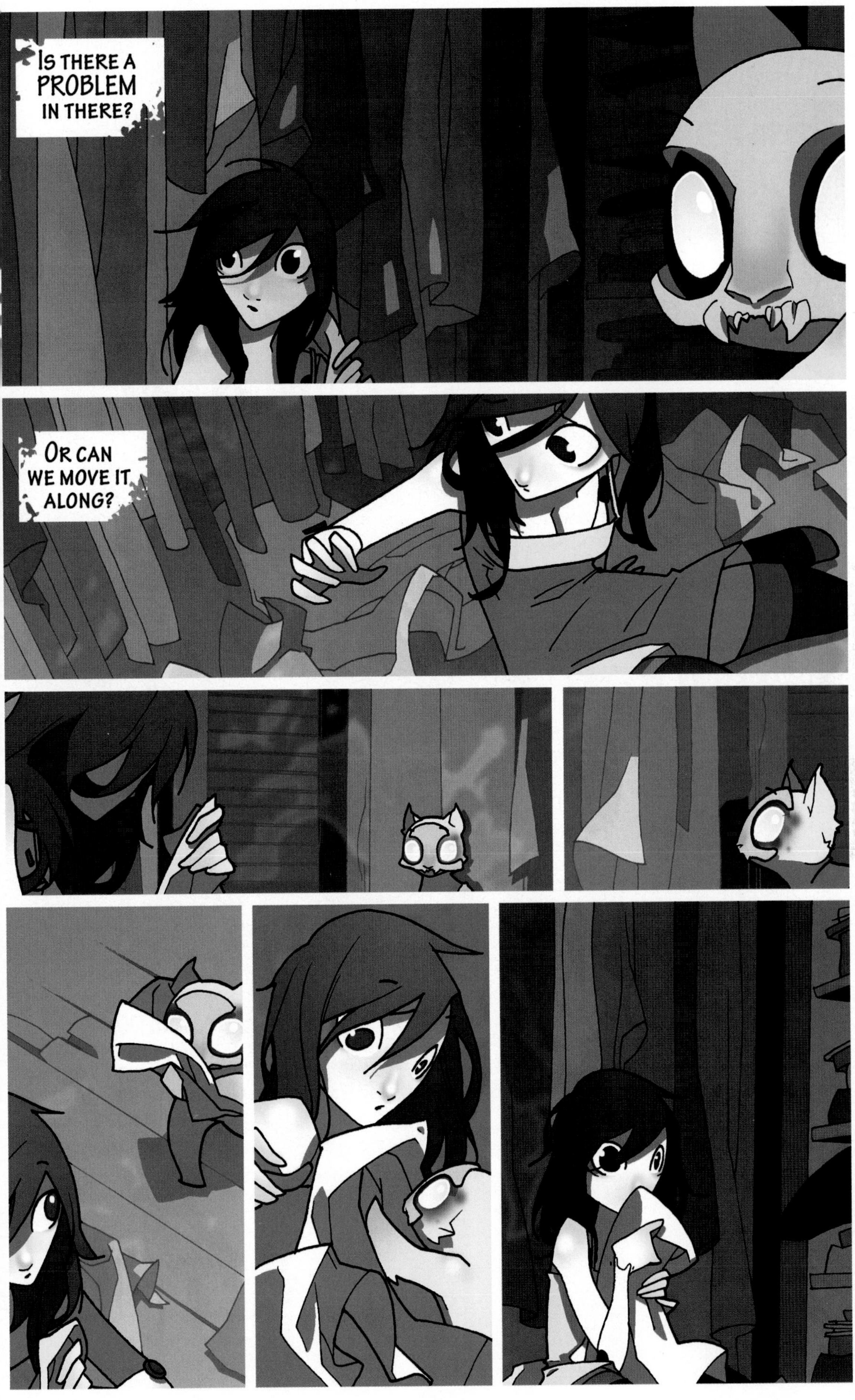
IS THERE A PROBLEM IN THERE?
OR CAN WE MOVE IT ALONG?

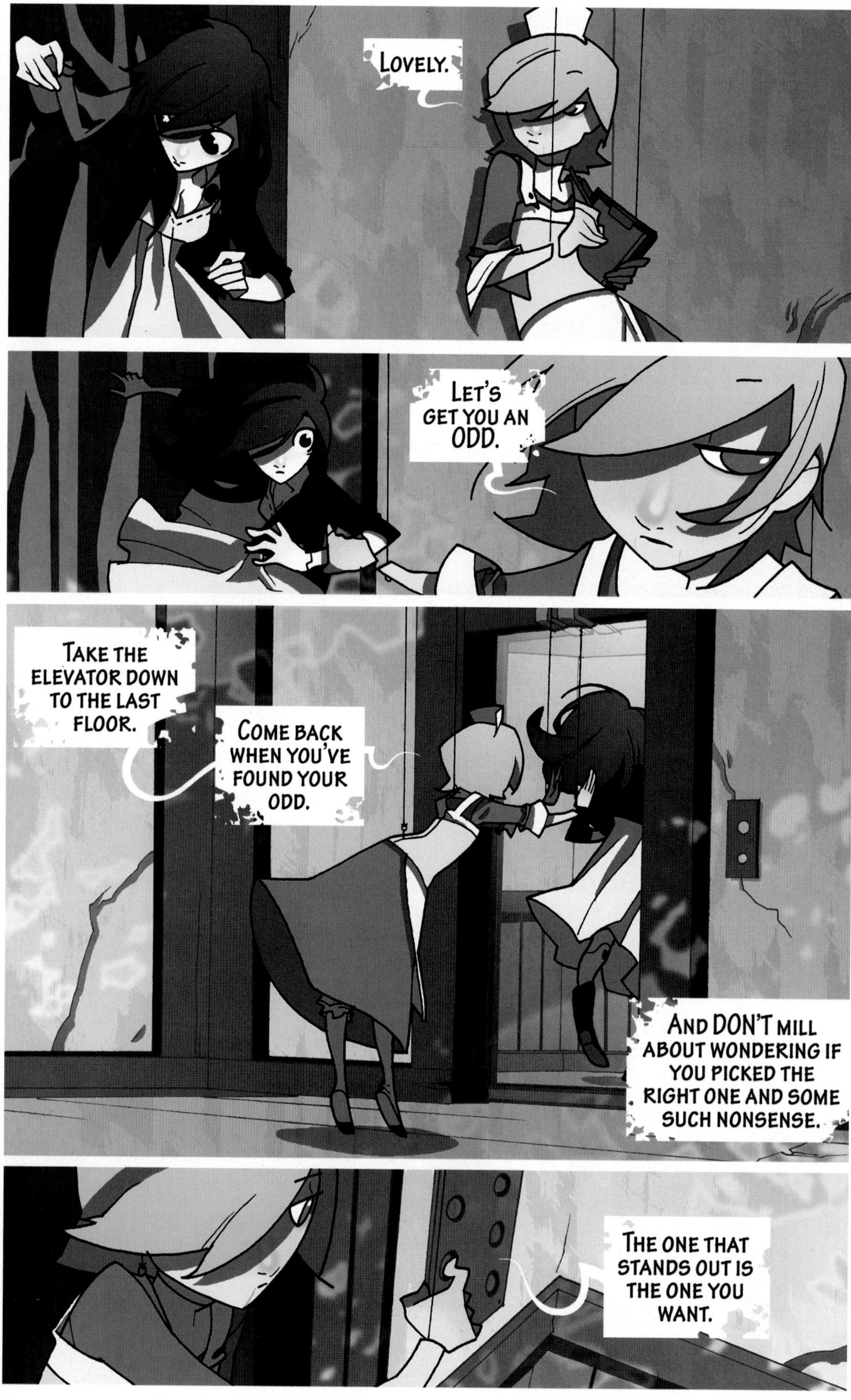
Lovely.
Let's get you an ODD.
Take the elevator down to the last floor.
Come back when you've found your odd.
And DON'T mill about wondering if you picked the right one and some such nonsense.
The one that stands out is the one you want.

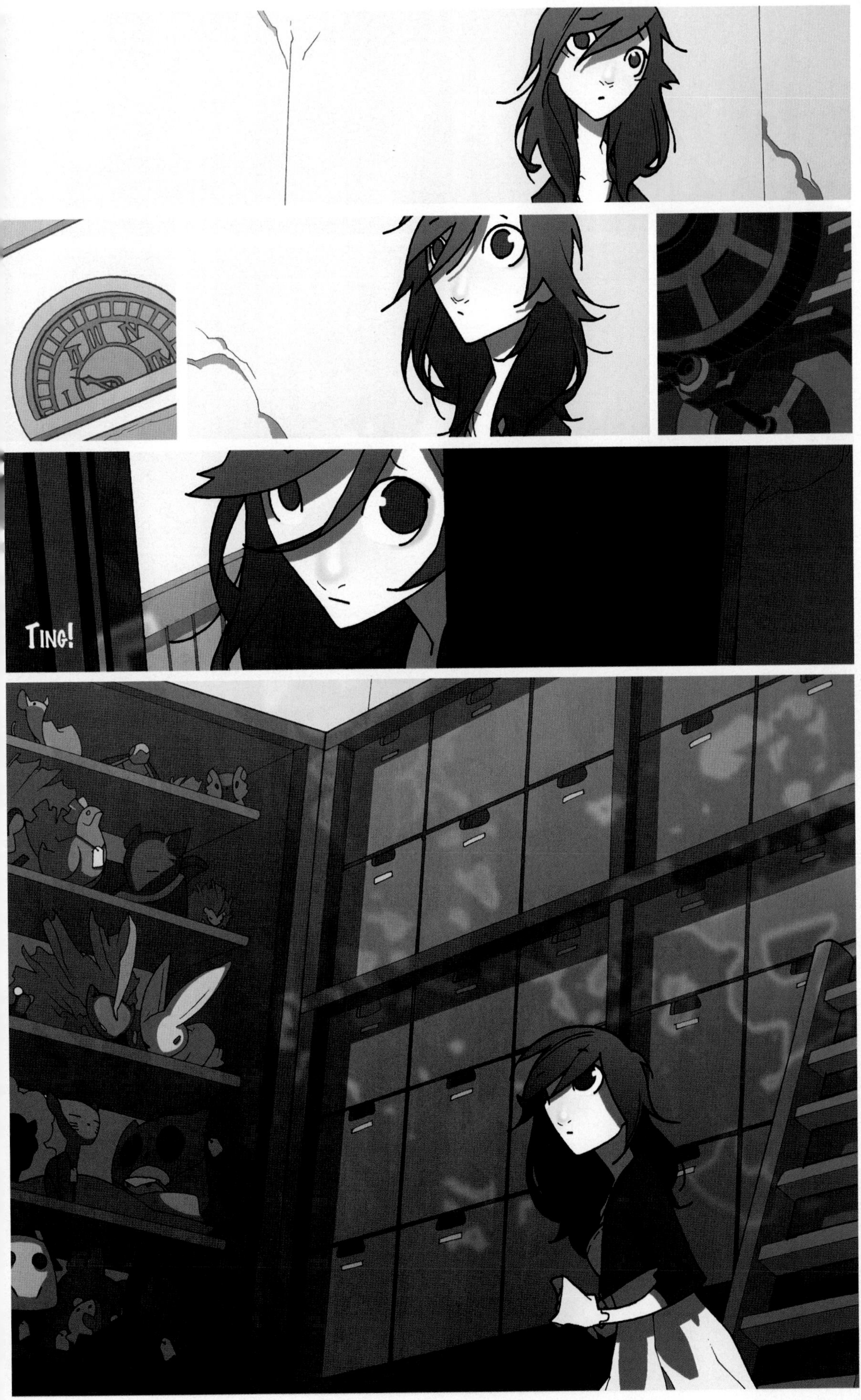
TING!

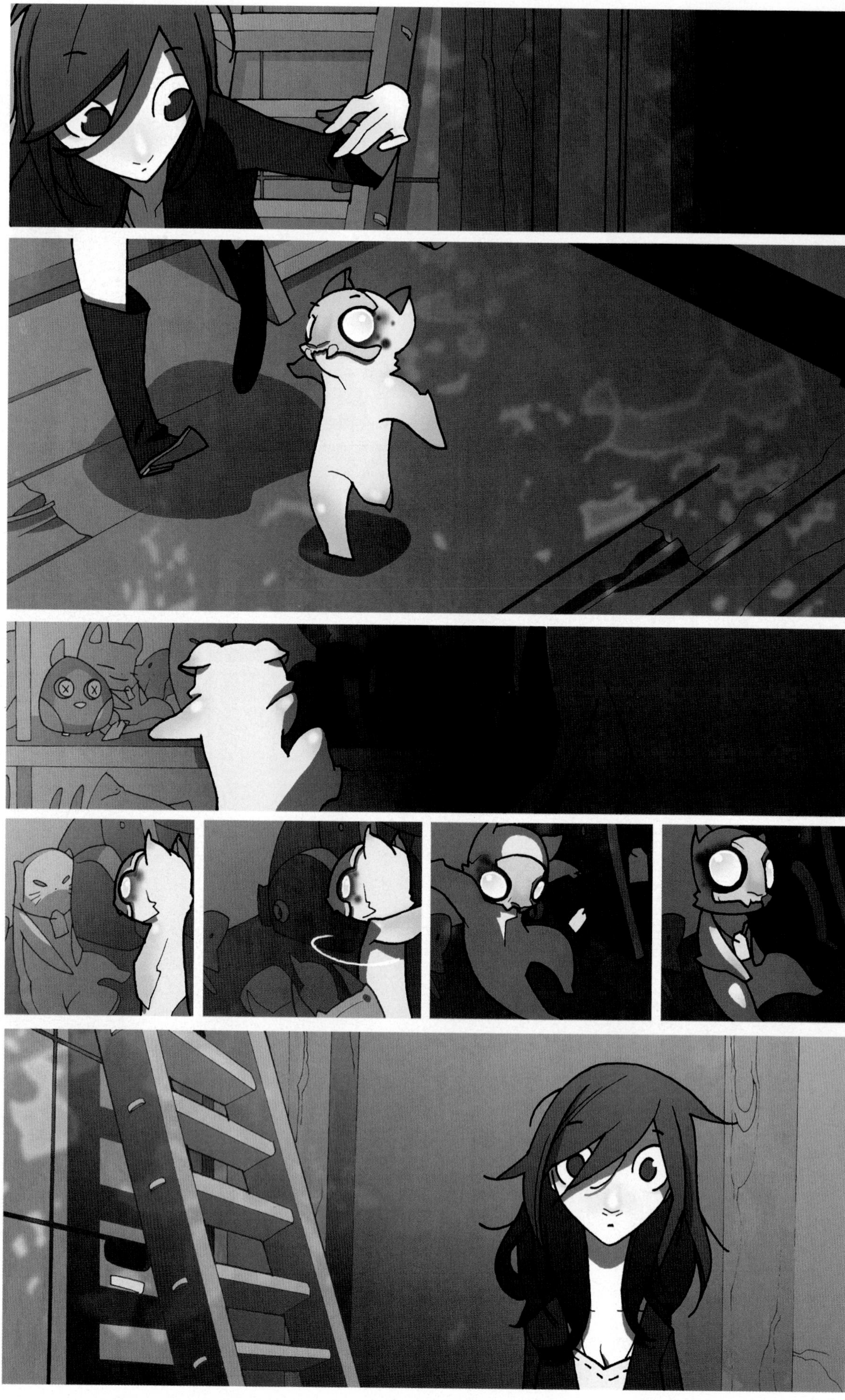

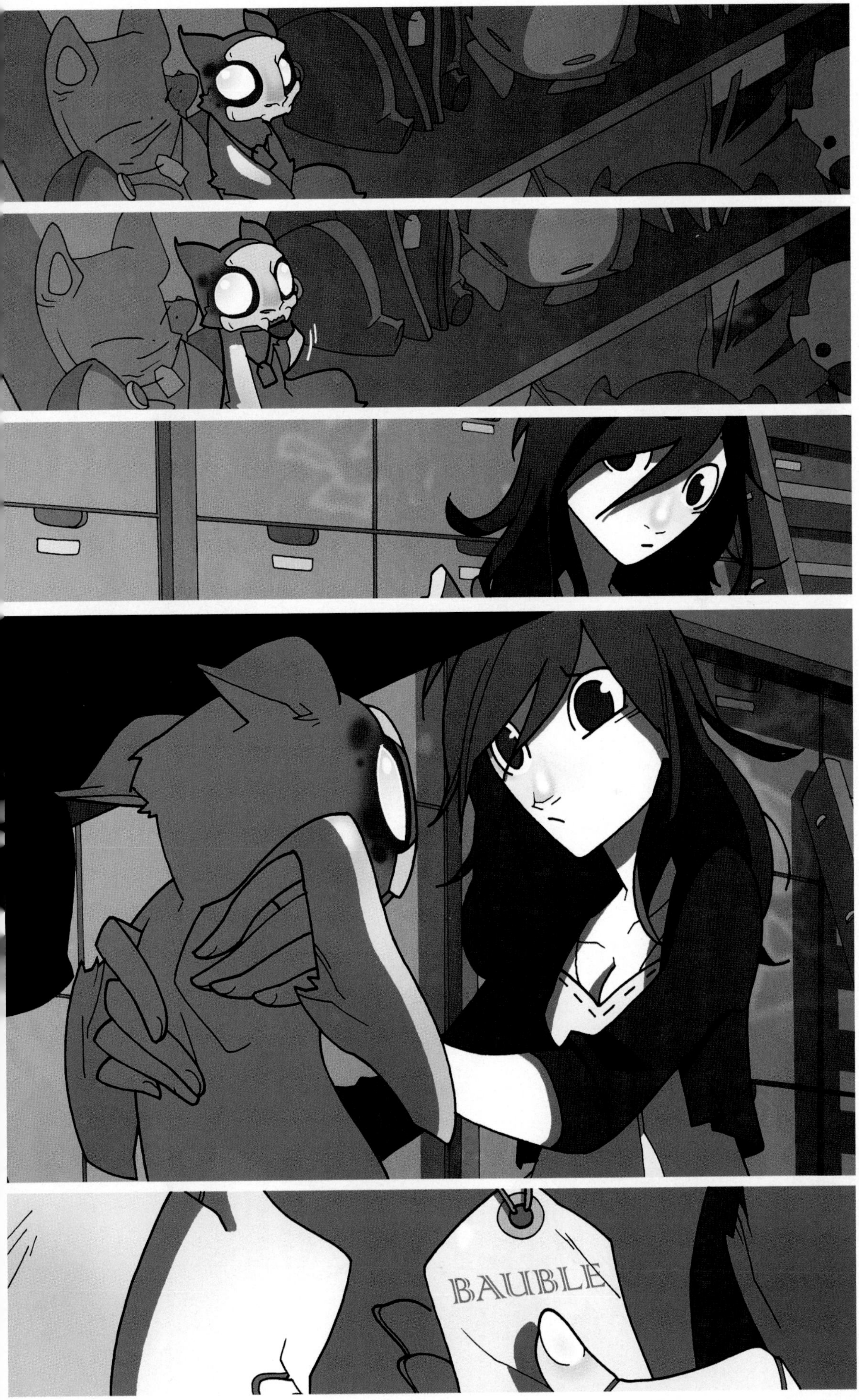
BAUBLE

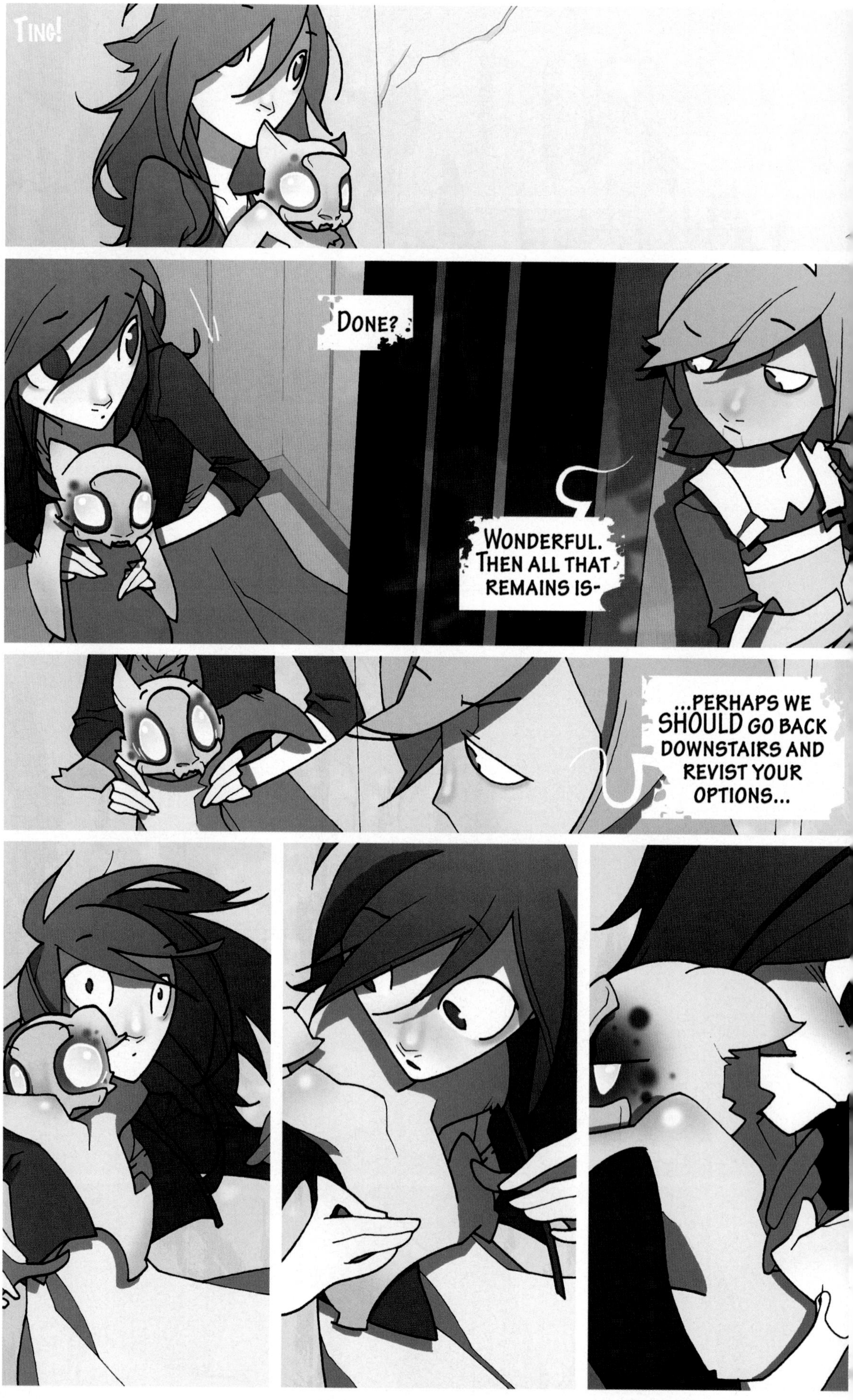

TING!
DONE?
WONDERFUL. THEN ALL THAT REMAINS IS-
...PERHAPS WE SHOULD GO BACK DOWNSTAIRS AND REVIST YOUR OPTIONS...

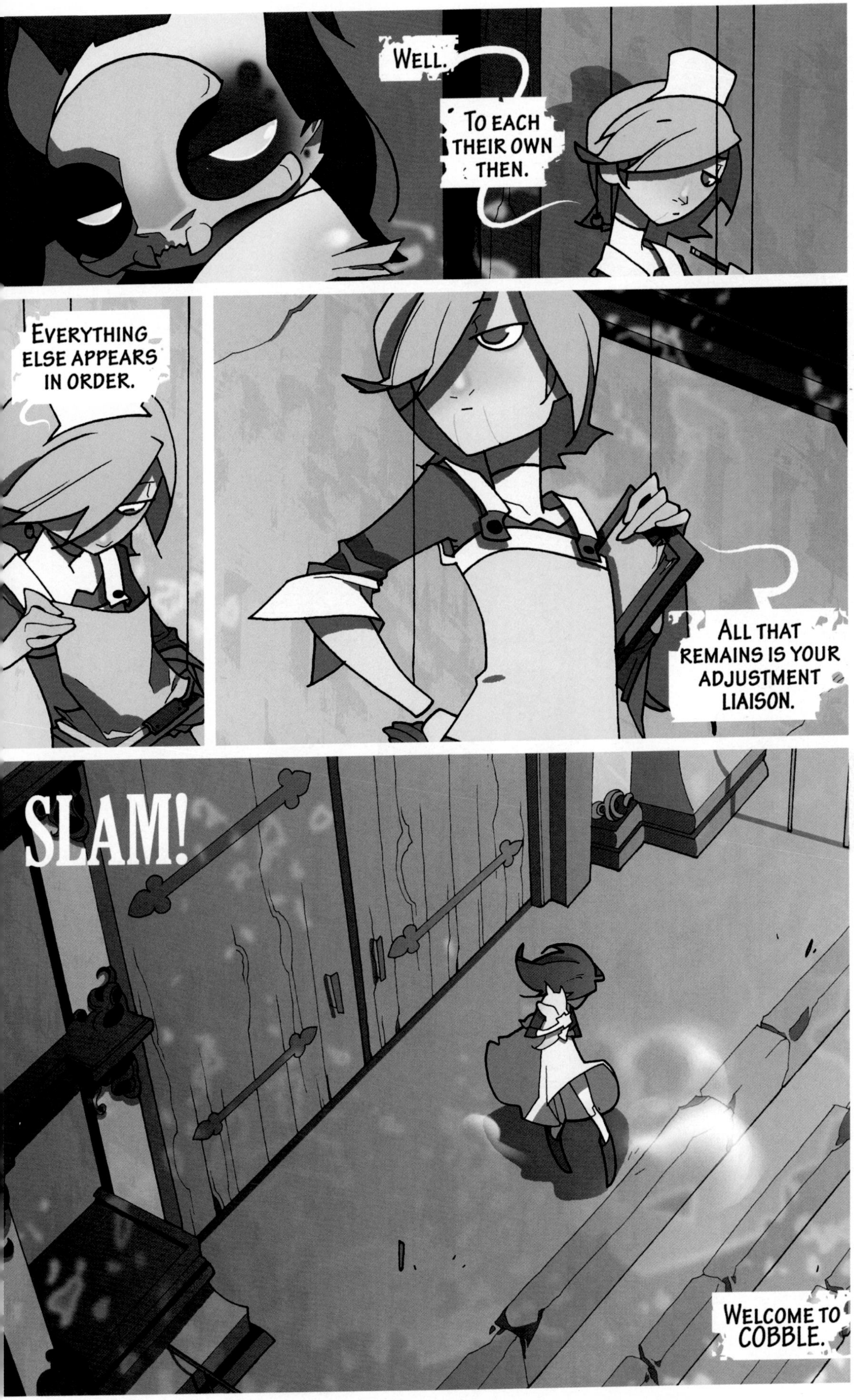

WELL.
TO EACH THEIR OWN THEN.
EVERYTHING ELSE APPEARS IN ORDER.
ALL THAT REMAINS IS YOUR ADJUSTMENT LIAISON.
SLAM!
WELCOME TO COBBLE.

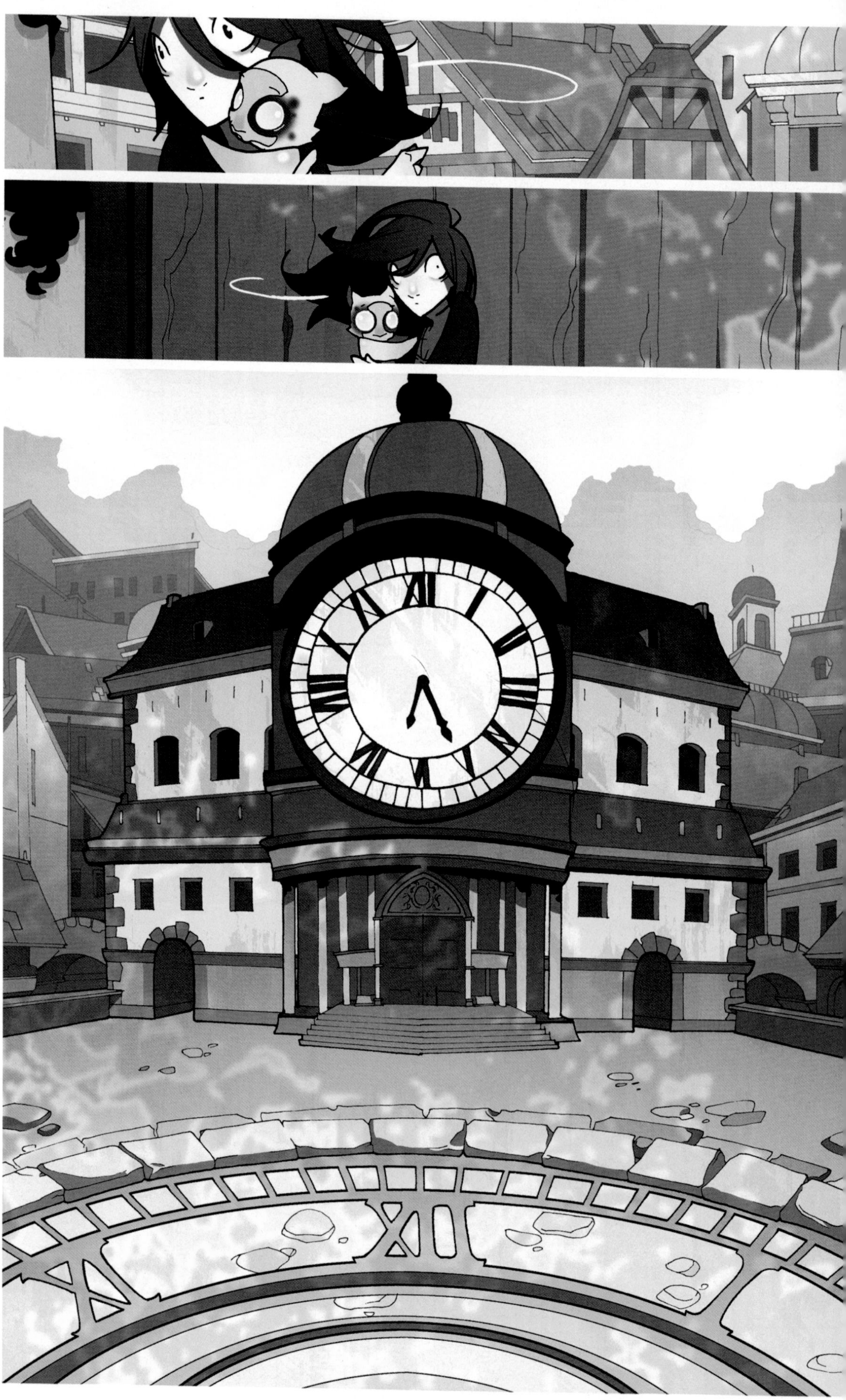

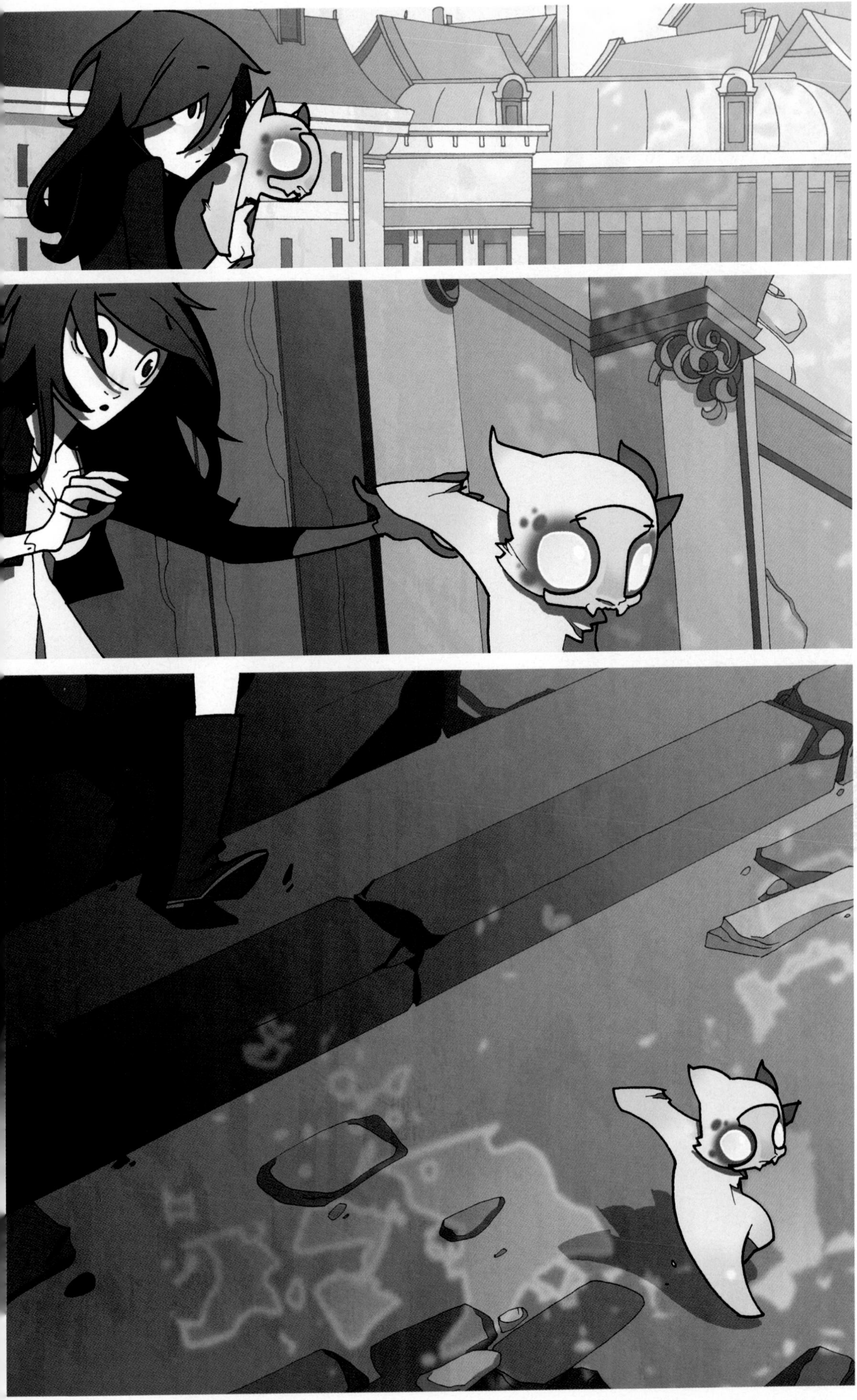

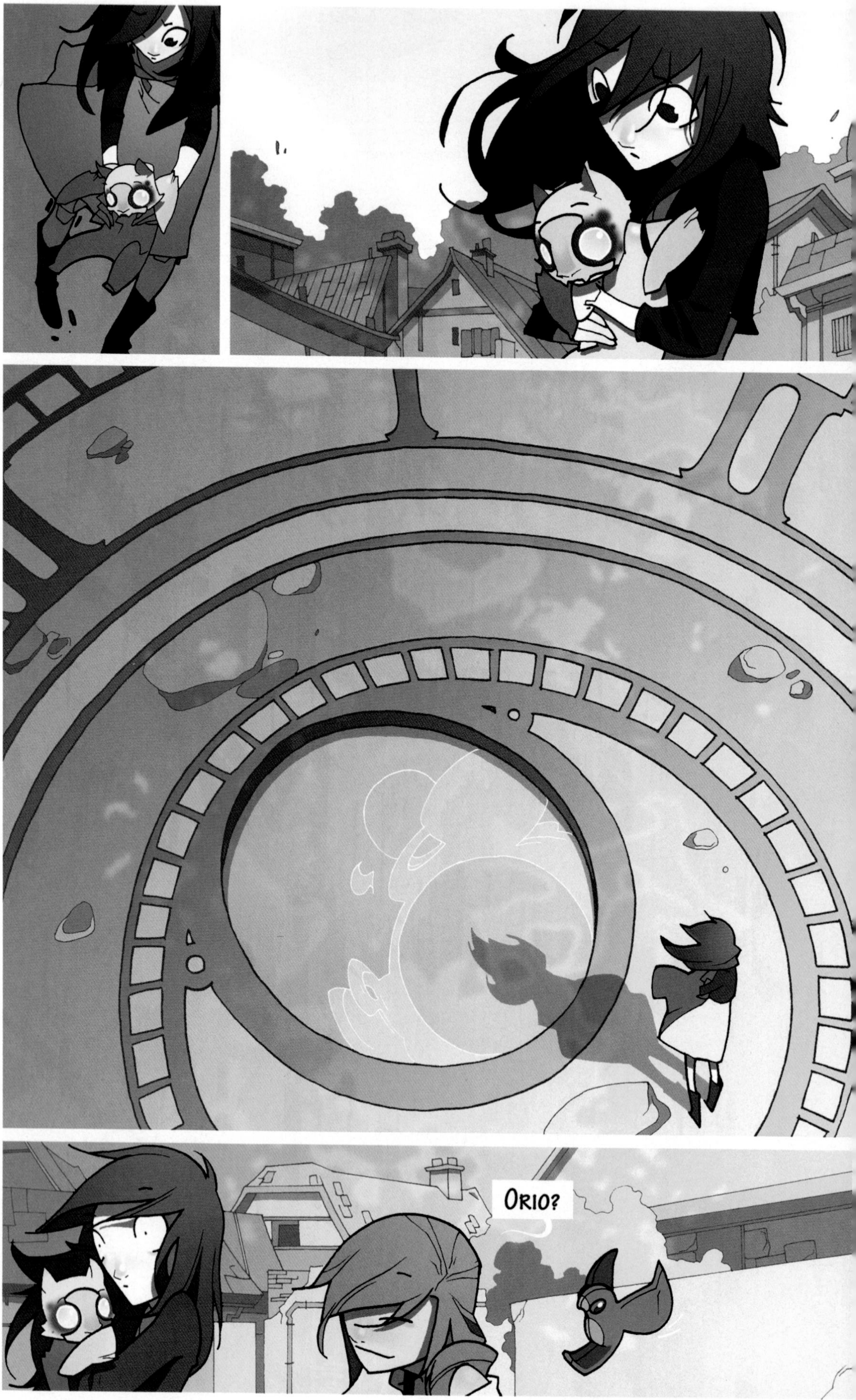
ORIO?

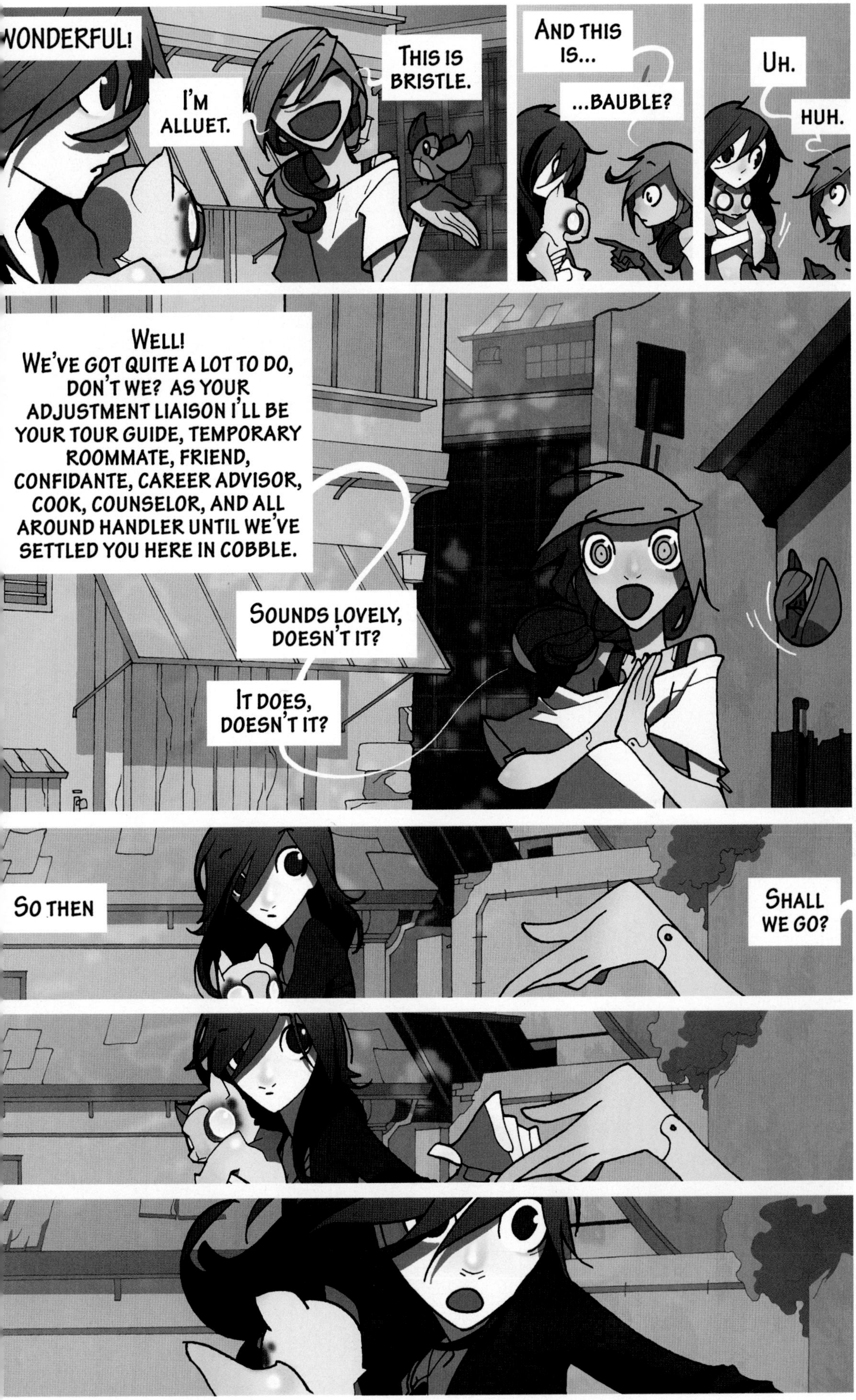

WONDERFUL!
I'M ALLUET.
THIS IS BRISTLE.
AND THIS IS...
...BAUBLE?
UH.
HUH.
WELL! WE'VE GOT QUITE A LOT TO DO, DON'T WE? AS YOUR ADJUSTMENT LIAISON I'LL BE YOUR TOUR GUIDE, TEMPORARY ROOMMATE, FRIEND, CONFIDANTE, CAREER ADVISOR, COOK, COUNSELOR, AND ALL AROUND HANDLER UNTIL WE'VE SETTLED YOU HERE IN COBBLE.
SOUNDS LOVELY, DOESN'T IT?
IT DOES, DOESN'T IT?
SO THEN
SHALL WE GO?

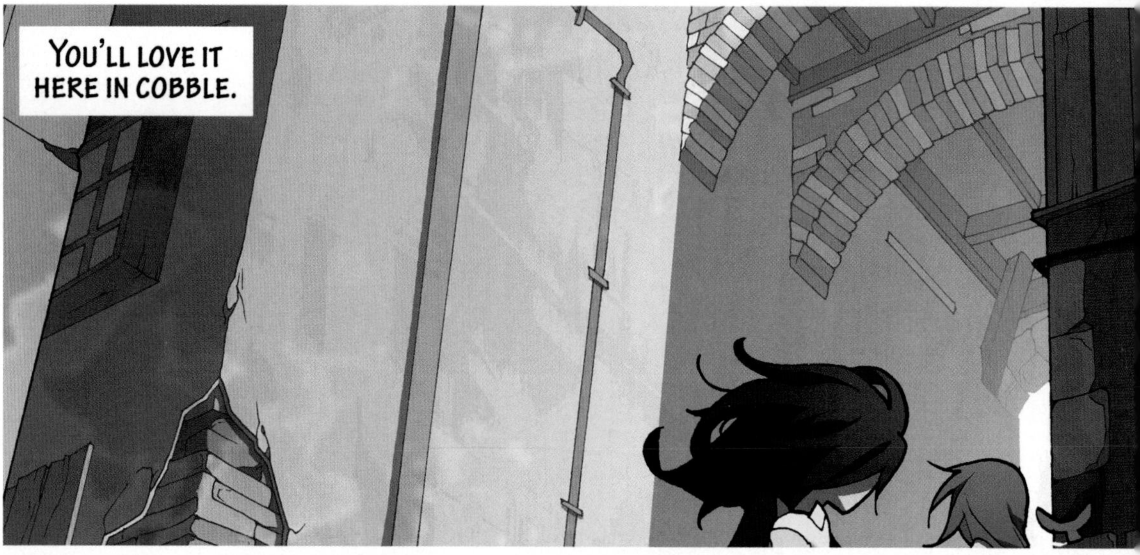
YOU'LL LOVE IT HERE IN COBBLE.

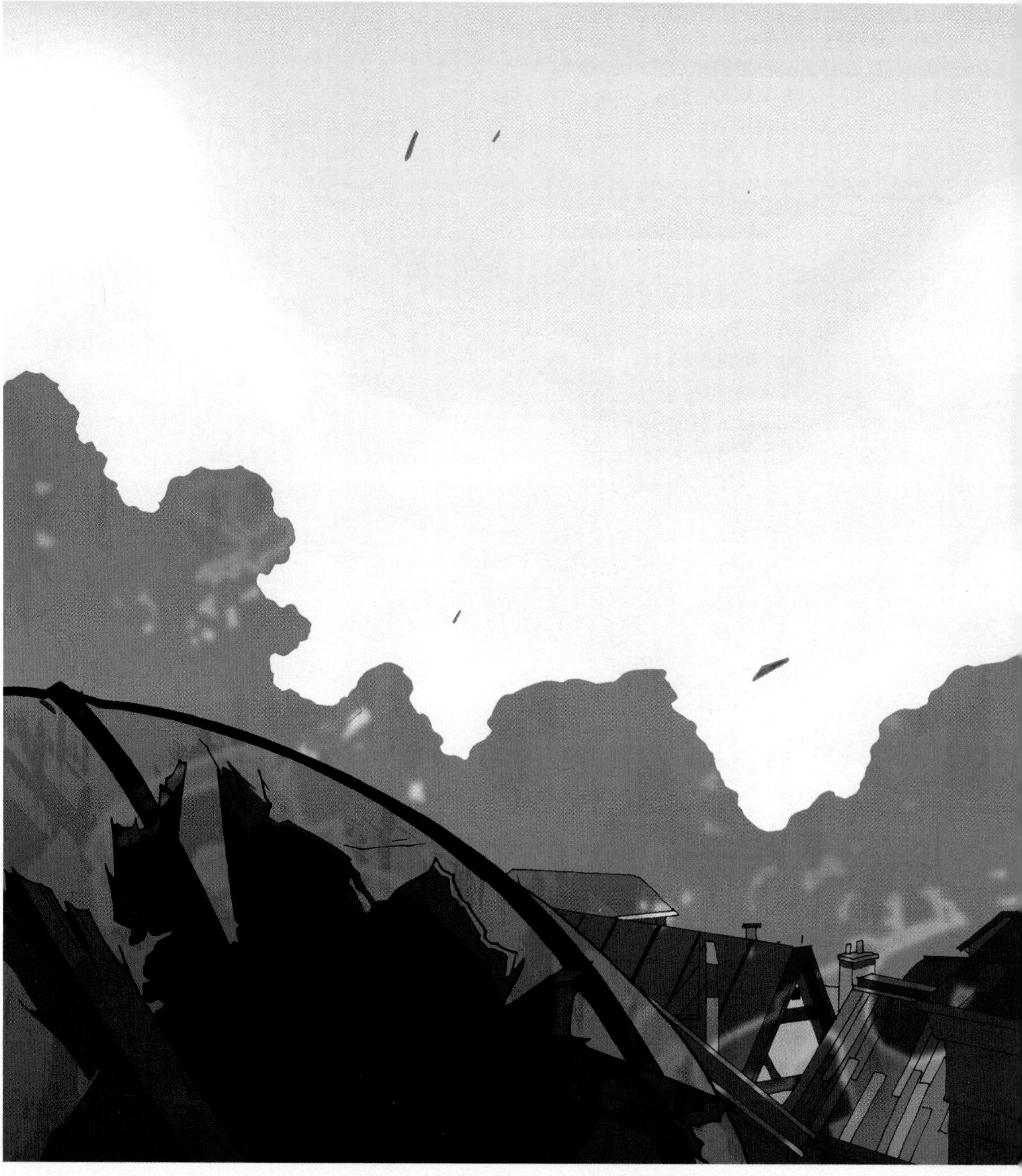

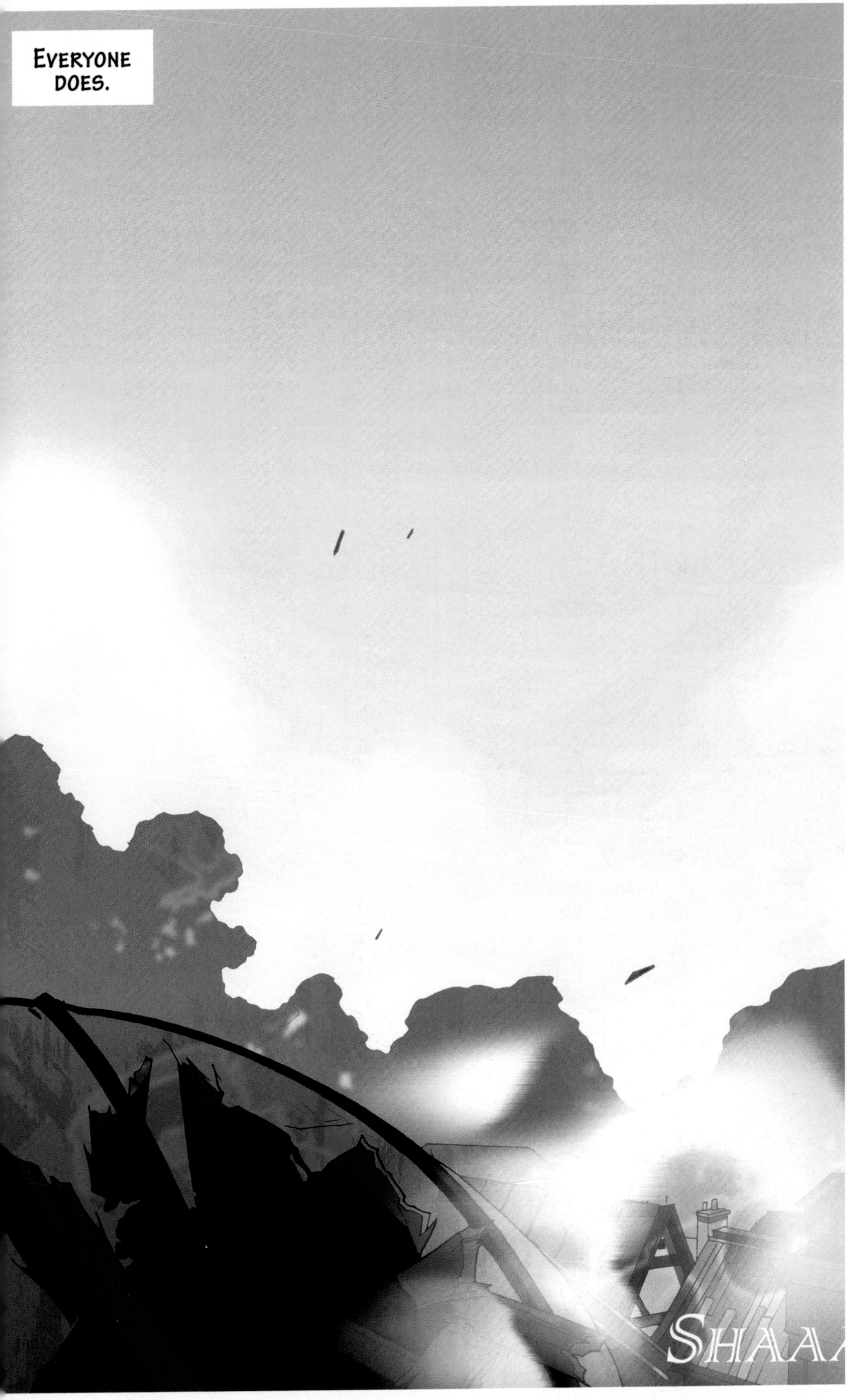

EVERYONE
DOES.

SHAA

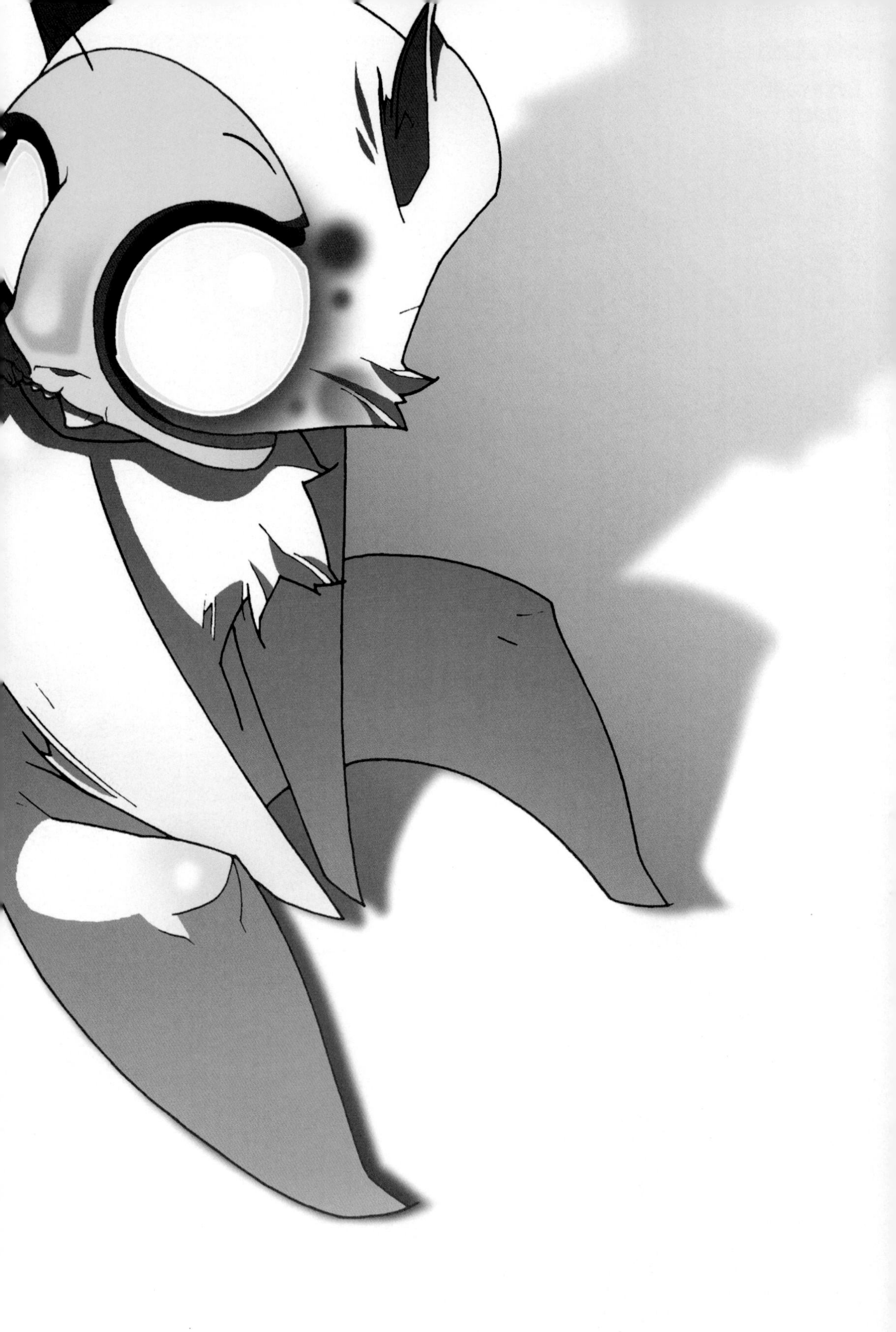

HINGES
CHAPTER 2

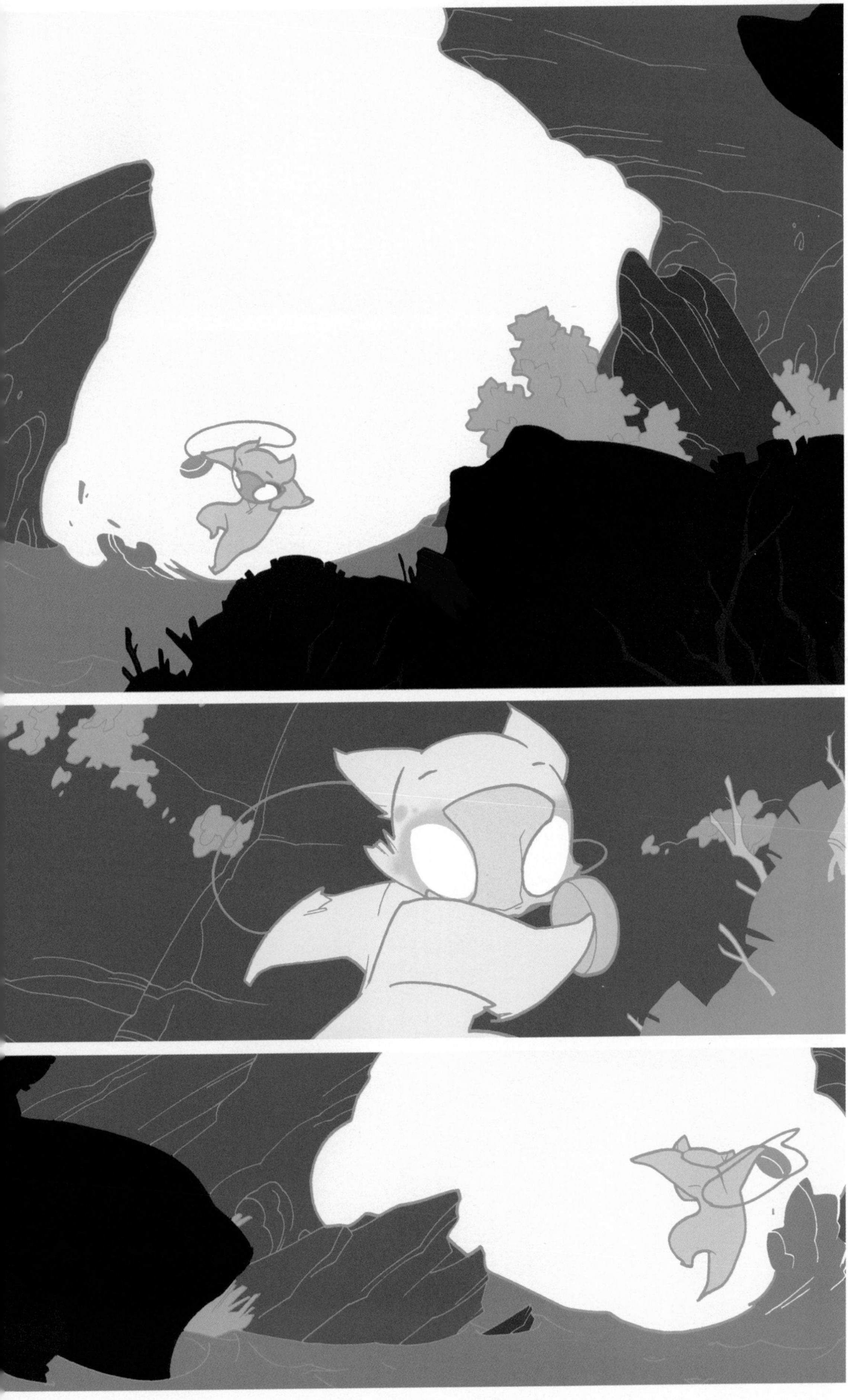

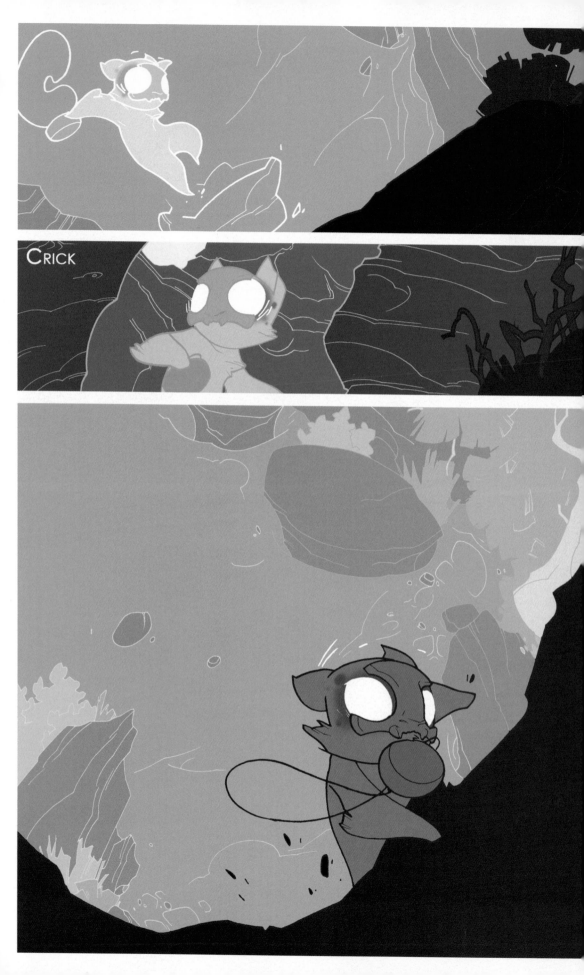

CRICK

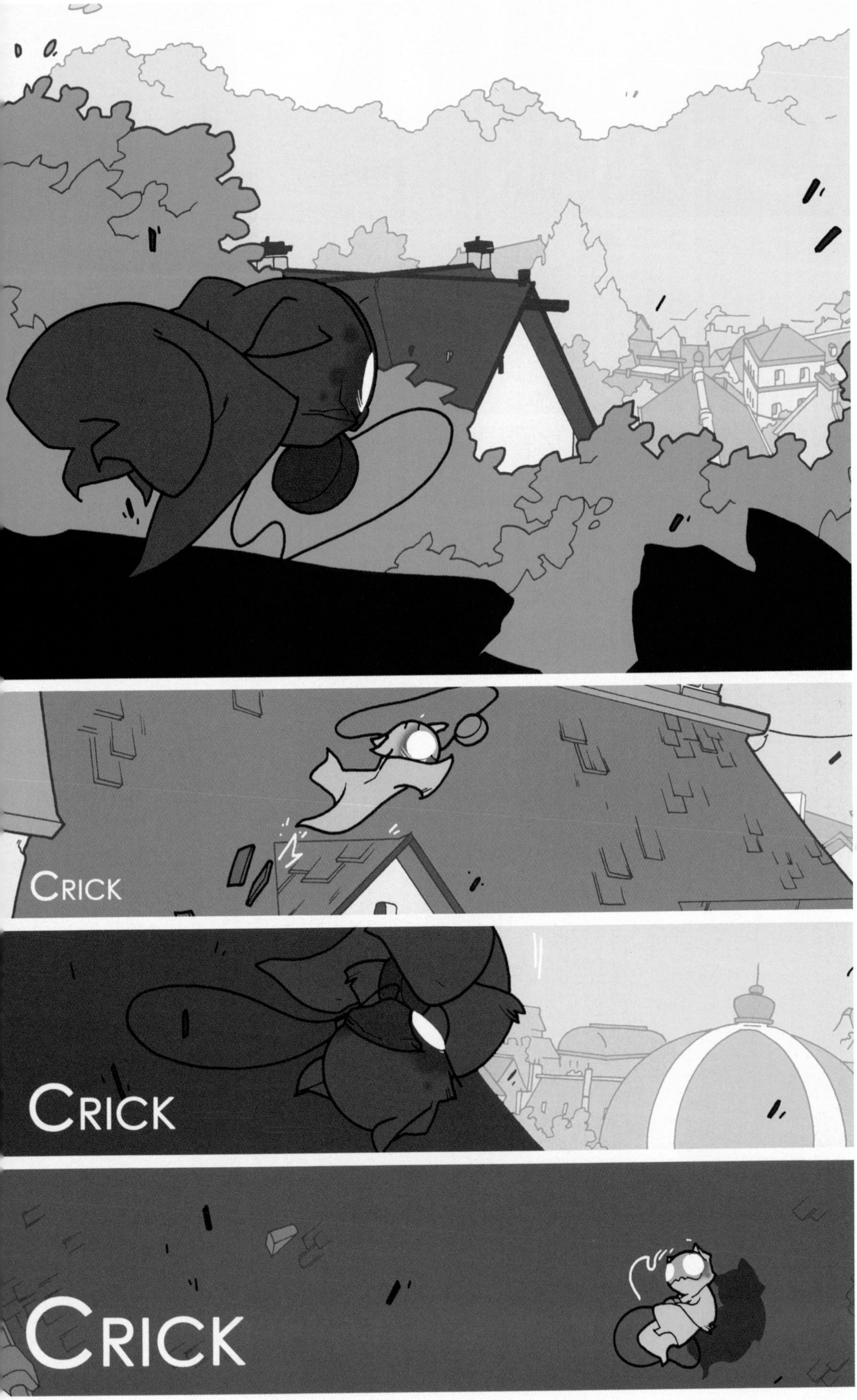
CRICK
CRICK
CRICK

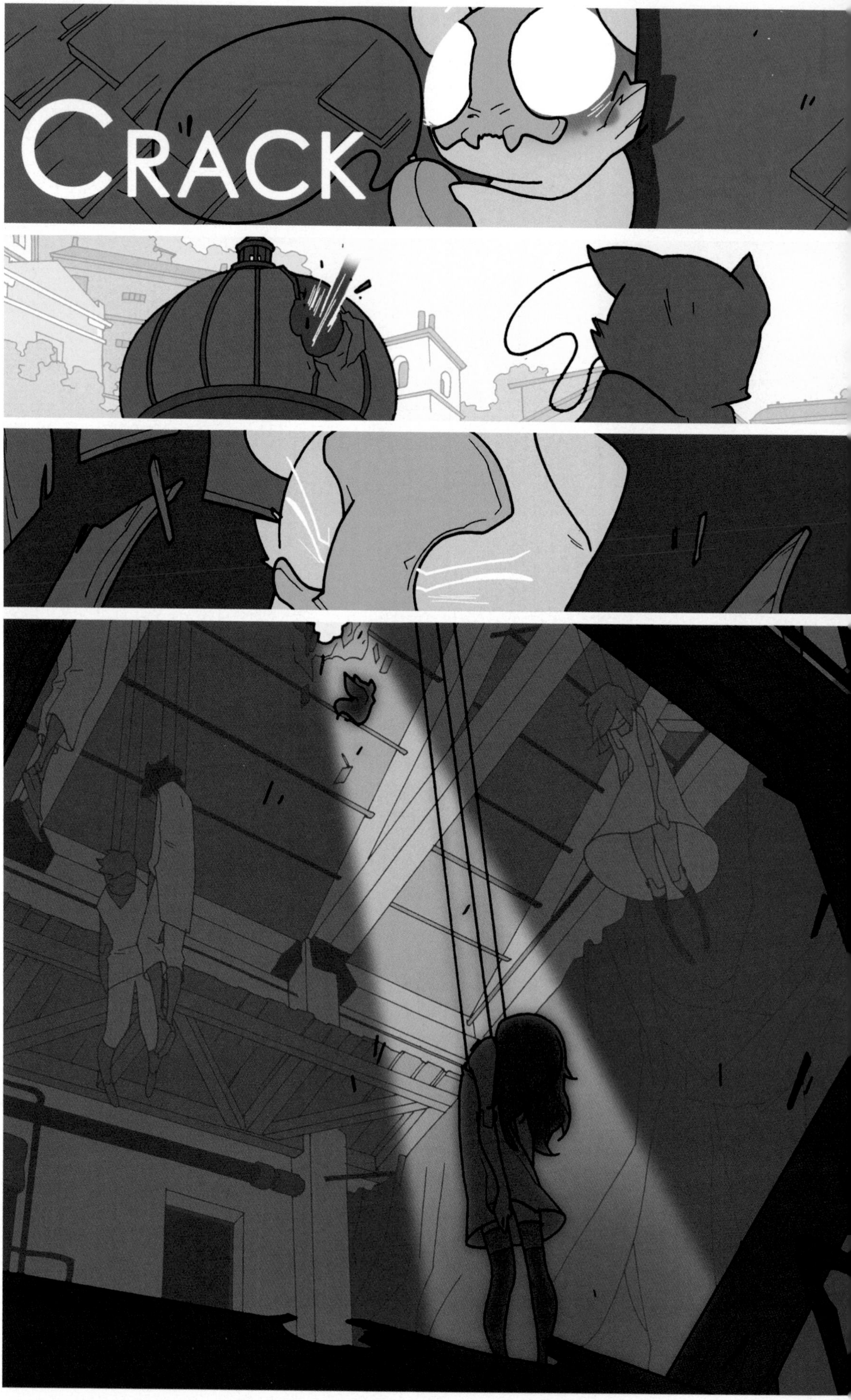
CRACK

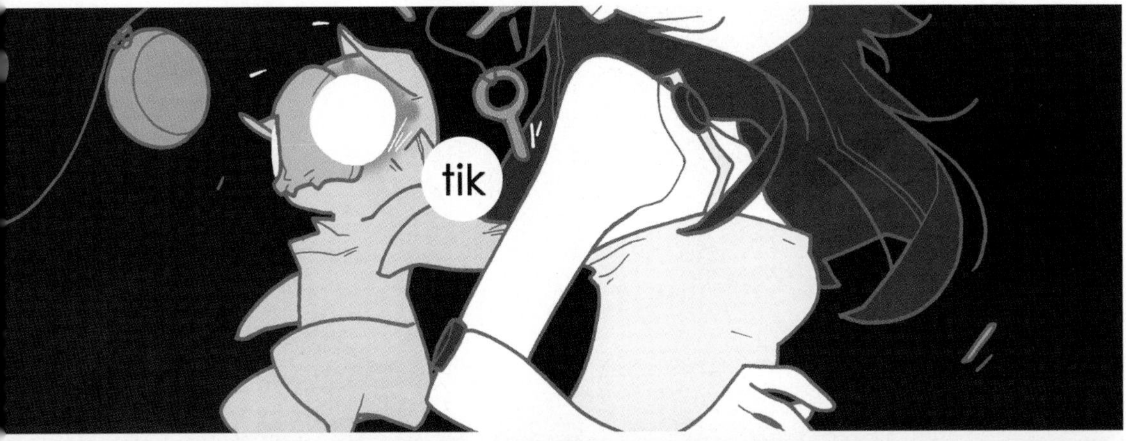
tik

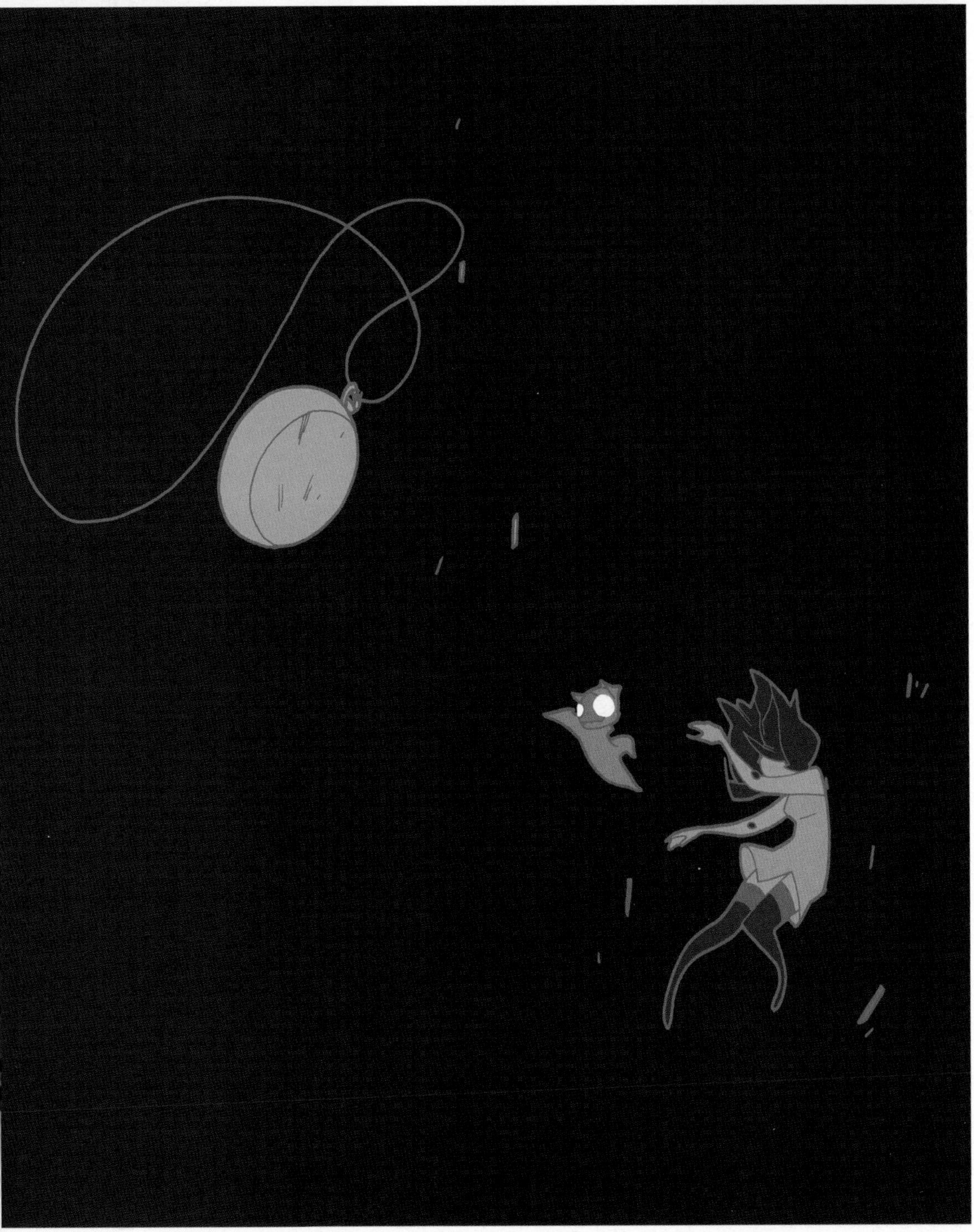

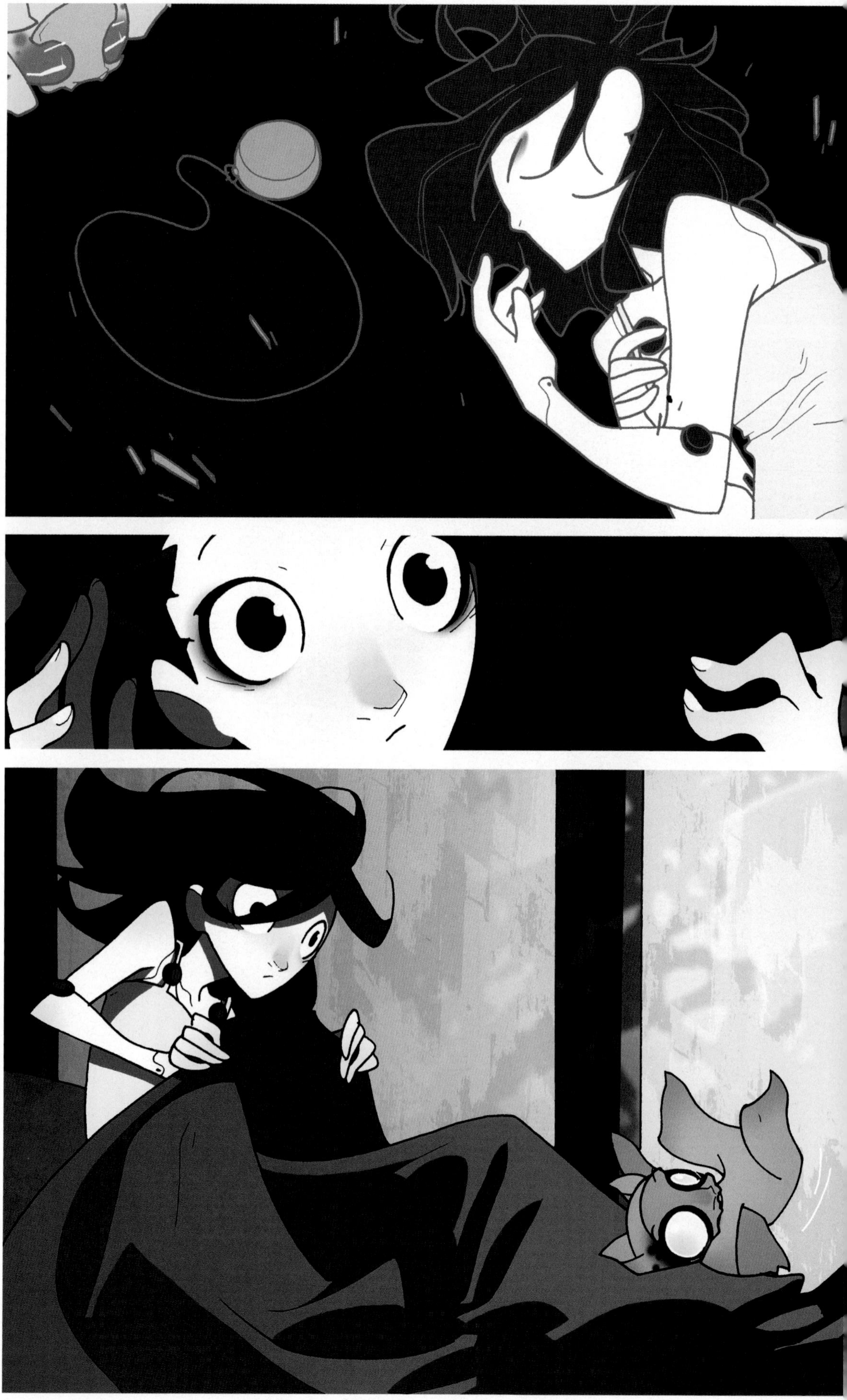

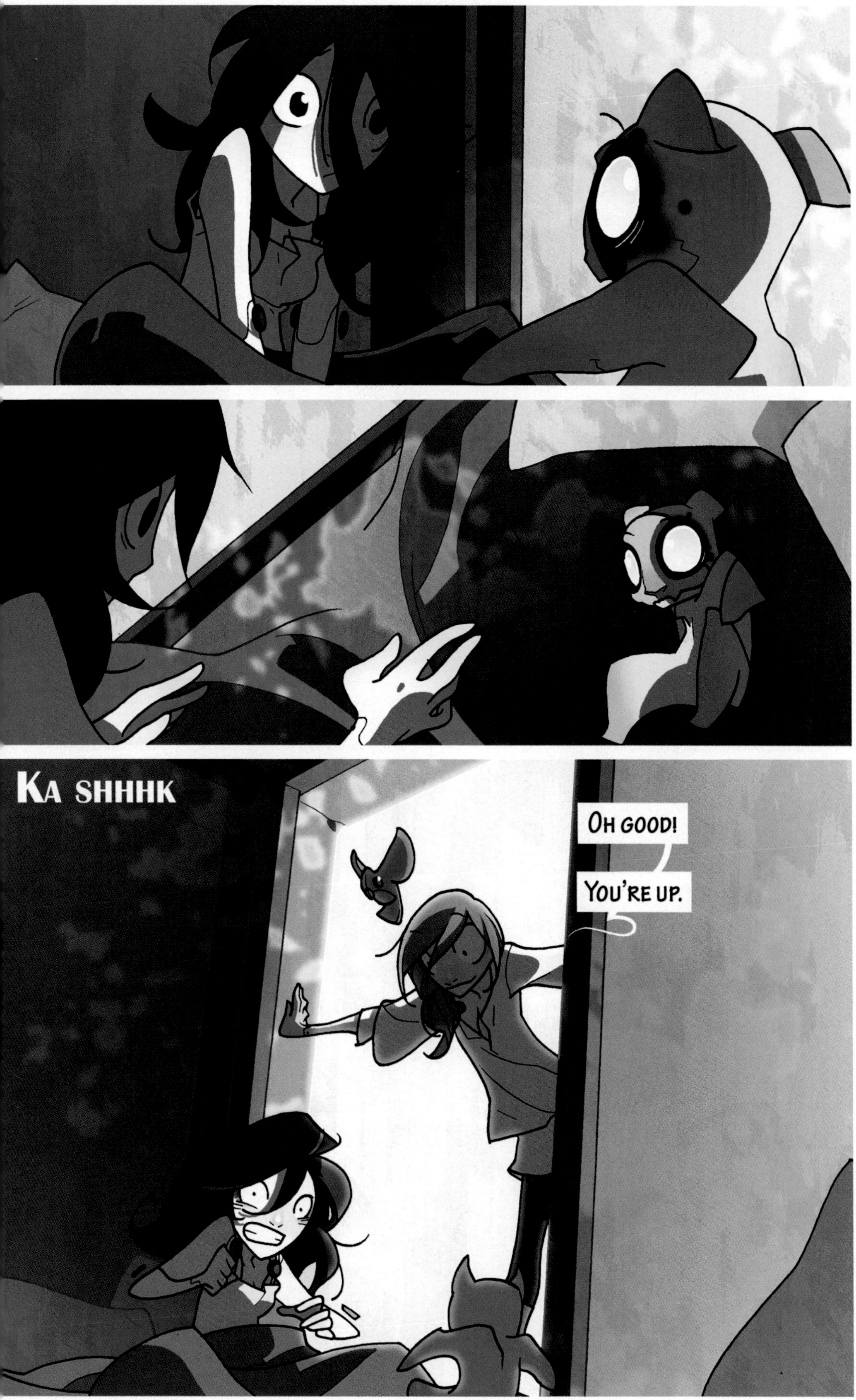
KA SHHHK
OH GOOD!
YOU'RE UP.

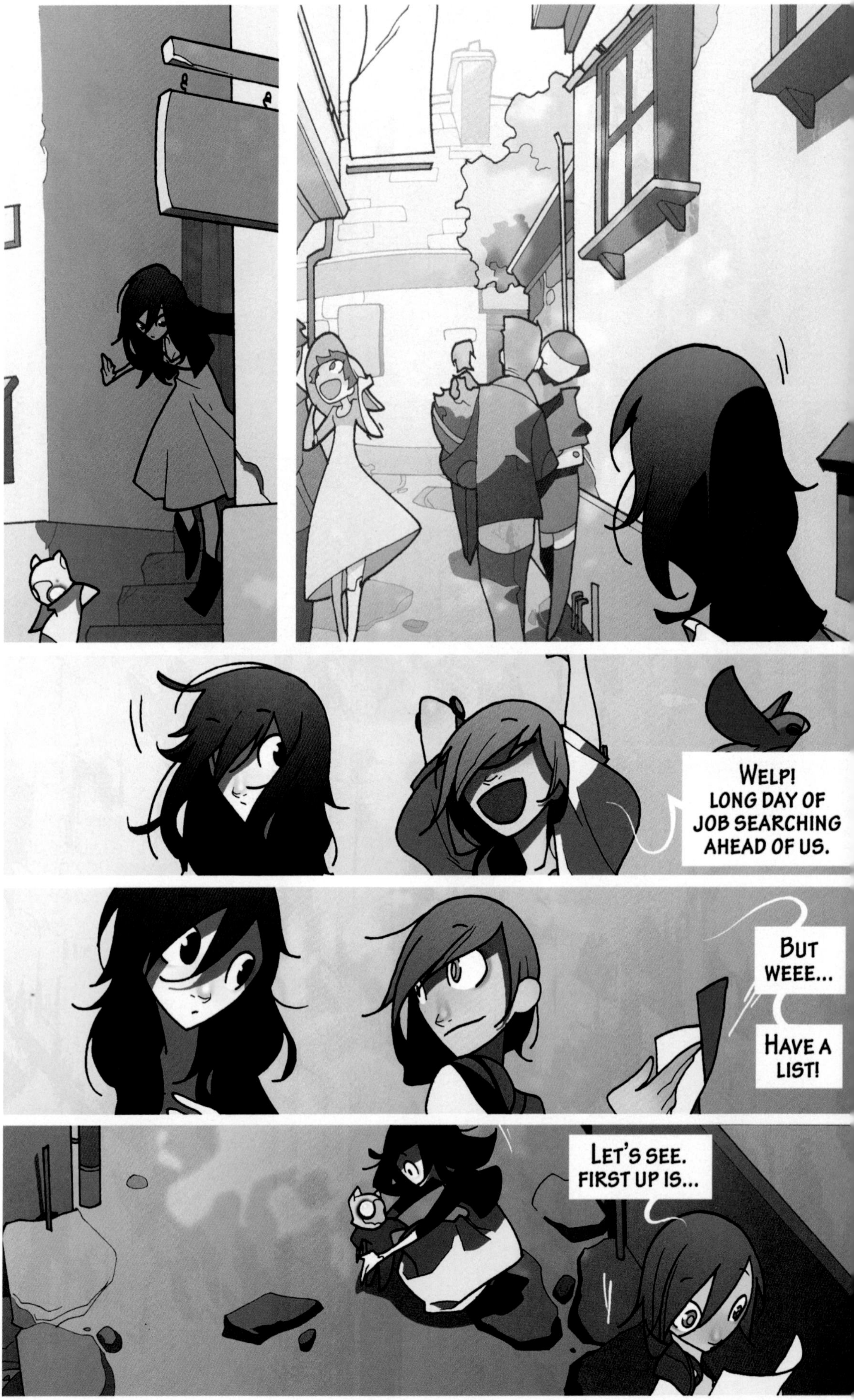
WELP!
LONG DAY OF
JOB SEARCHING
AHEAD OF US.
BUT
WEEE...
HAVE A
LIST!
LET'S SEE.
FIRST UP IS...

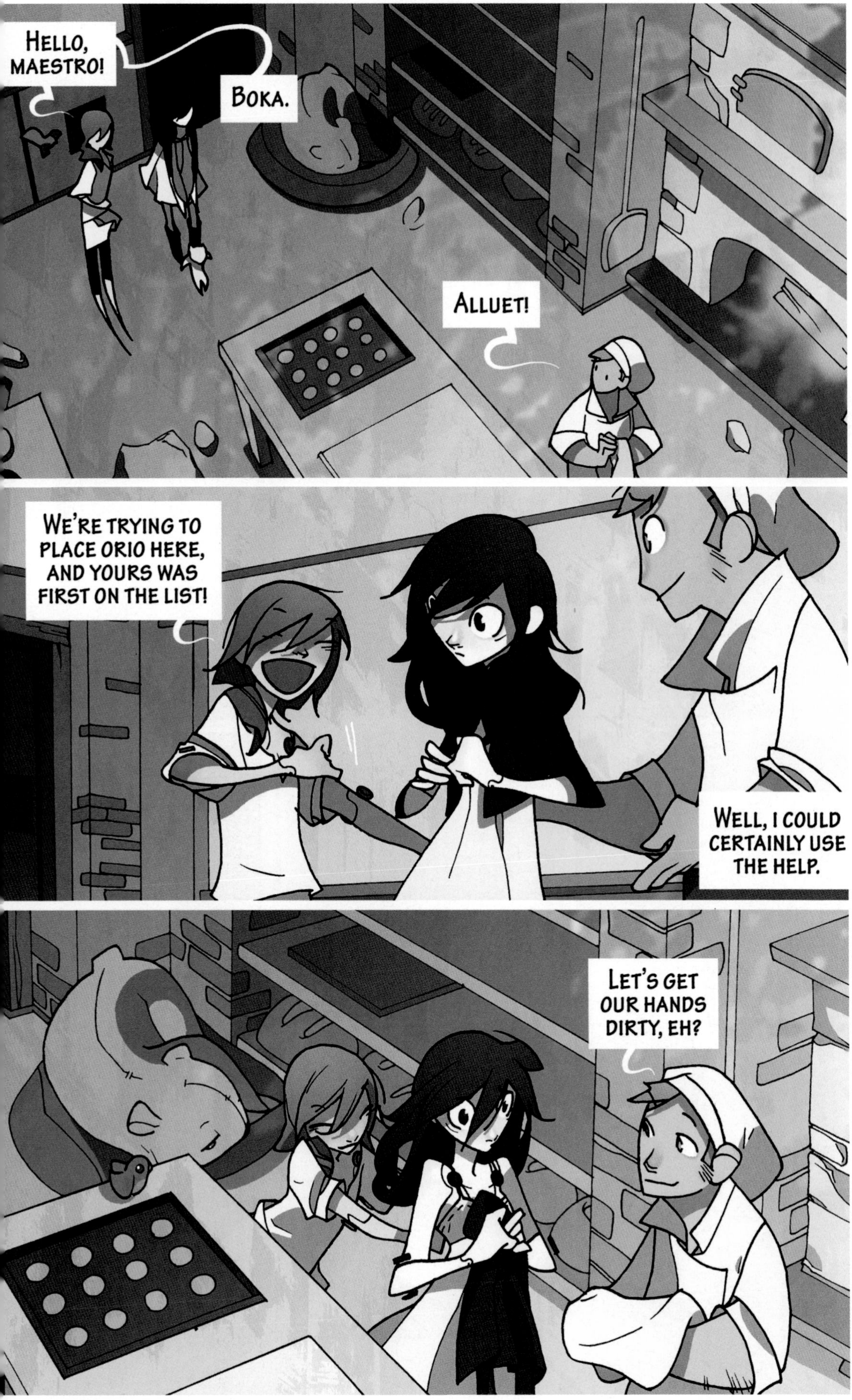
HELLO, MAESTRO!
BOKA.
ALLUET!
WE'RE TRYING TO PLACE ORIO HERE, AND YOURS WAS FIRST ON THE LIST!
WELL, I COULD CERTAINLY USE THE HELP.
LET'S GET OUR HANDS DIRTY, EH?

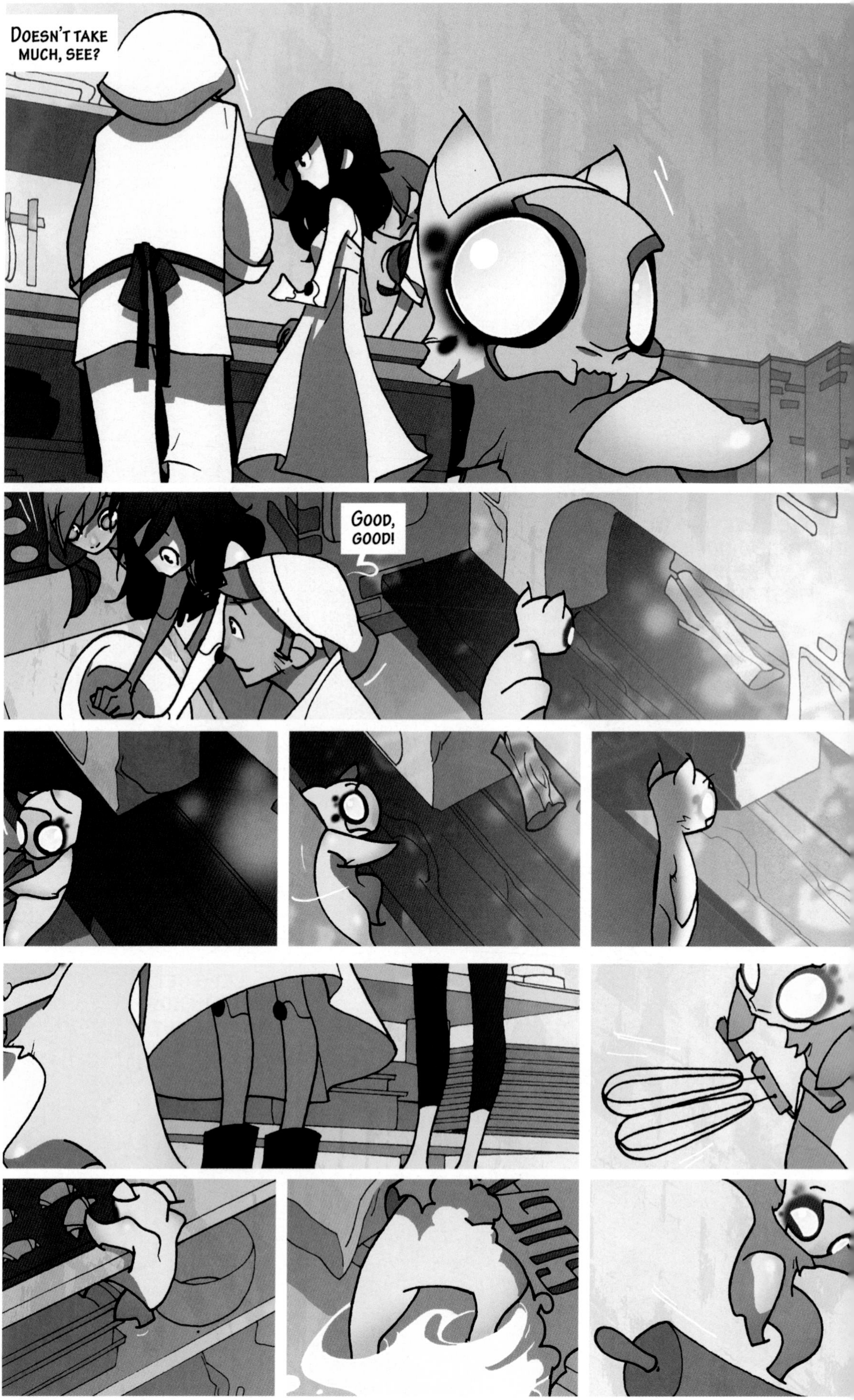
DOESN'T TAKE MUCH, SEE?
GOOD, GOOD!

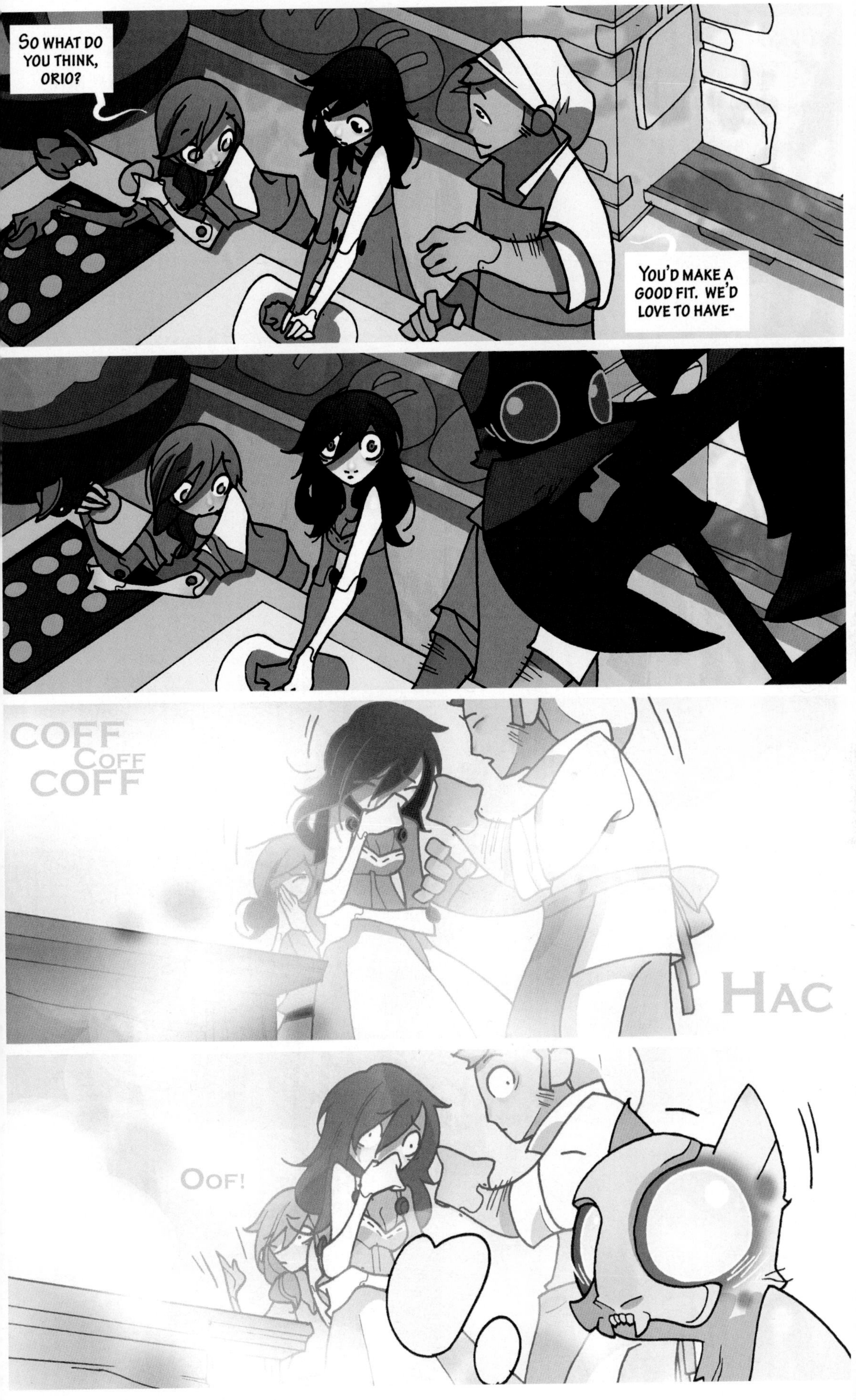

SO WHAT DO YOU THINK, ORIO?
YOU'D MAKE A GOOD FIT. WE'D LOVE TO HAVE-
COFF
COFF
COFF
HAC
OOF!

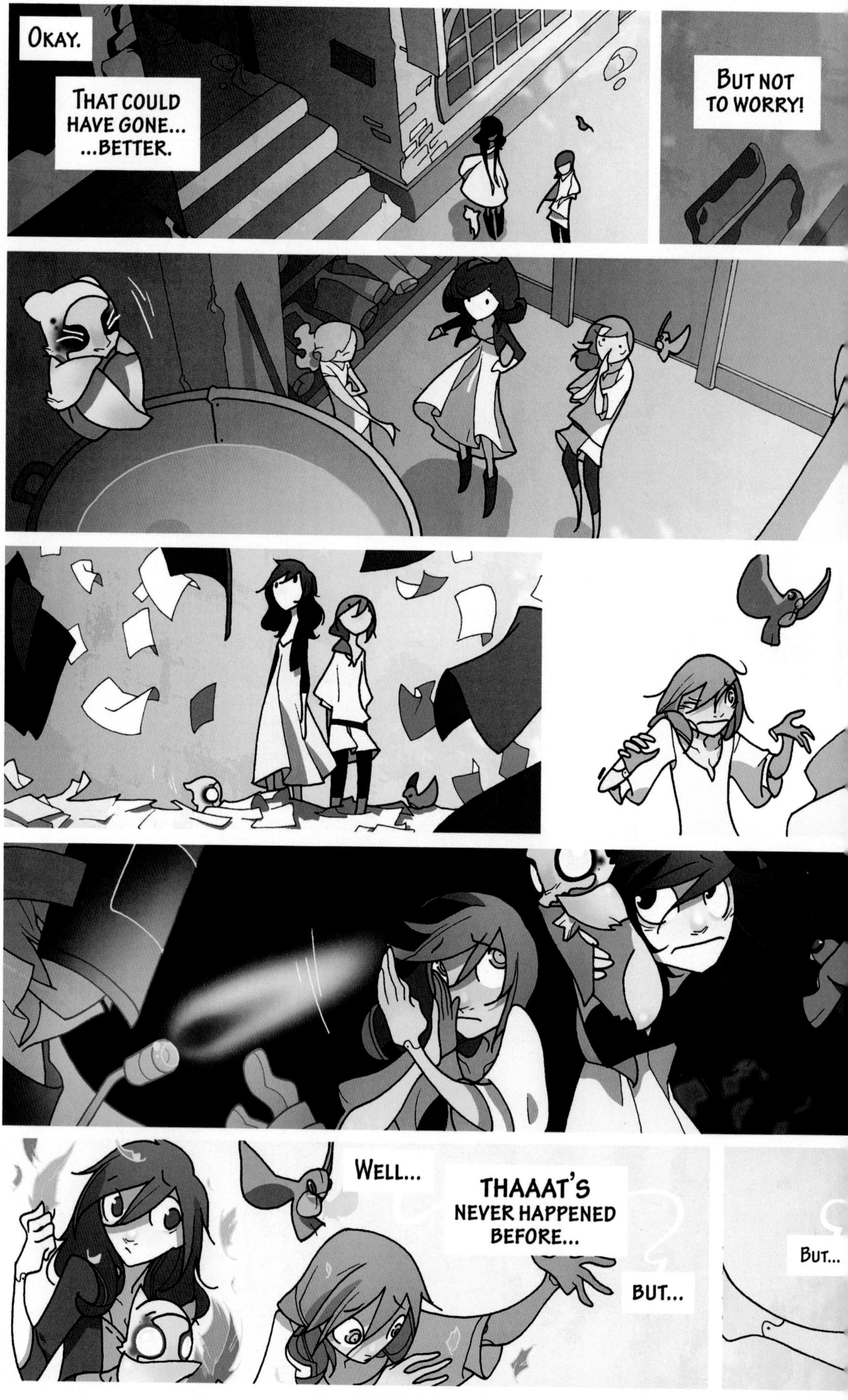
Okay.
That could have gone... ...better.
But not to worry!
Well...
Thaaat's never happened before...
But...
But...

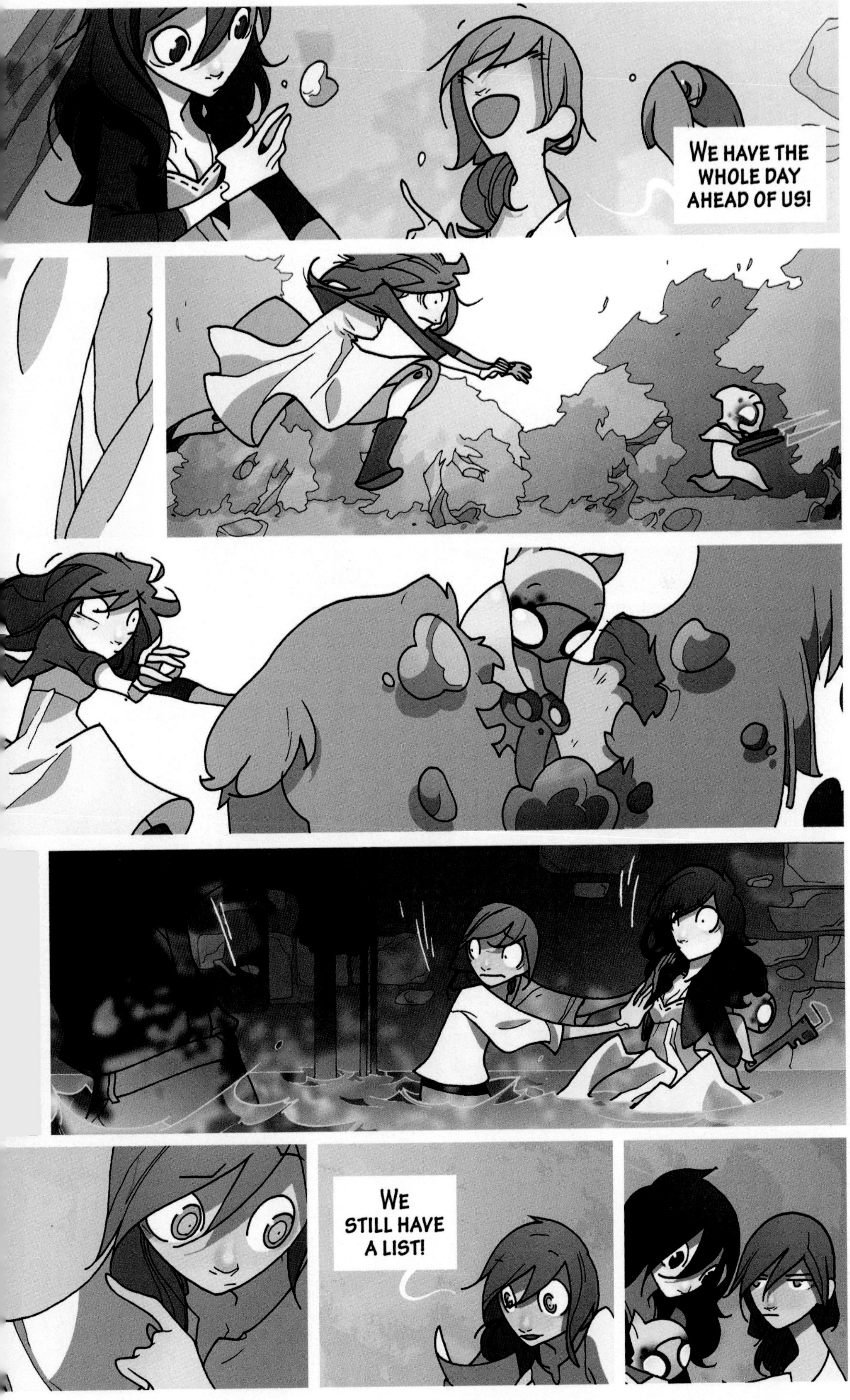
WE HAVE THE WHOLE DAY AHEAD OF US!
WE STILL HAVE A LIST!

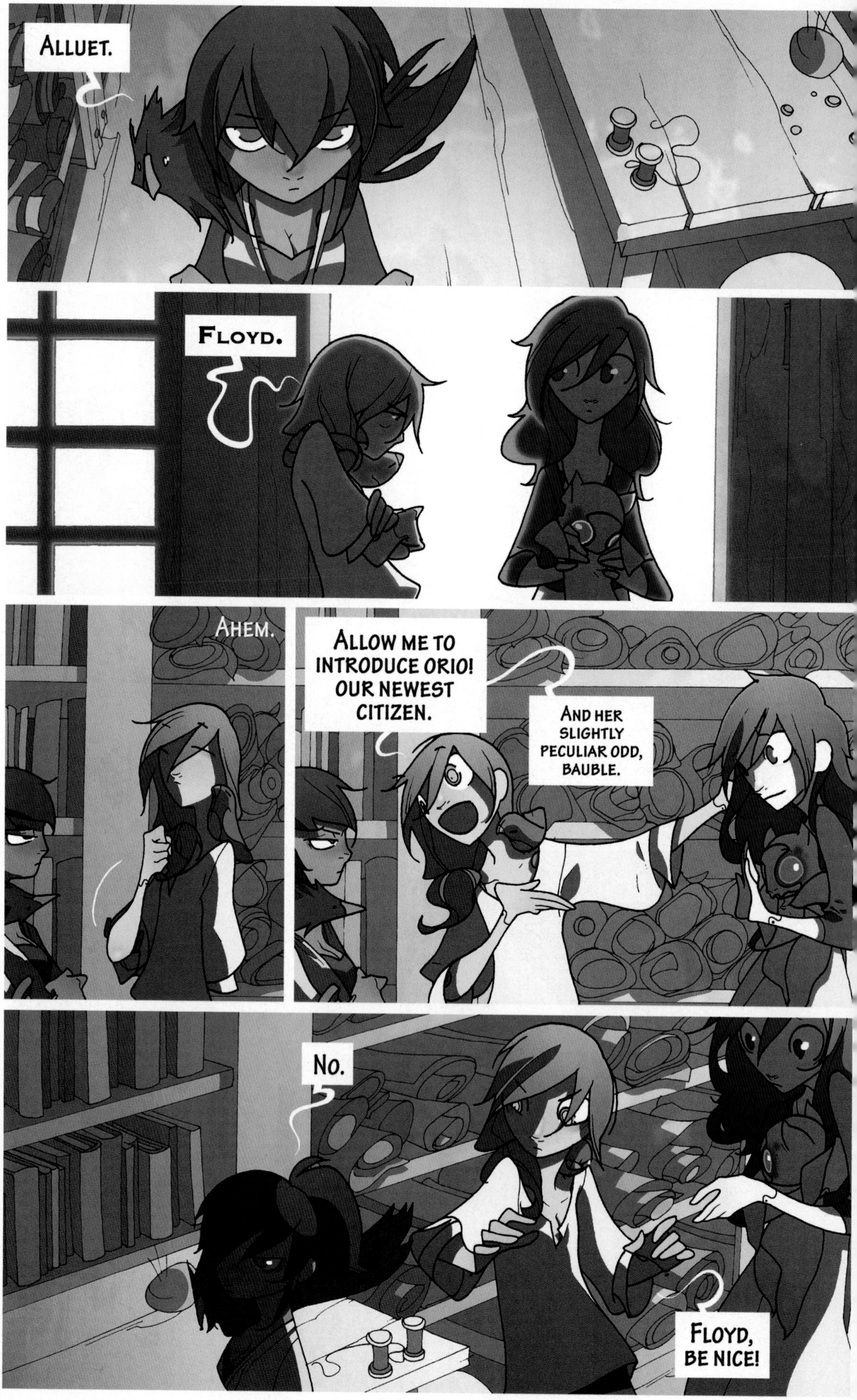
ALLUET.
FLOYD.
AHEM.
ALLOW ME TO INTRODUCE ORIO! OUR NEWEST CITIZEN.
AND HER SLIGHTLY PECULIAR ODD, BAUBLE.
NO.
FLOYD, BE NICE!

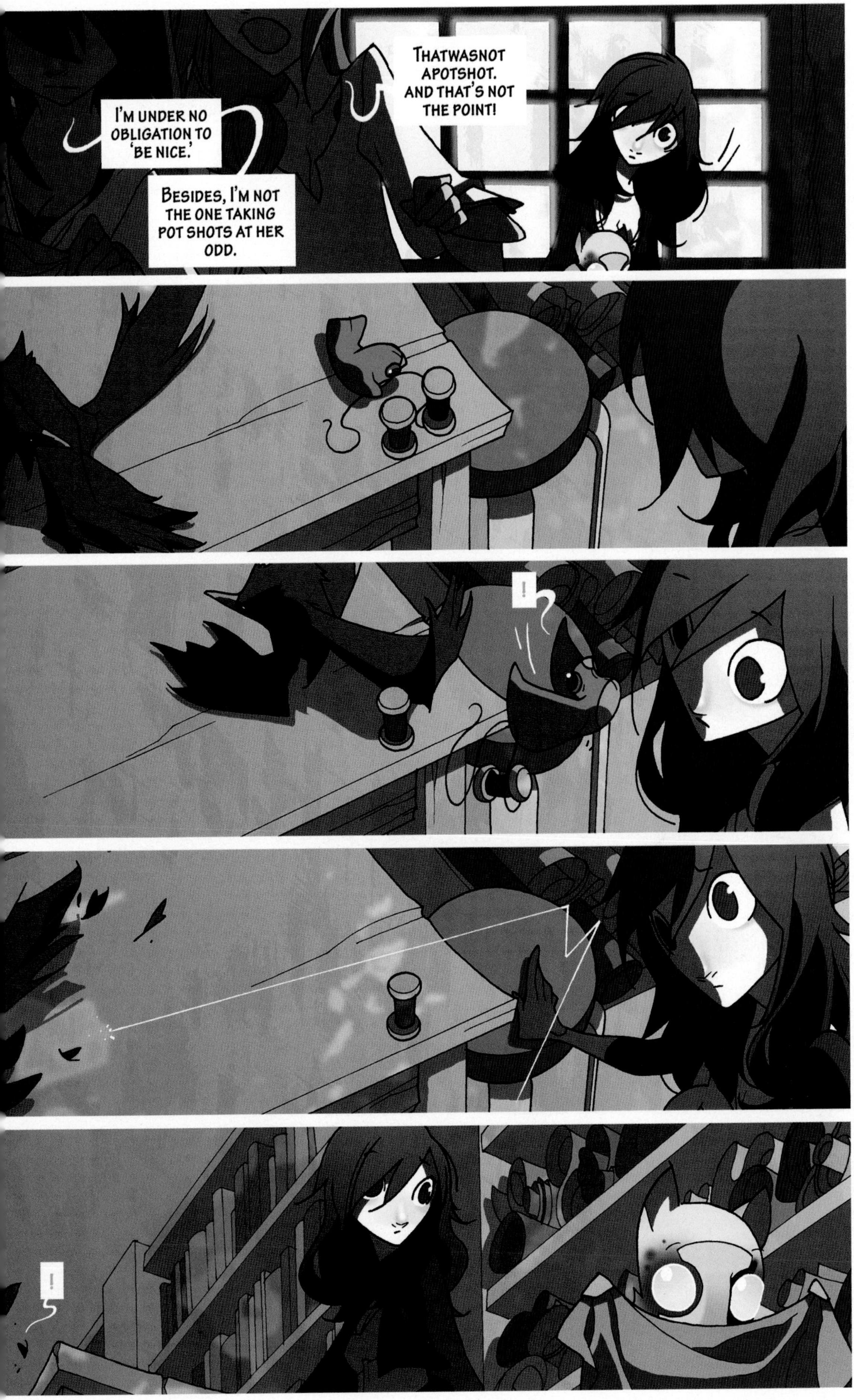
I'M UNDER NO OBLIGATION TO 'BE NICE.'
BESIDES, I'M NOT THE ONE TAKING POT SHOTS AT HER ODD.
THATWASNOT APOTSHOT. AND THAT'S NOT THE POINT!
!
!

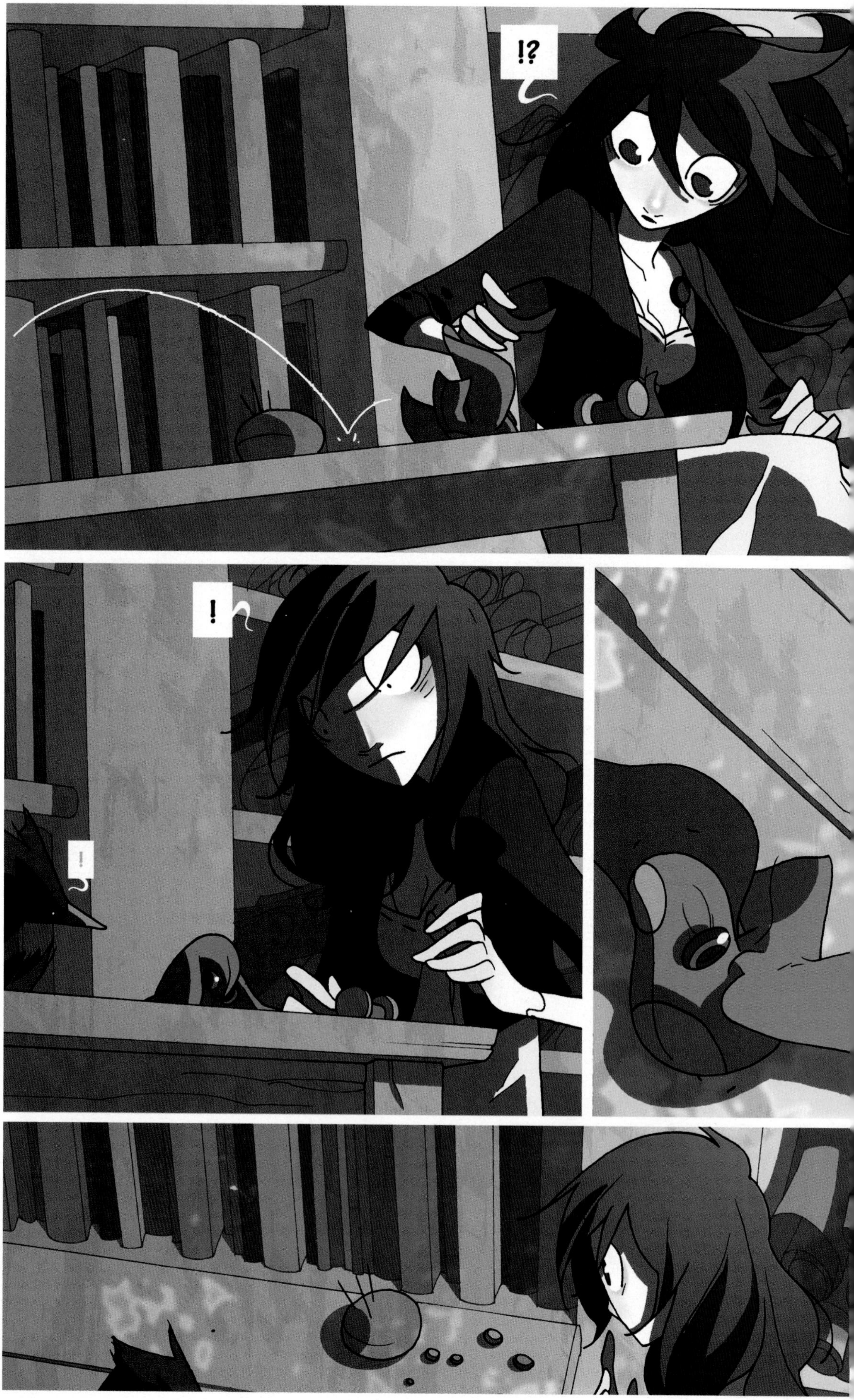

!?
!
!

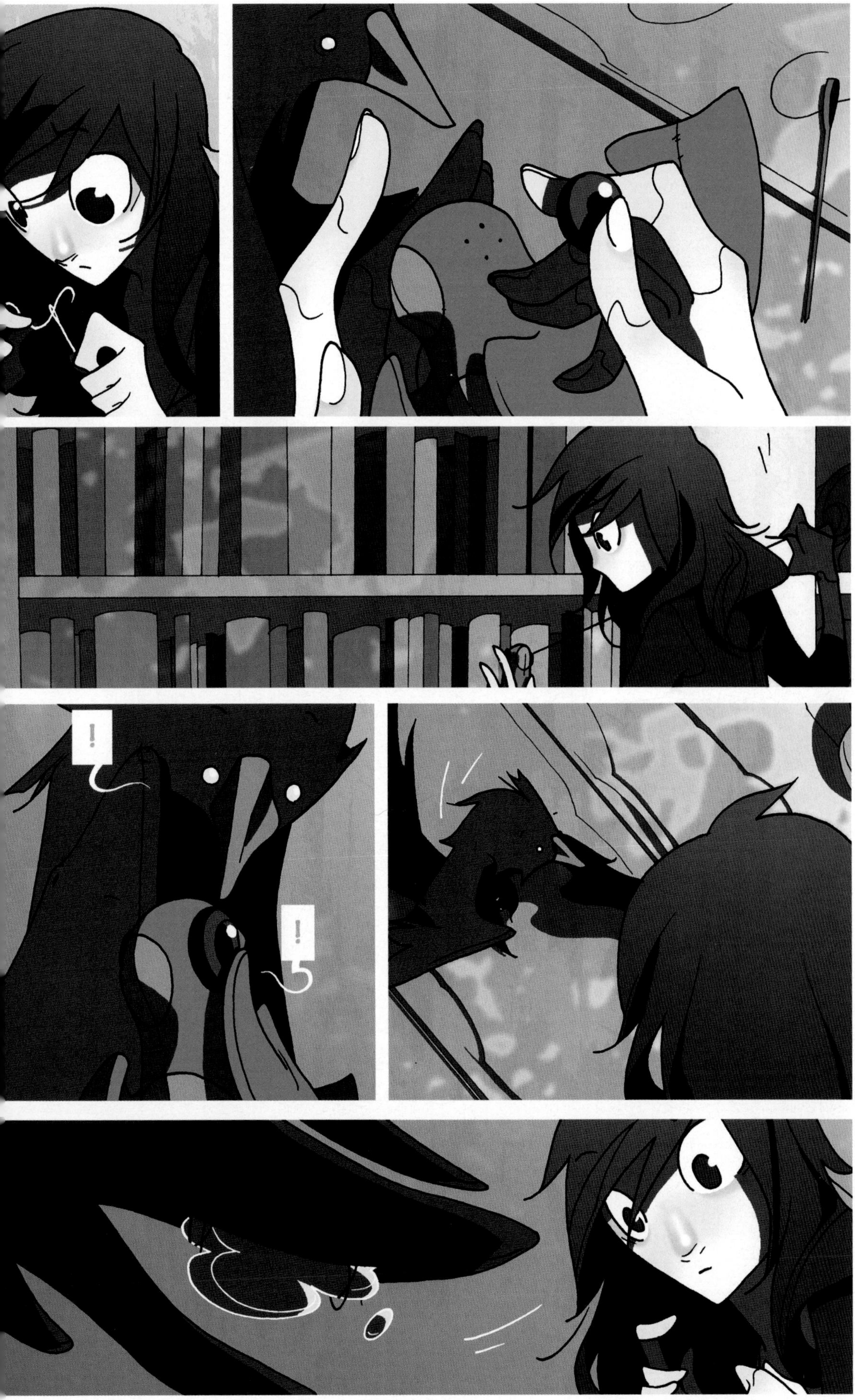
!
!

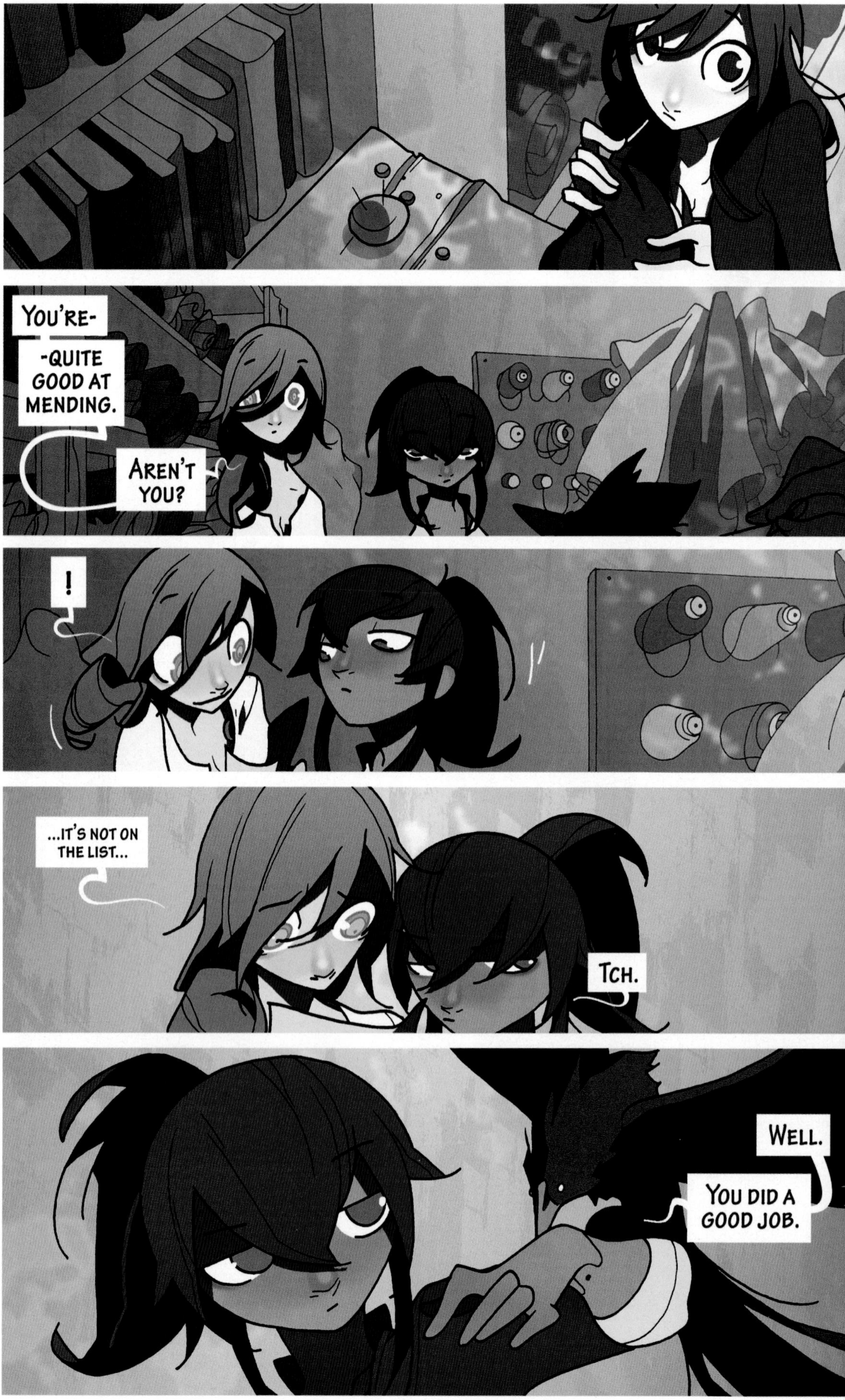
You're-
-quite good at mending.
Aren't you?
!
...it's not on the list...
Tch.
Well.
You did a good job.

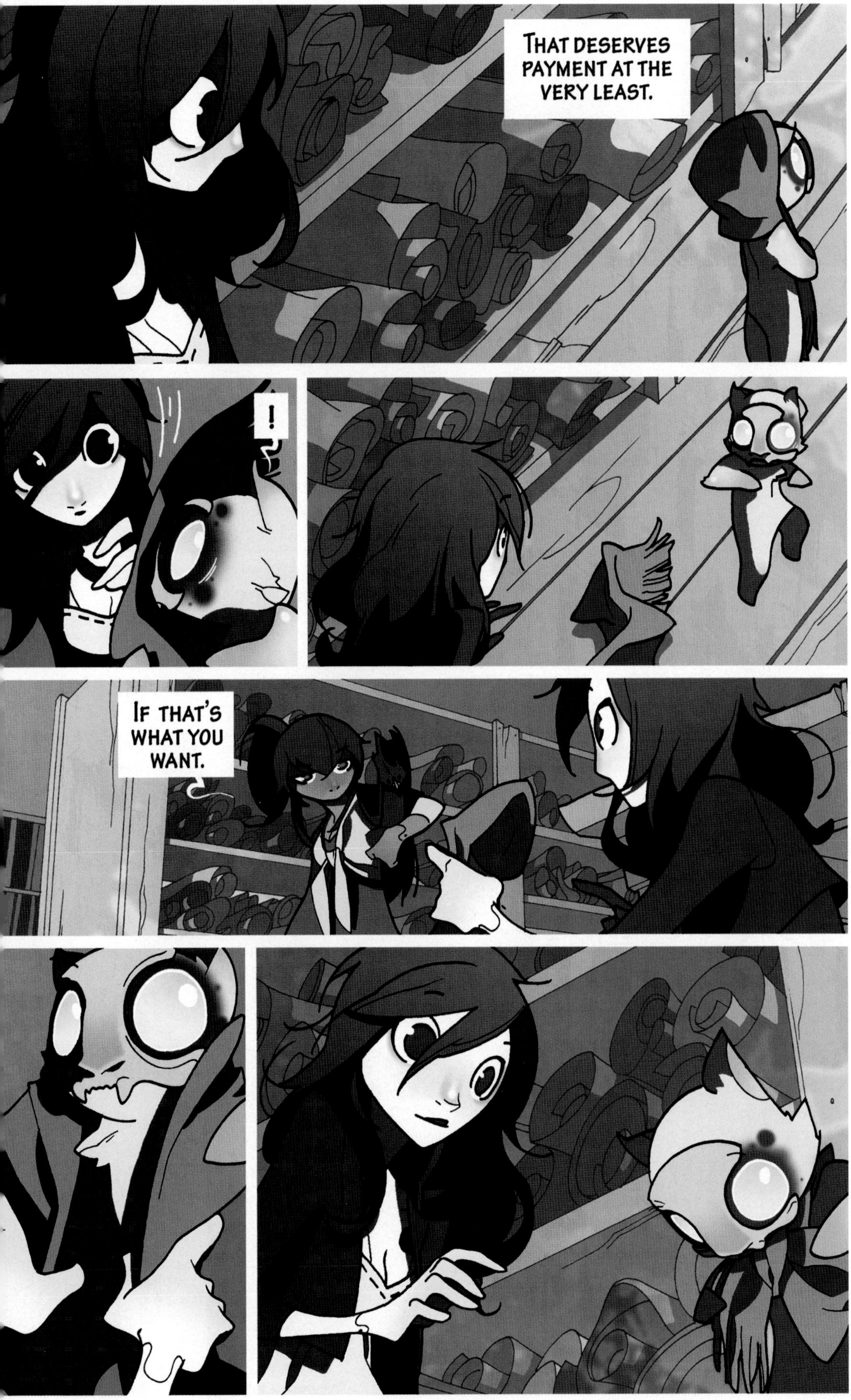
THAT DESERVES PAYMENT AT THE VERY LEAST.
!
IF THAT'S WHAT YOU WANT.

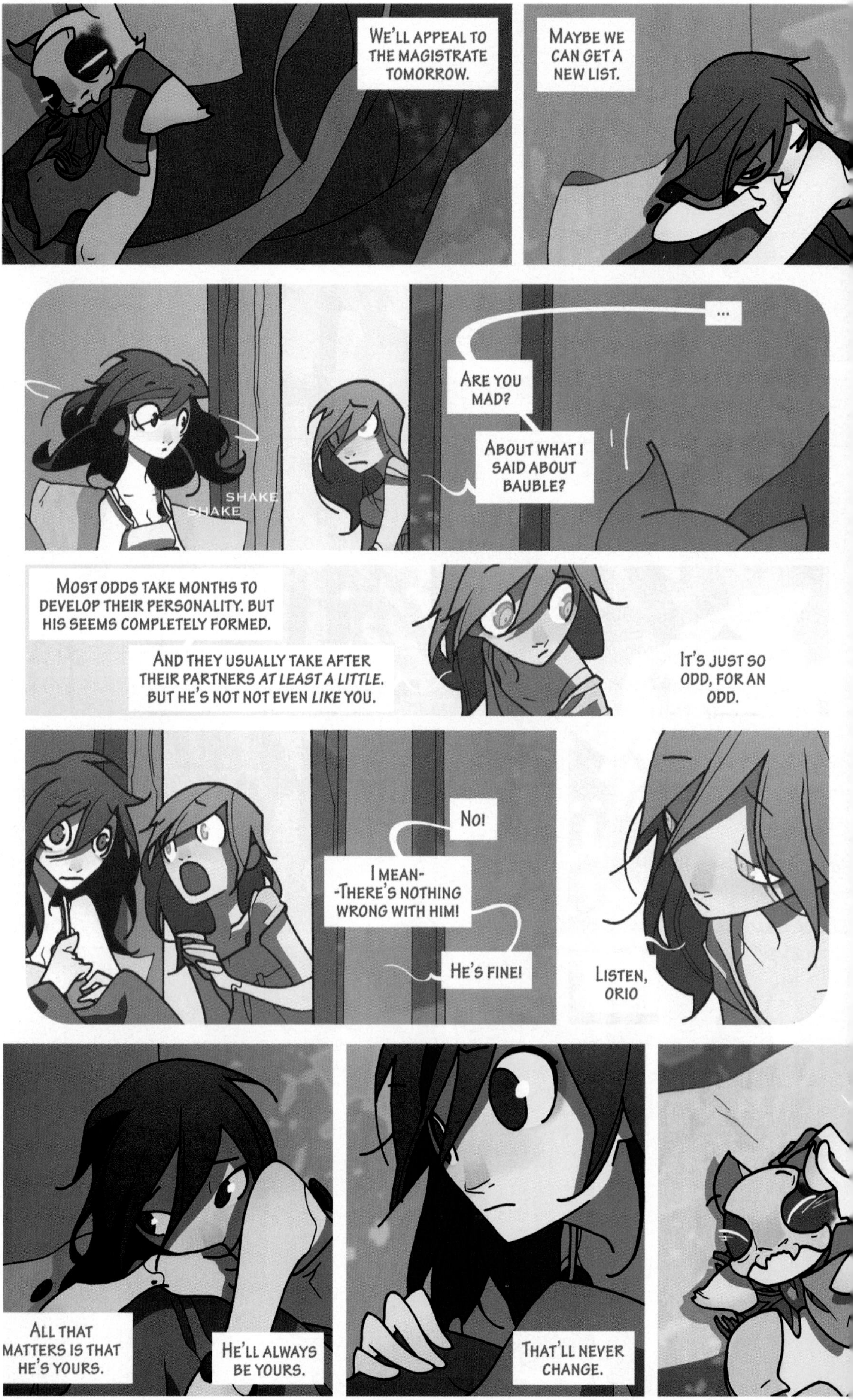
We'll appeal to the magistrate tomorrow.
Maybe we can get a new list.
...
Are you mad?
About what I said about Bauble?
SHAKE SHAKE
Most odds take months to develop their personality. But his seems completely formed.
And they usually take after their partners *at least a little*. But he's not not even *like* you.
It's just so odd, for an odd.
No!
I mean- -There's nothing wrong with him!
He's fine!
Listen, Orio
All that matters is that he's yours.
He'll always be yours.
That'll never change.

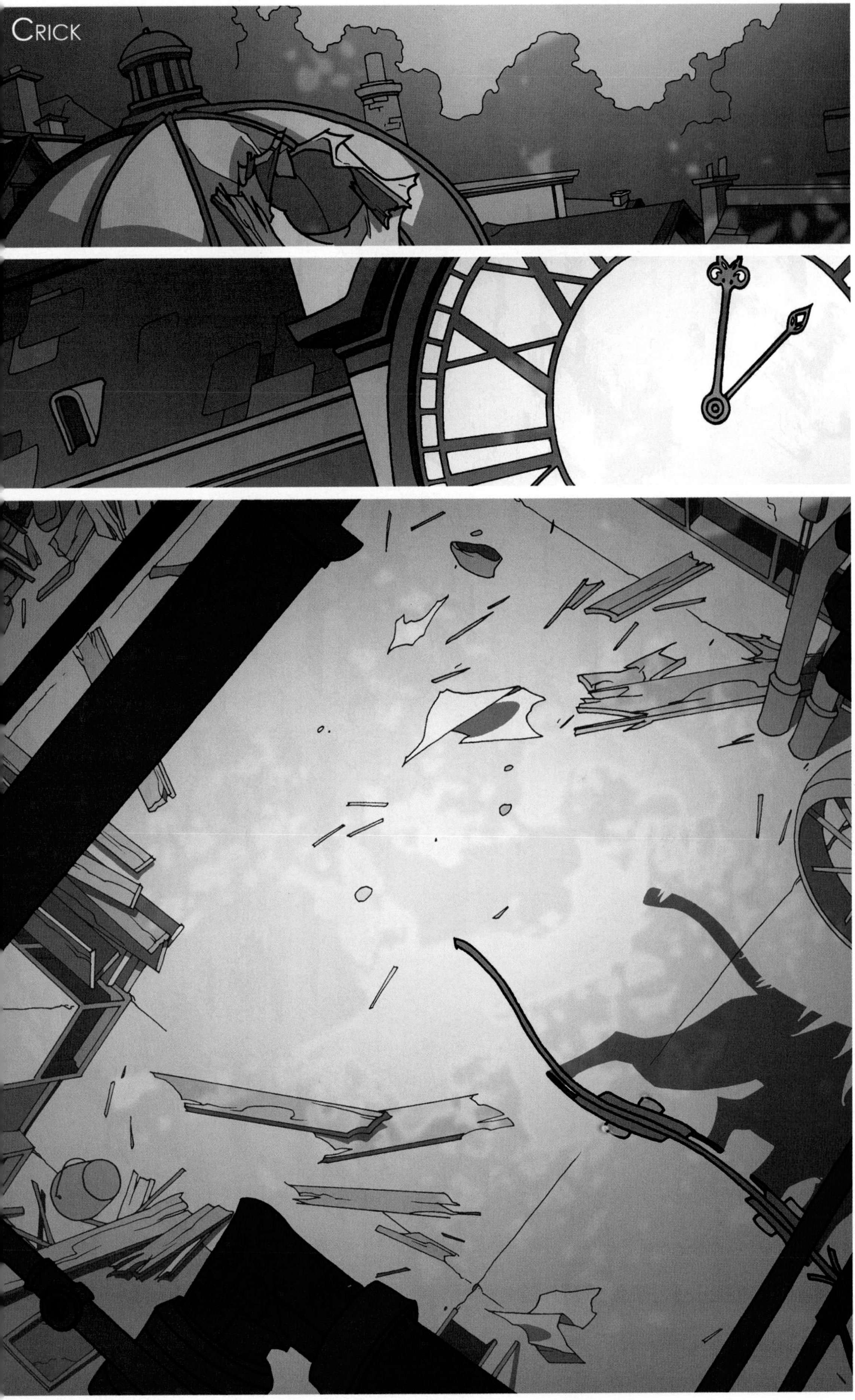
CRICK

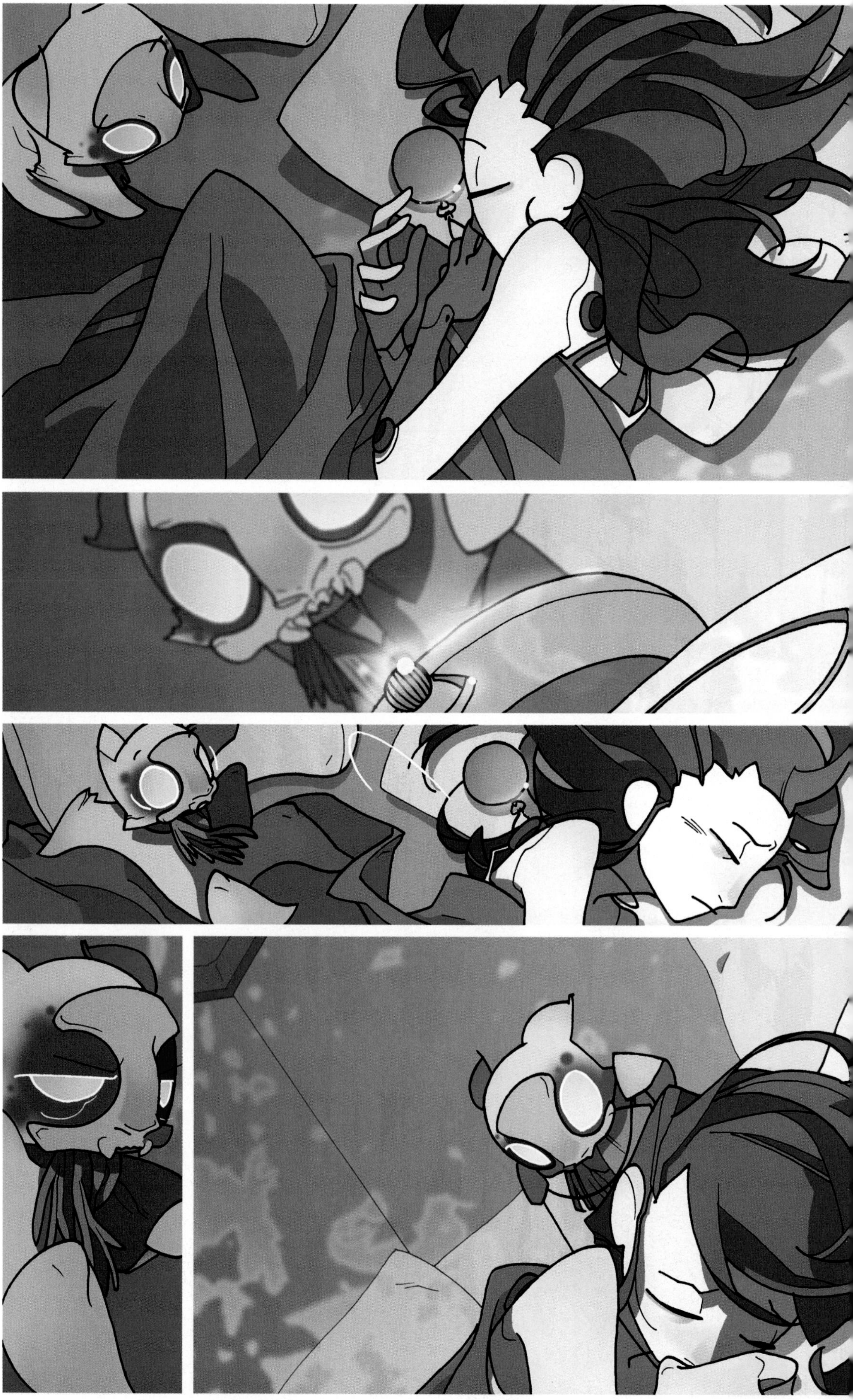

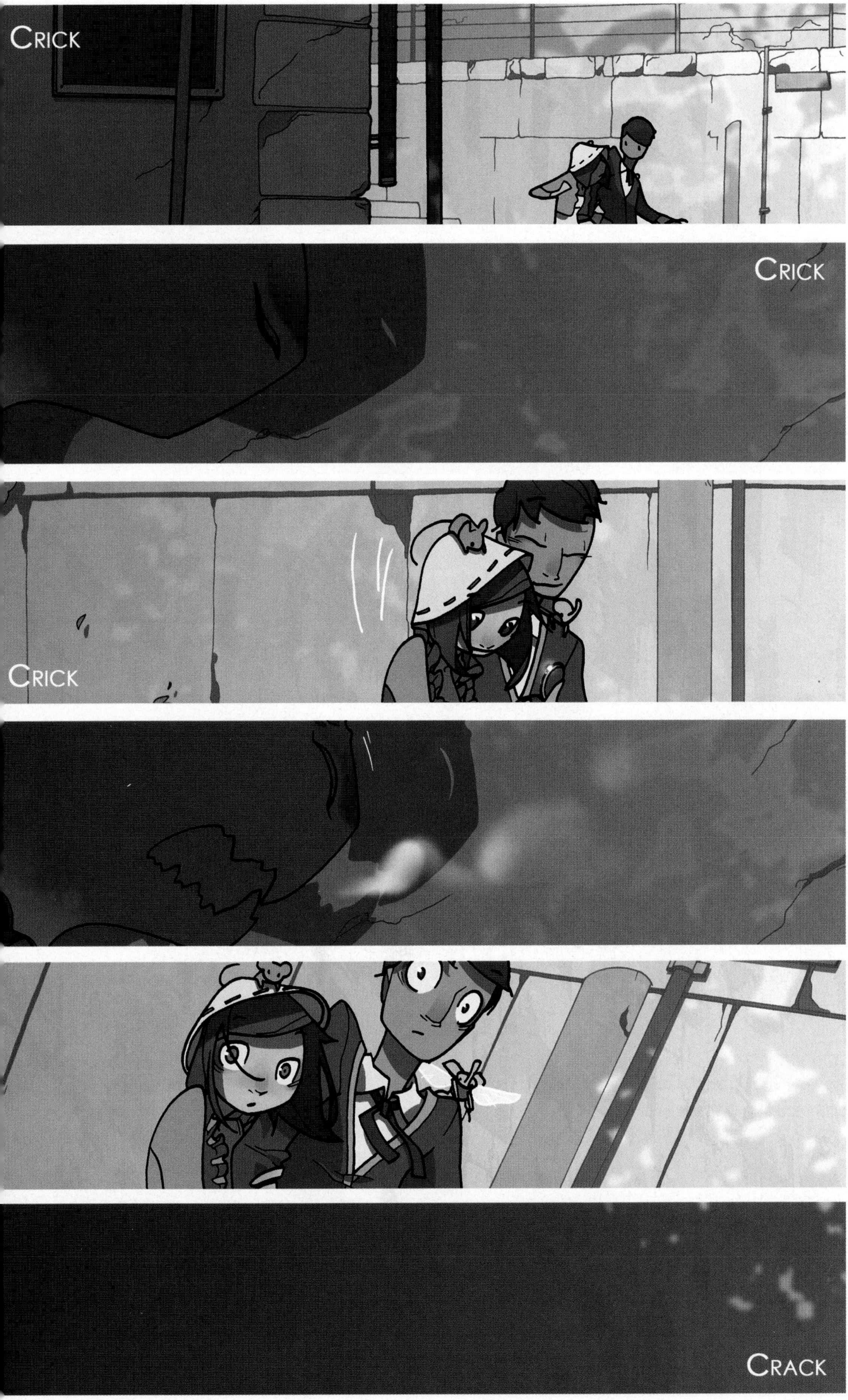
CRICK
CRICK
CRICK
CRACK

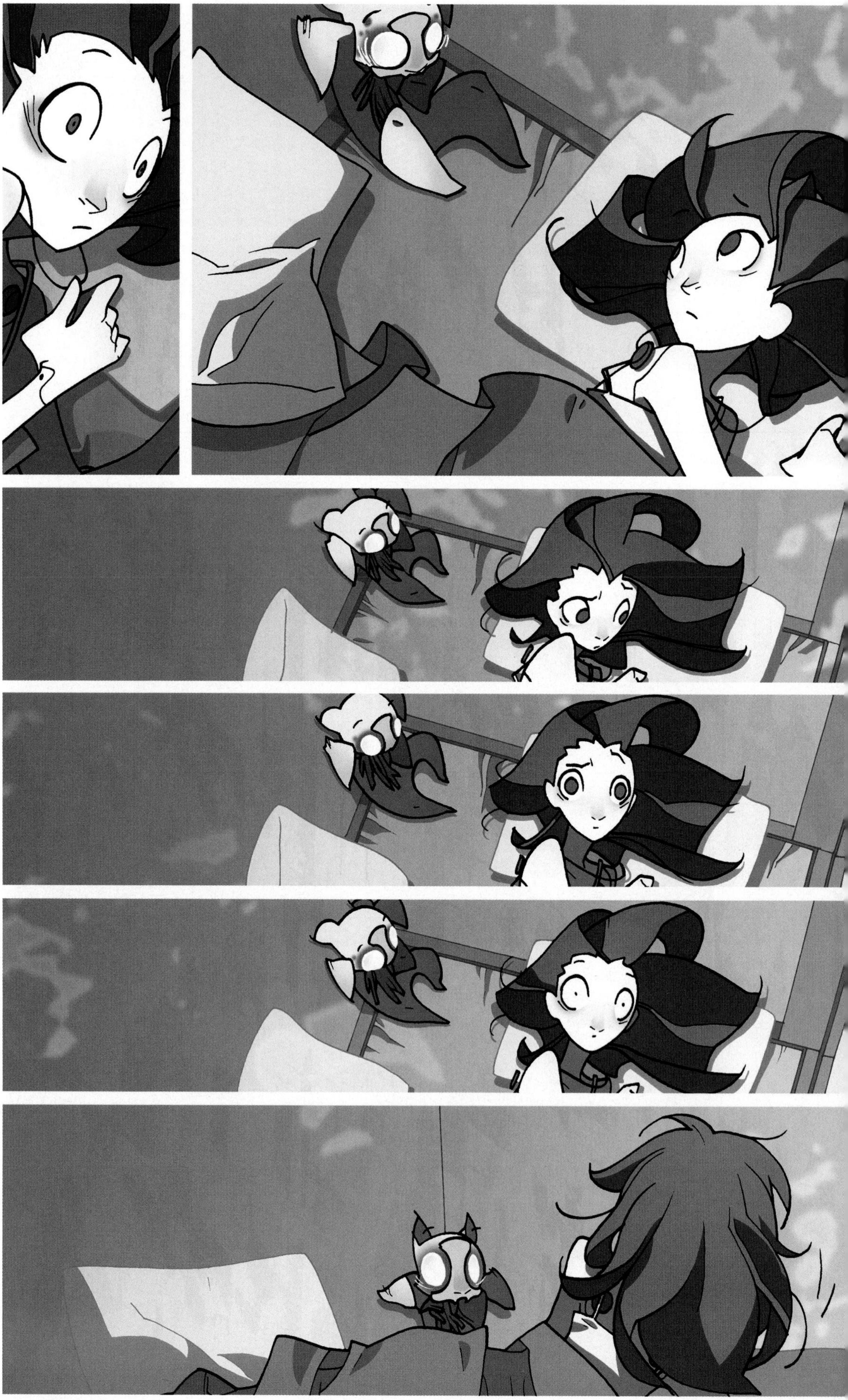

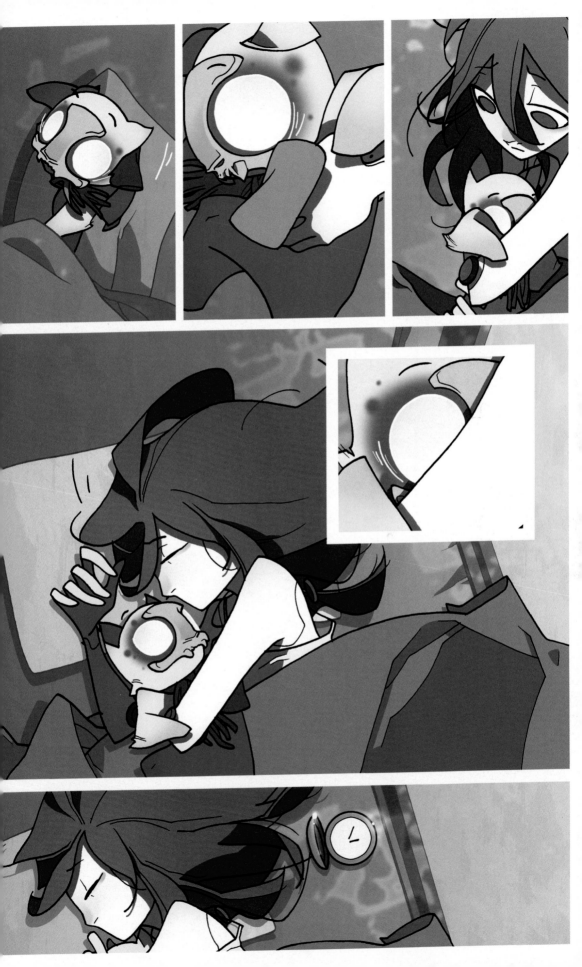

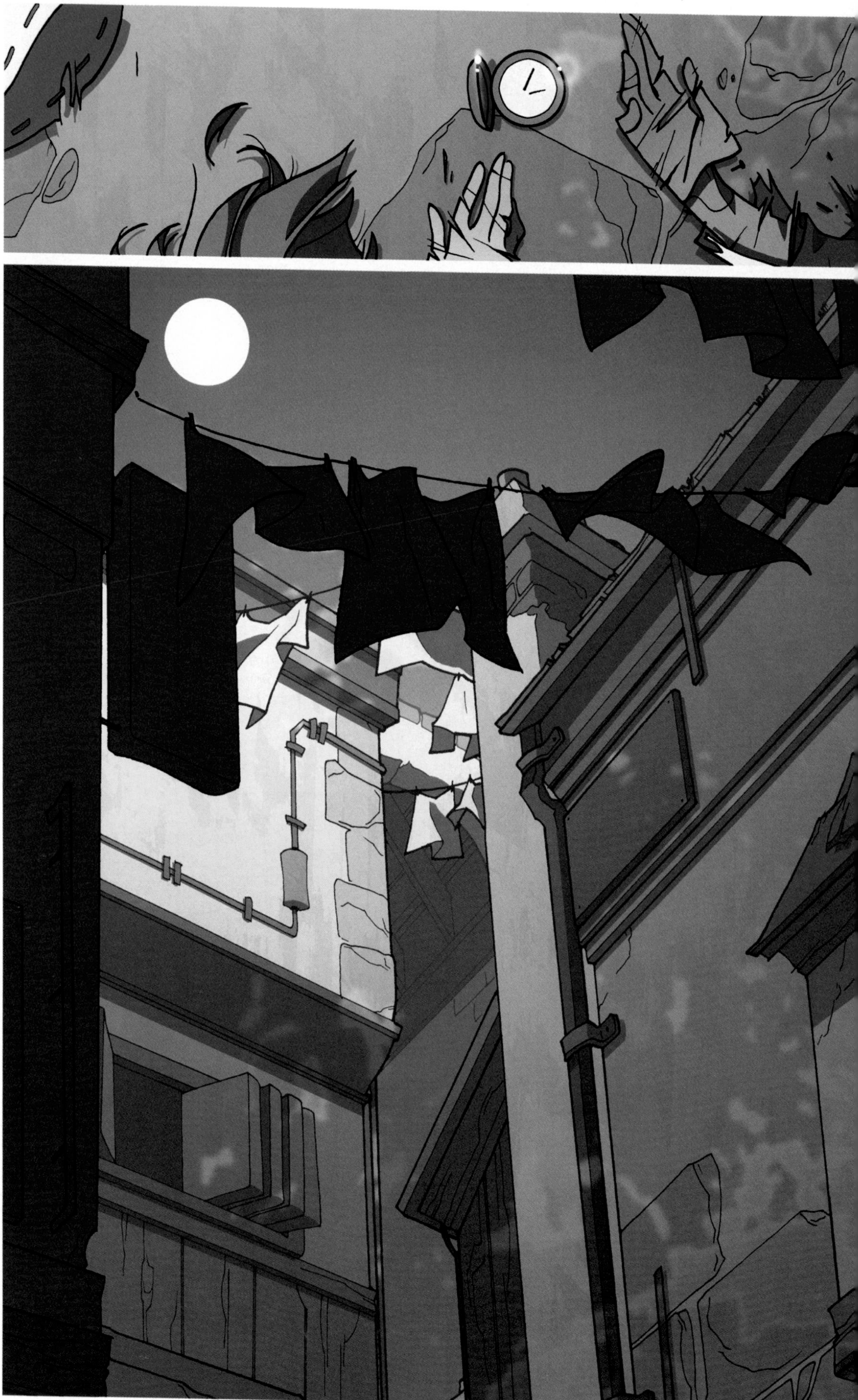

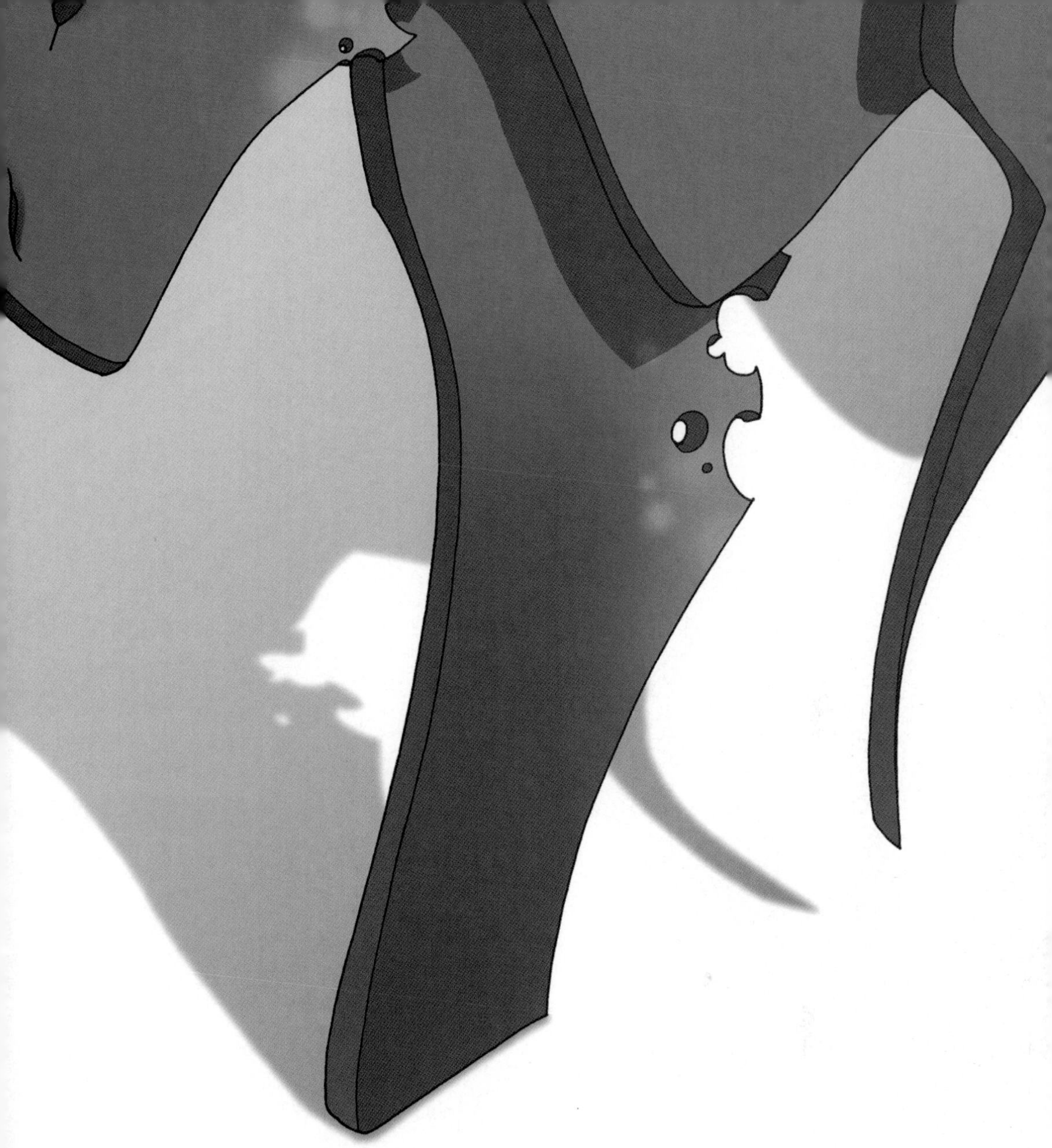

HINGES
CHAPTER 3

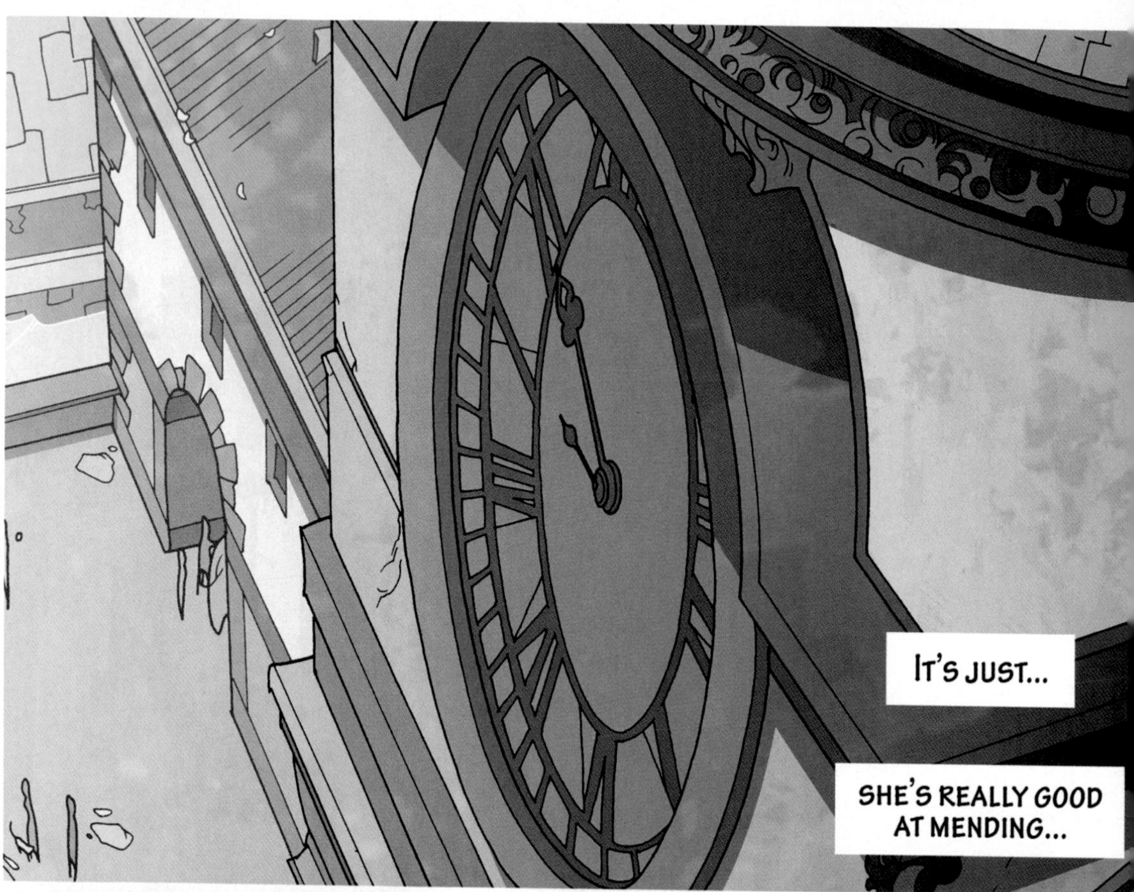
It's just...
She's really good at mending...

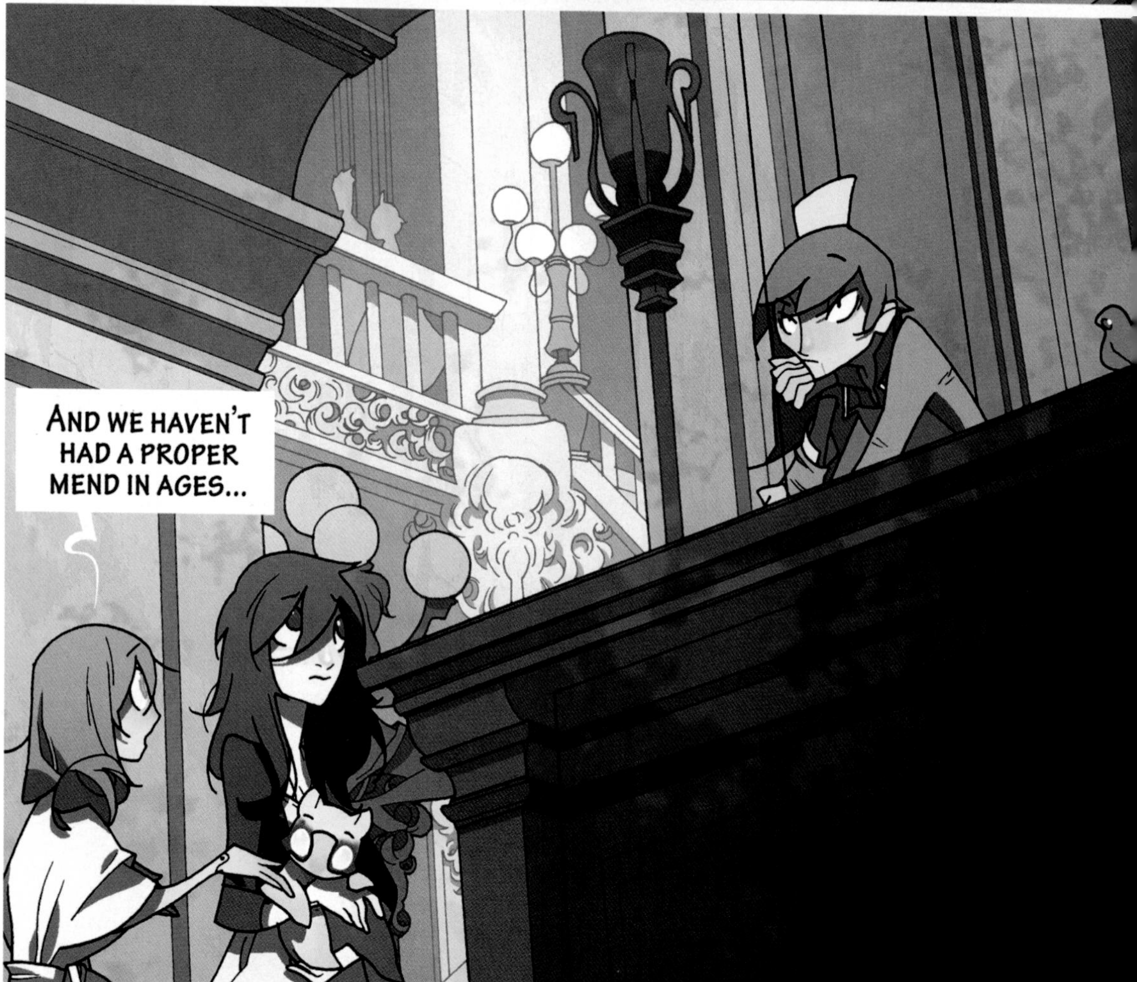
And we haven't had a proper mend in ages...

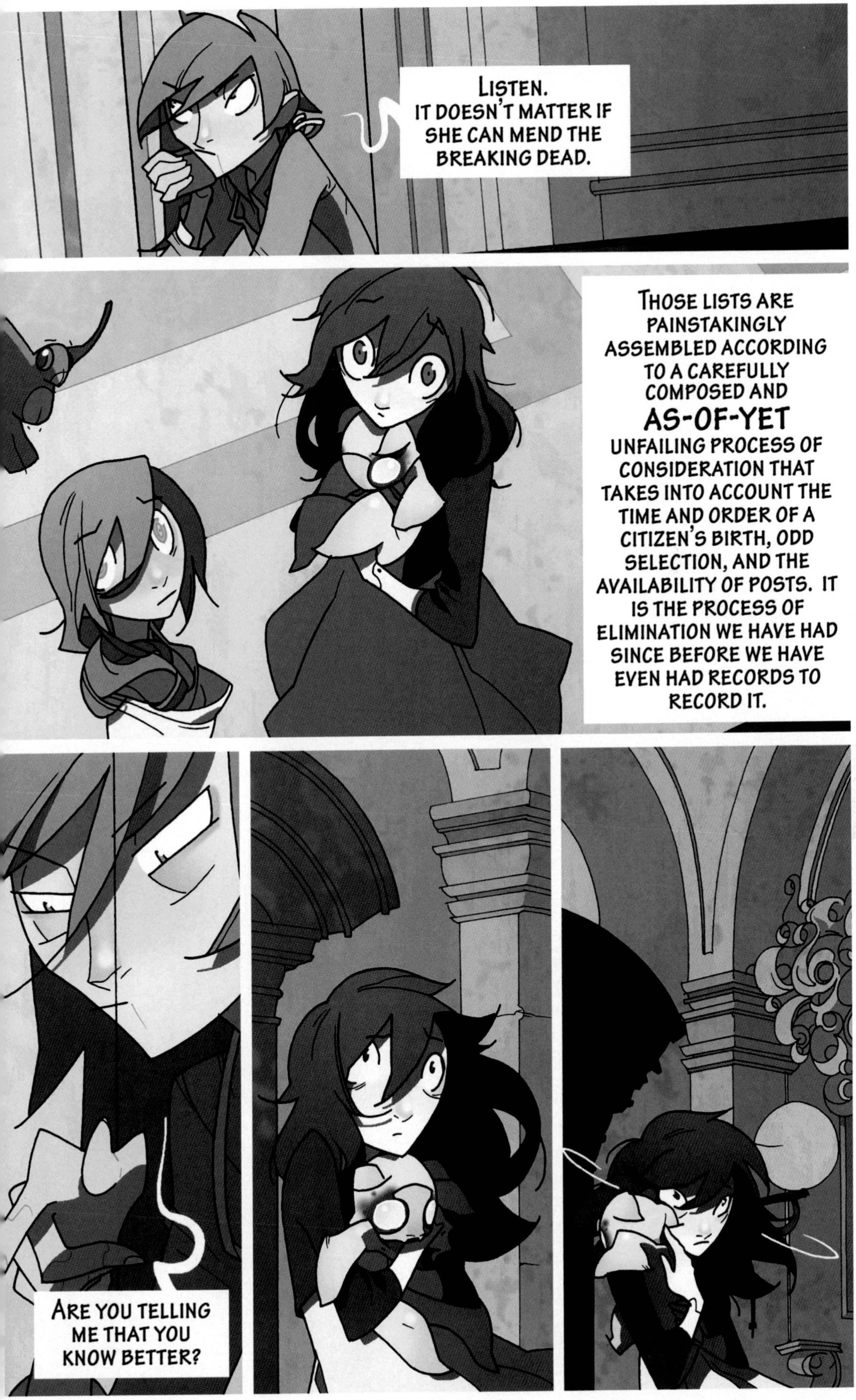
LISTEN. IT DOESN'T MATTER IF SHE CAN MEND THE BREAKING DEAD.
THOSE LISTS ARE PAINSTAKINGLY ASSEMBLED ACCORDING TO A CAREFULLY COMPOSED AND AS-OF-YET UNFAILING PROCESS OF CONSIDERATION THAT TAKES INTO ACCOUNT THE TIME AND ORDER OF A CITIZEN'S BIRTH, ODD SELECTION, AND THE AVAILABILITY OF POSTS. IT IS THE PROCESS OF ELIMINATION WE HAVE HAD SINCE BEFORE WE HAVE EVEN HAD RECORDS TO RECORD IT.
ARE YOU TELLING ME THAT YOU KNOW BETTER?

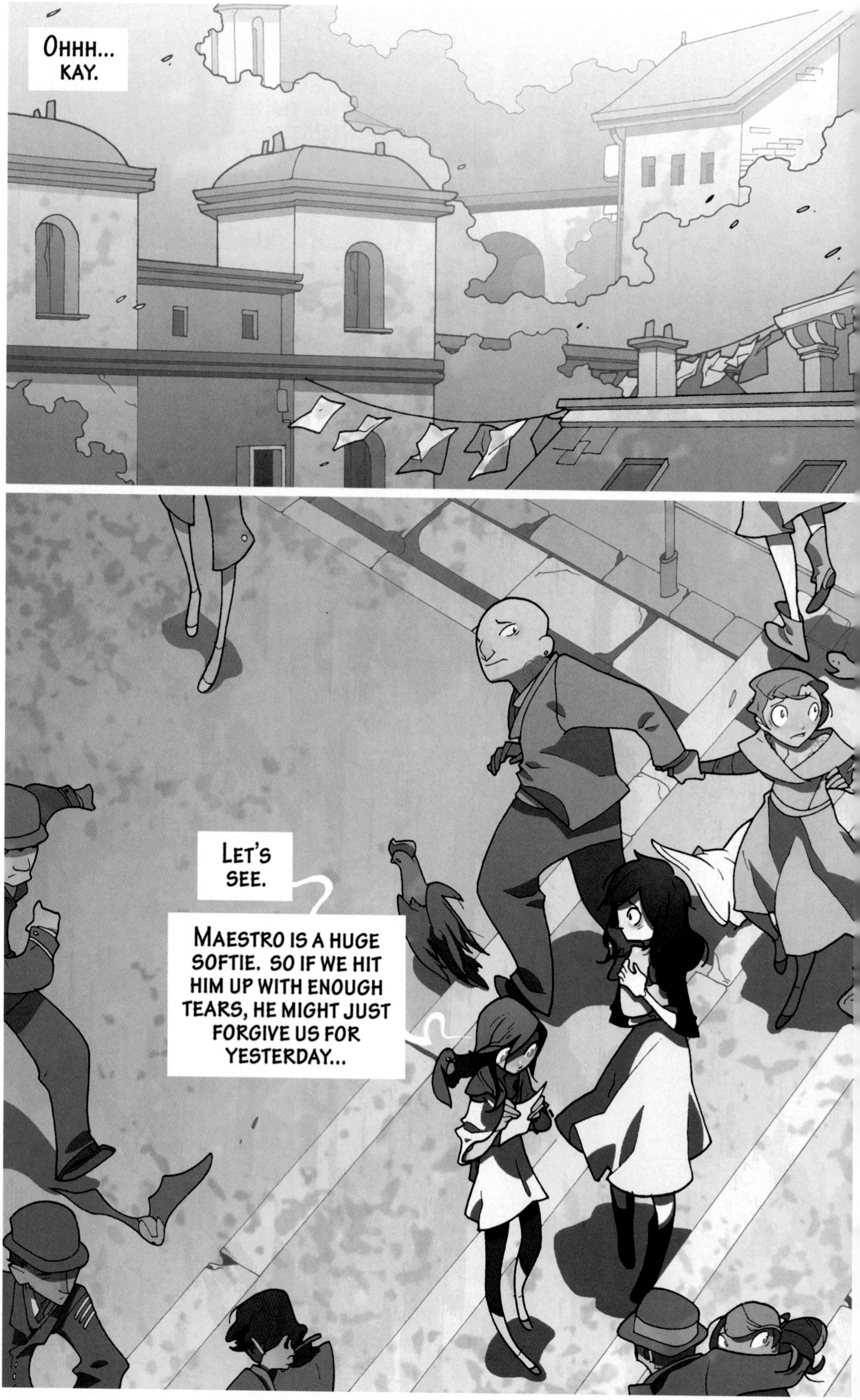
Ohhh... kay.
Let's see.
Maestro is a huge softie. So if we hit him up with enough tears, he might just forgive us for yesterday...

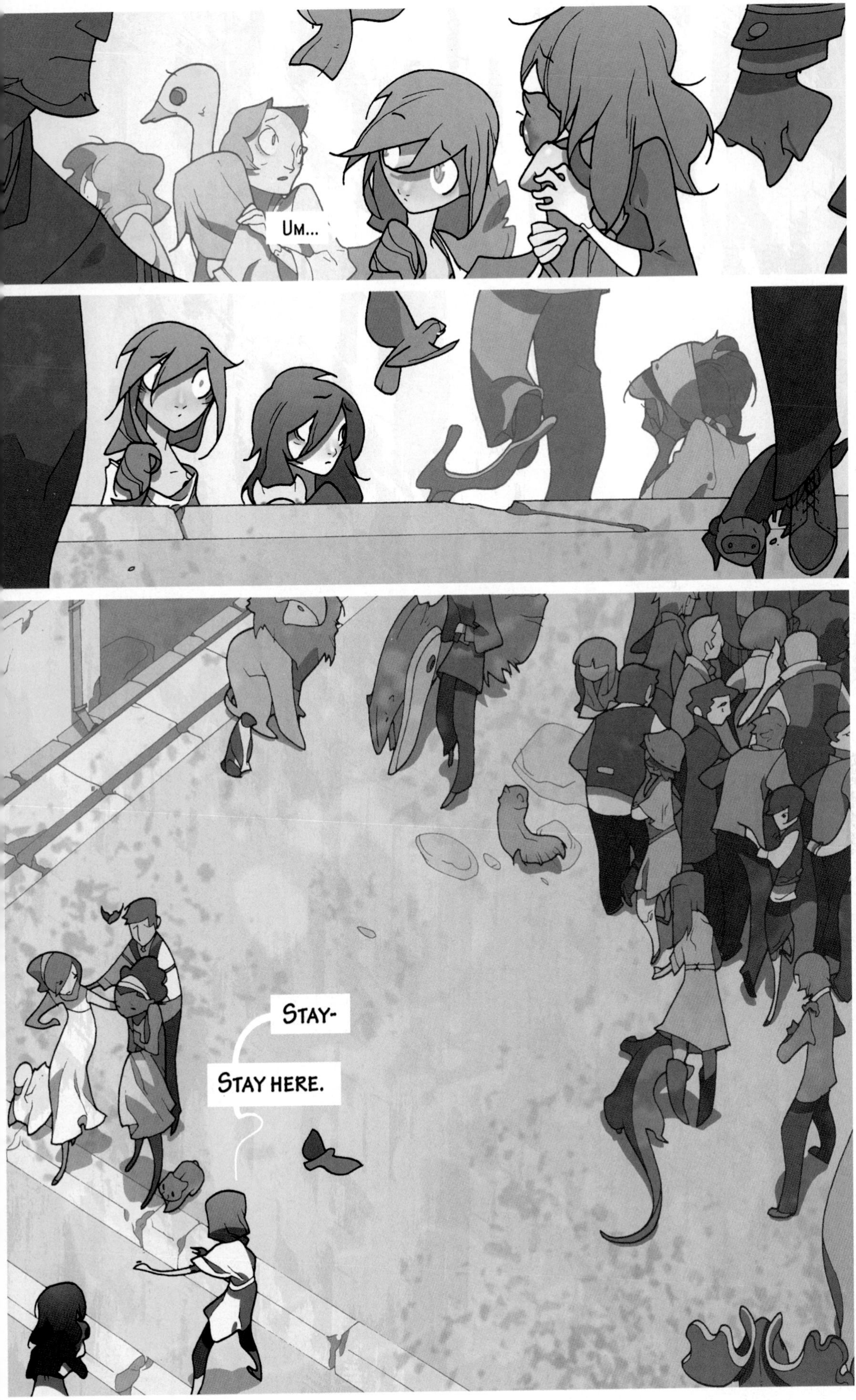
UM...
STAY-
STAY HERE.

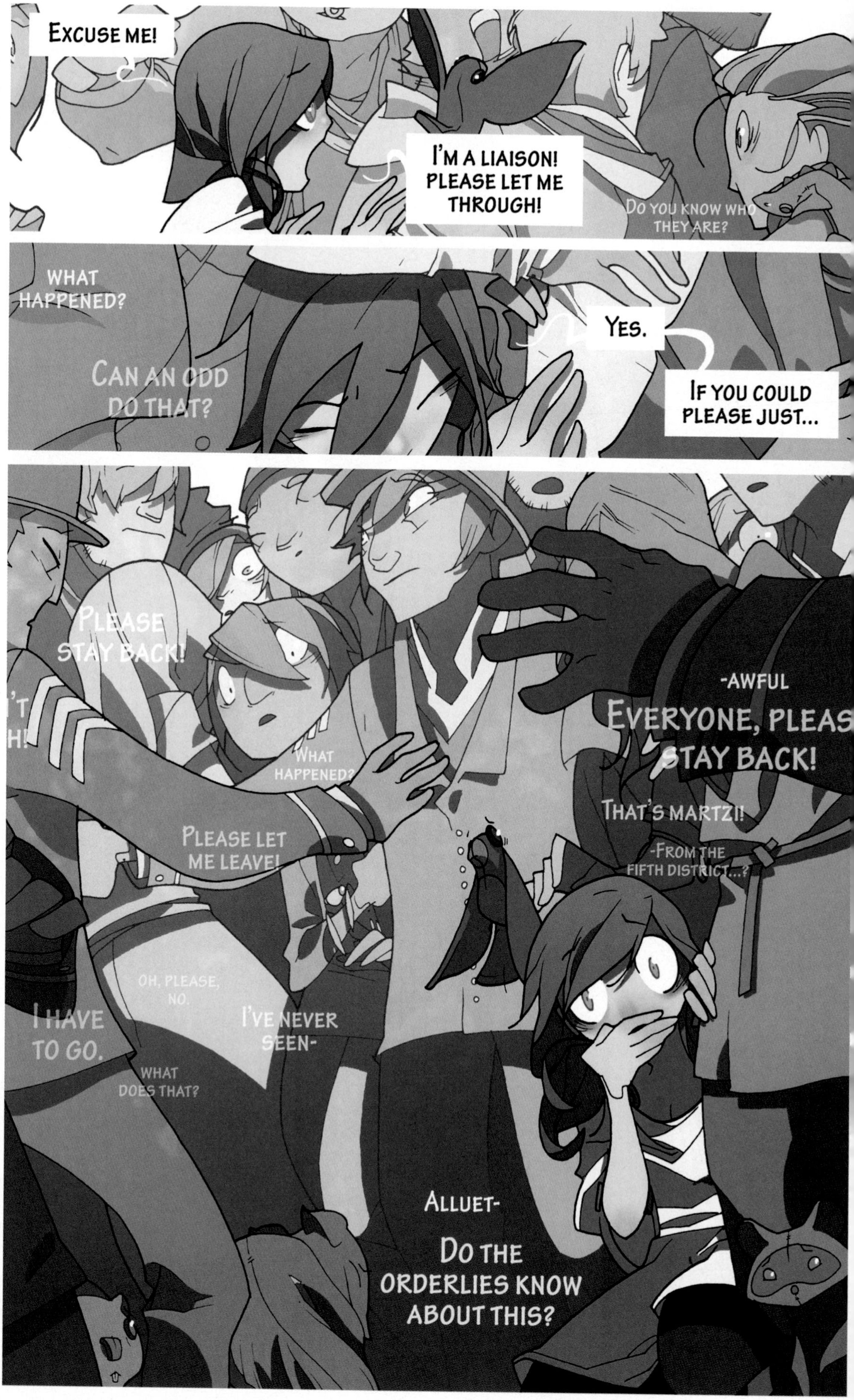

EXCUSE ME!
I'M A LIAISON! PLEASE LET ME THROUGH!
DO YOU KNOW WHO THEY ARE?
WHAT HAPPENED?
CAN AN ODD DO THAT?
YES.
IF YOU COULD PLEASE JUST...
PLEASE STAY BACK!
-AWFUL
EVERYONE, PLEAS STAY BACK!
WHAT HAPPENED?
THAT'S MARTZI!
PLEASE LET ME LEAVE!
-FROM THE FIFTH DISTRICT...?
OH, PLEASE, NO.
I HAVE TO GO.
I'VE NEVER SEEN-
WHAT DOES THAT?
ALLUET-
DO THE ORDERLIES KNOW ABOUT THIS?

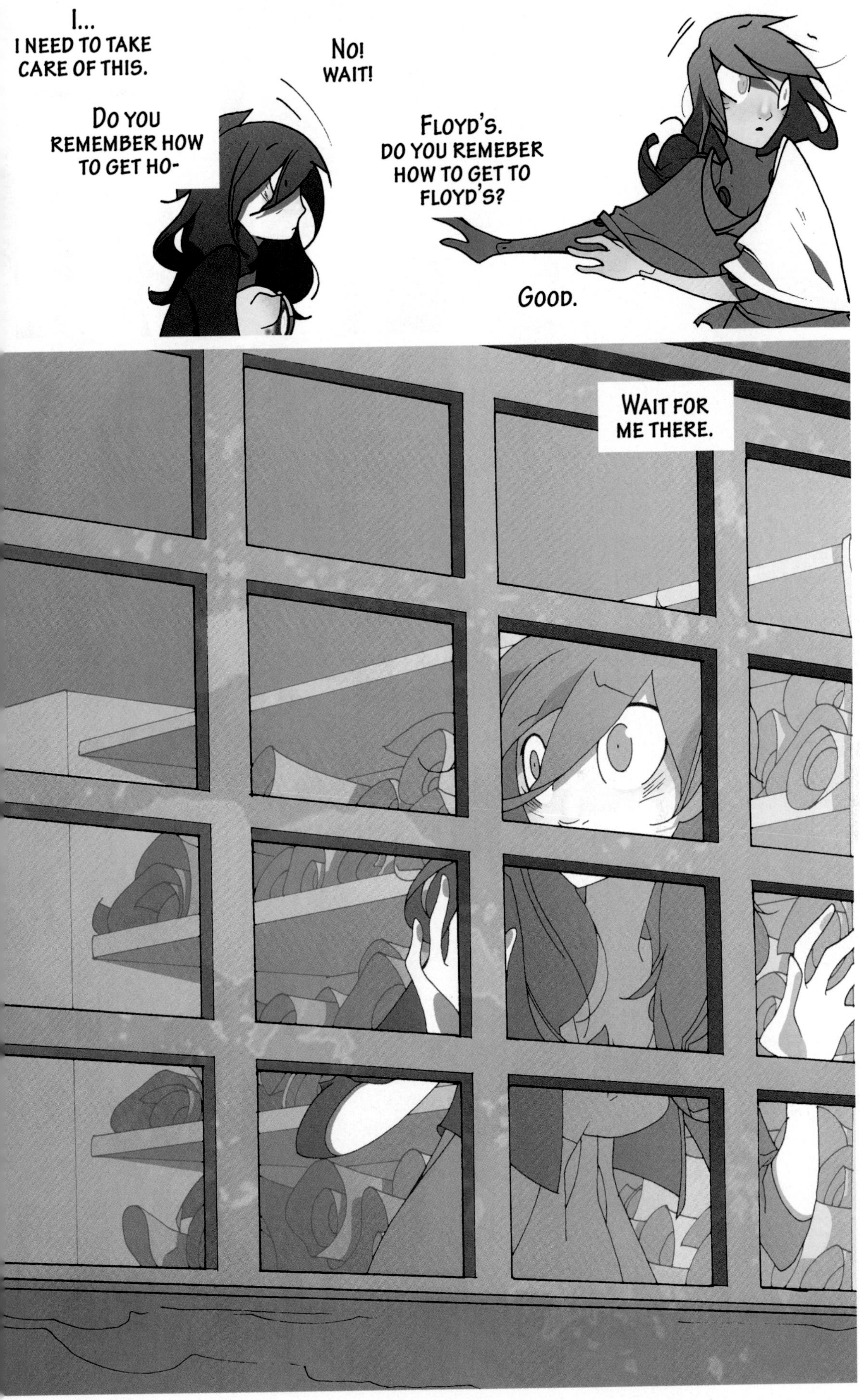
I...
I NEED TO TAKE CARE OF THIS.
DO YOU REMEMBER HOW TO GET HO-
NO! WAIT!
FLOYD'S. DO YOU REMEBER HOW TO GET TO FLOYD'S?
GOOD.
WAIT FOR ME THERE.

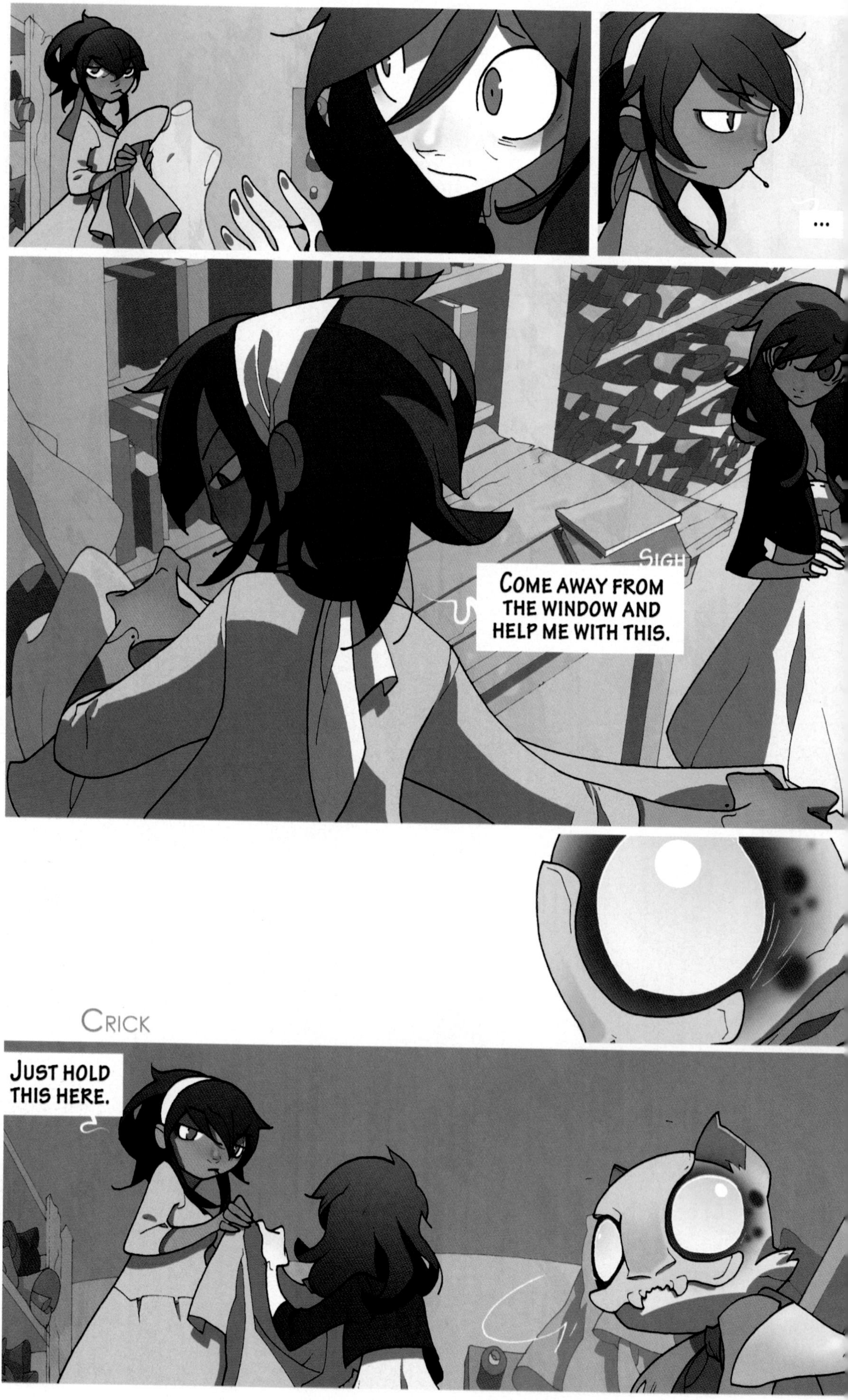
...
SIGH
COME AWAY FROM THE WINDOW AND HELP ME WITH THIS.
CRICK
JUST HOLD THIS HERE.

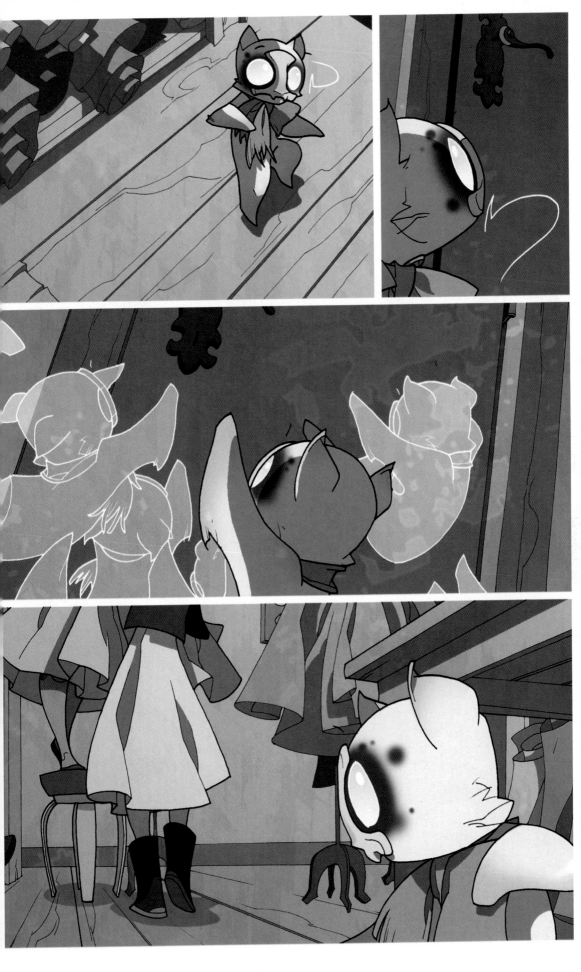

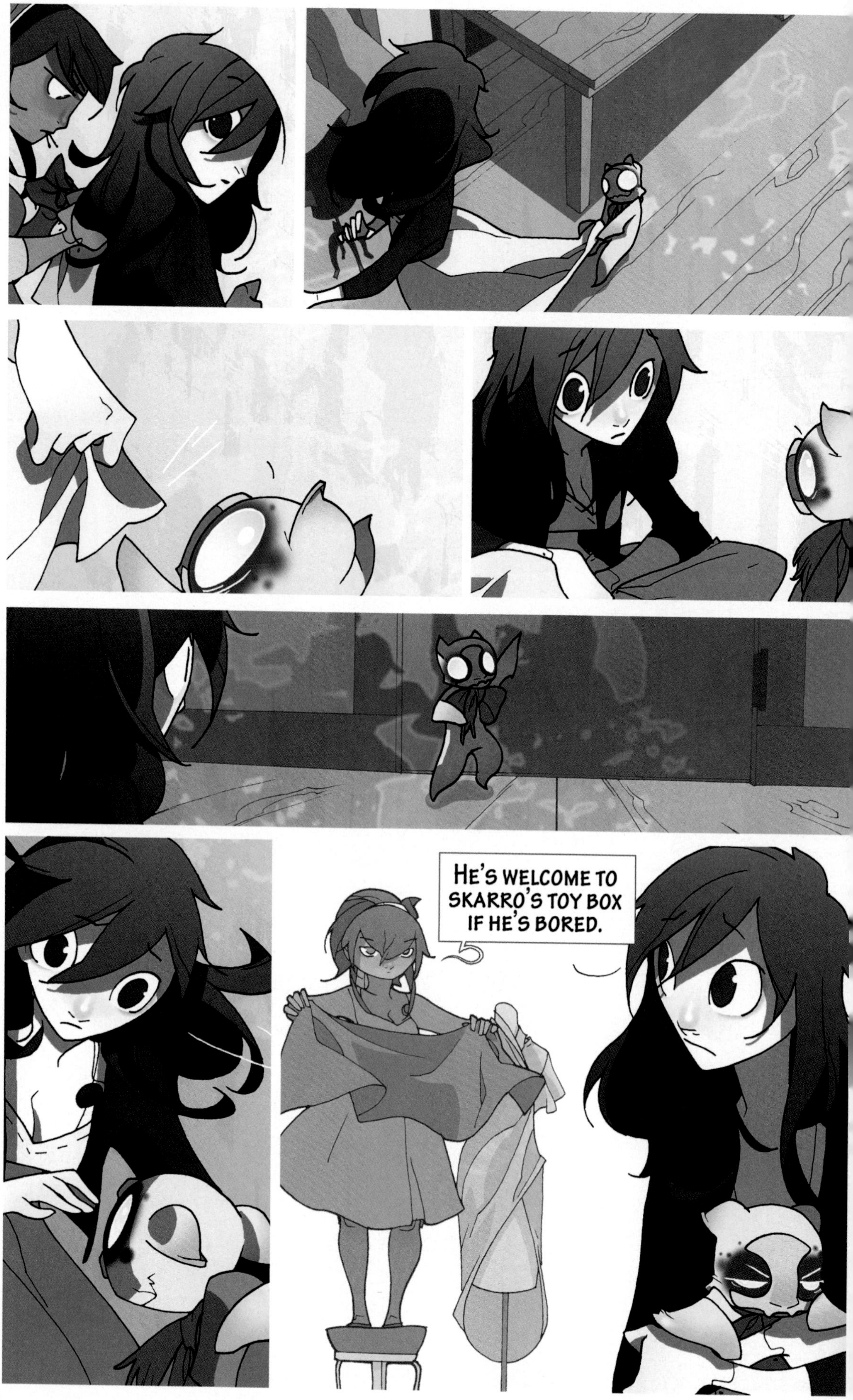
HE'S WELCOME TO SKARRO'S TOY BOX IF HE'S BORED.

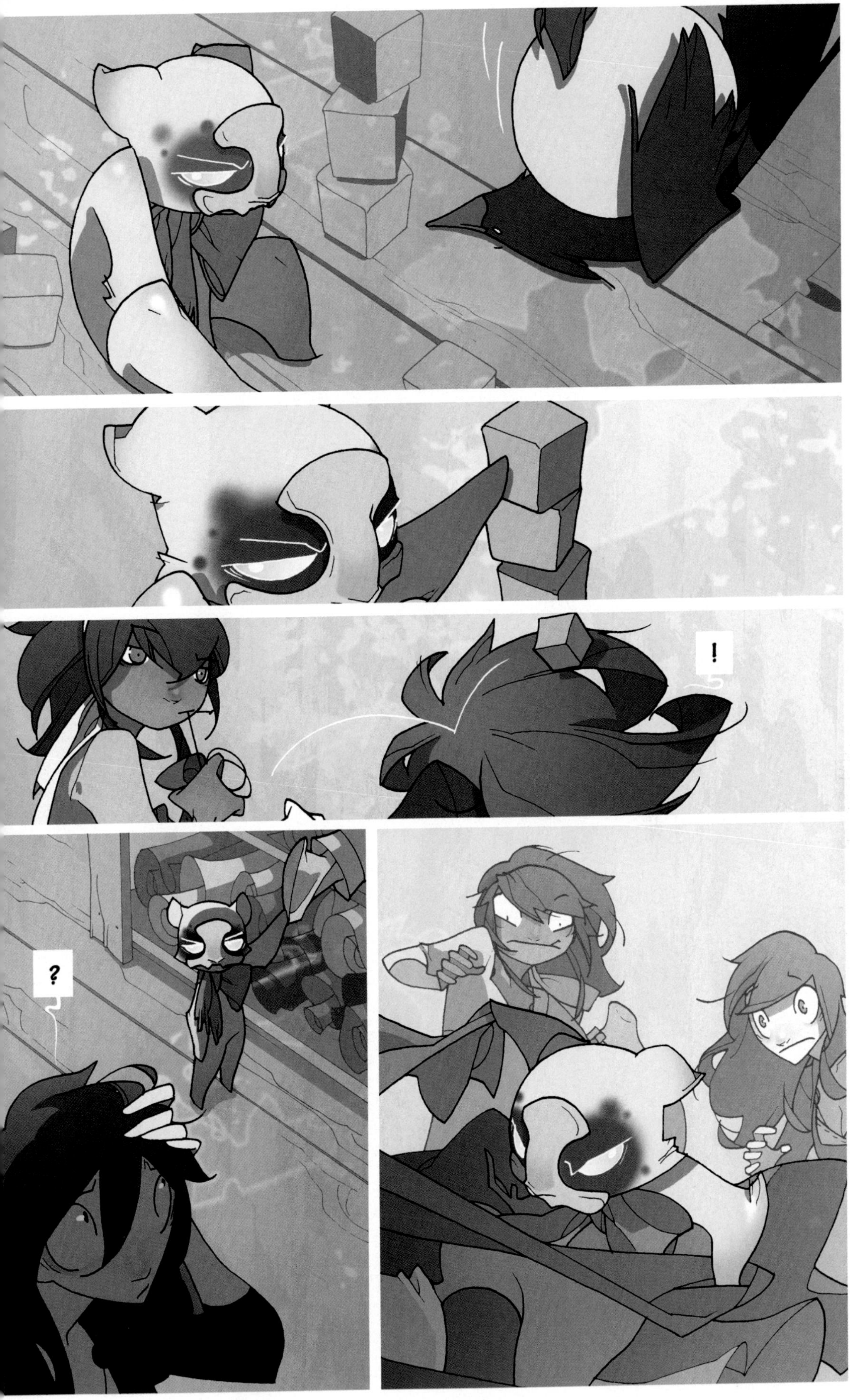
!
?

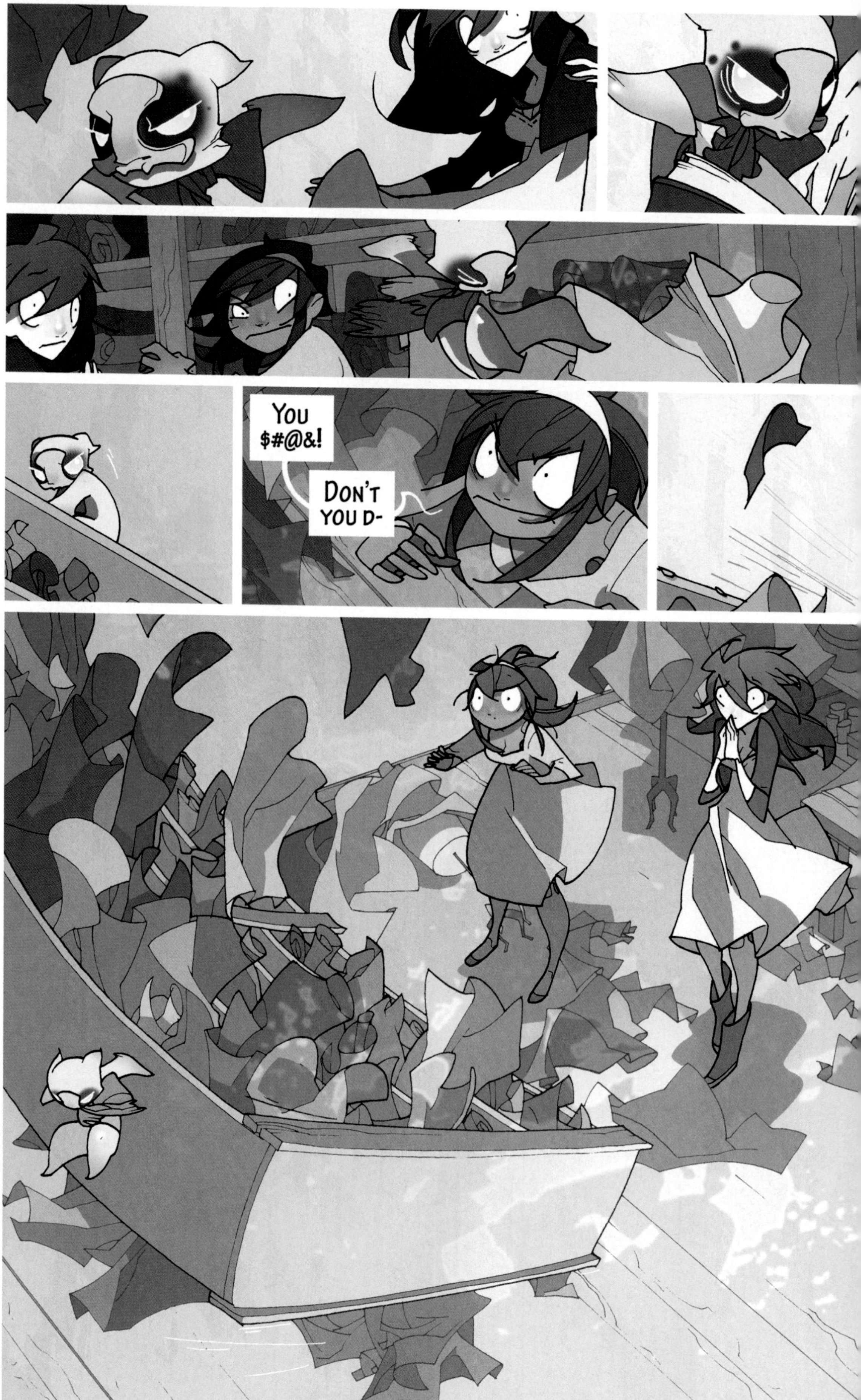

YOU $#@&!
DON'T YOU D-

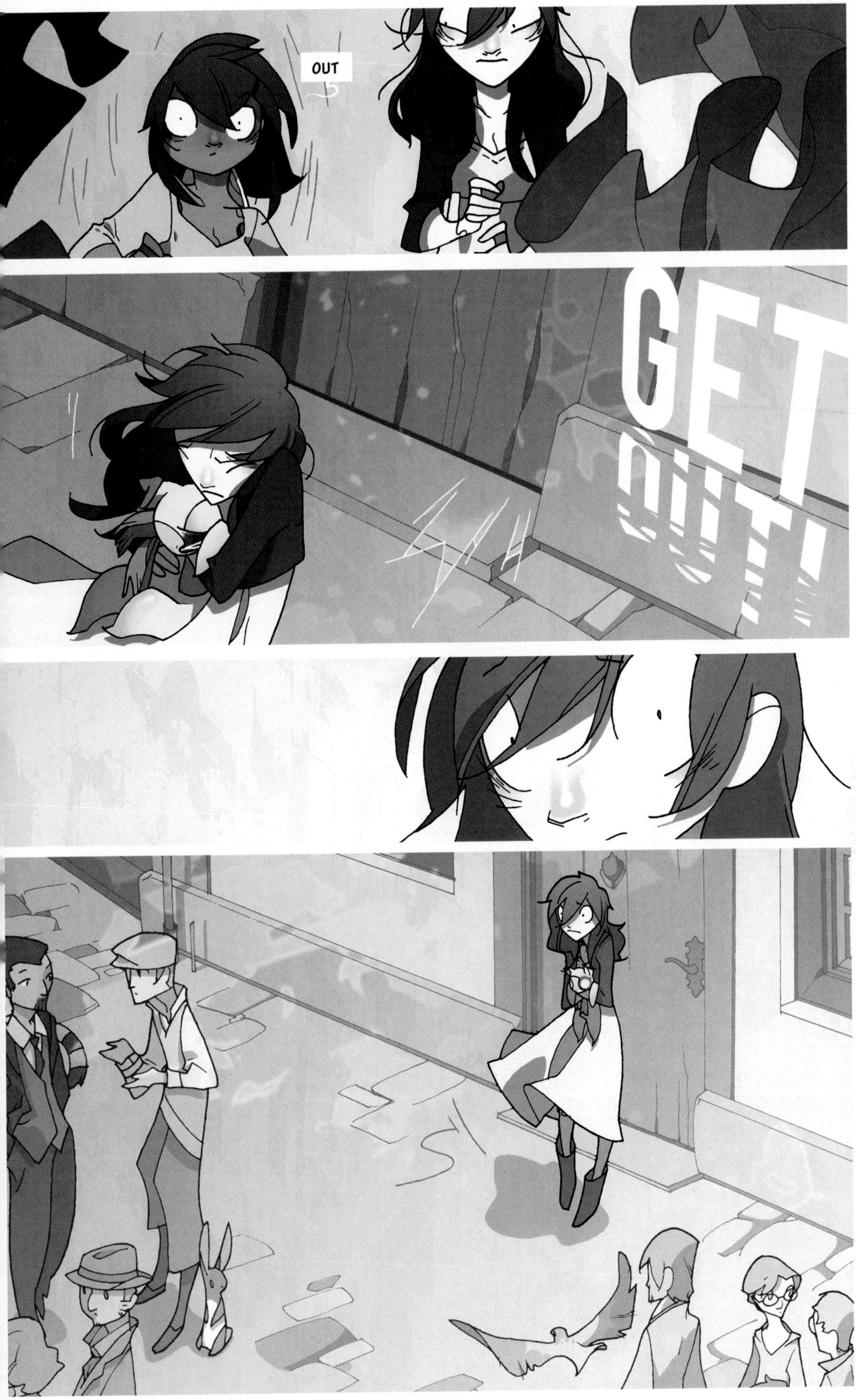
OUT
GET OUT!!

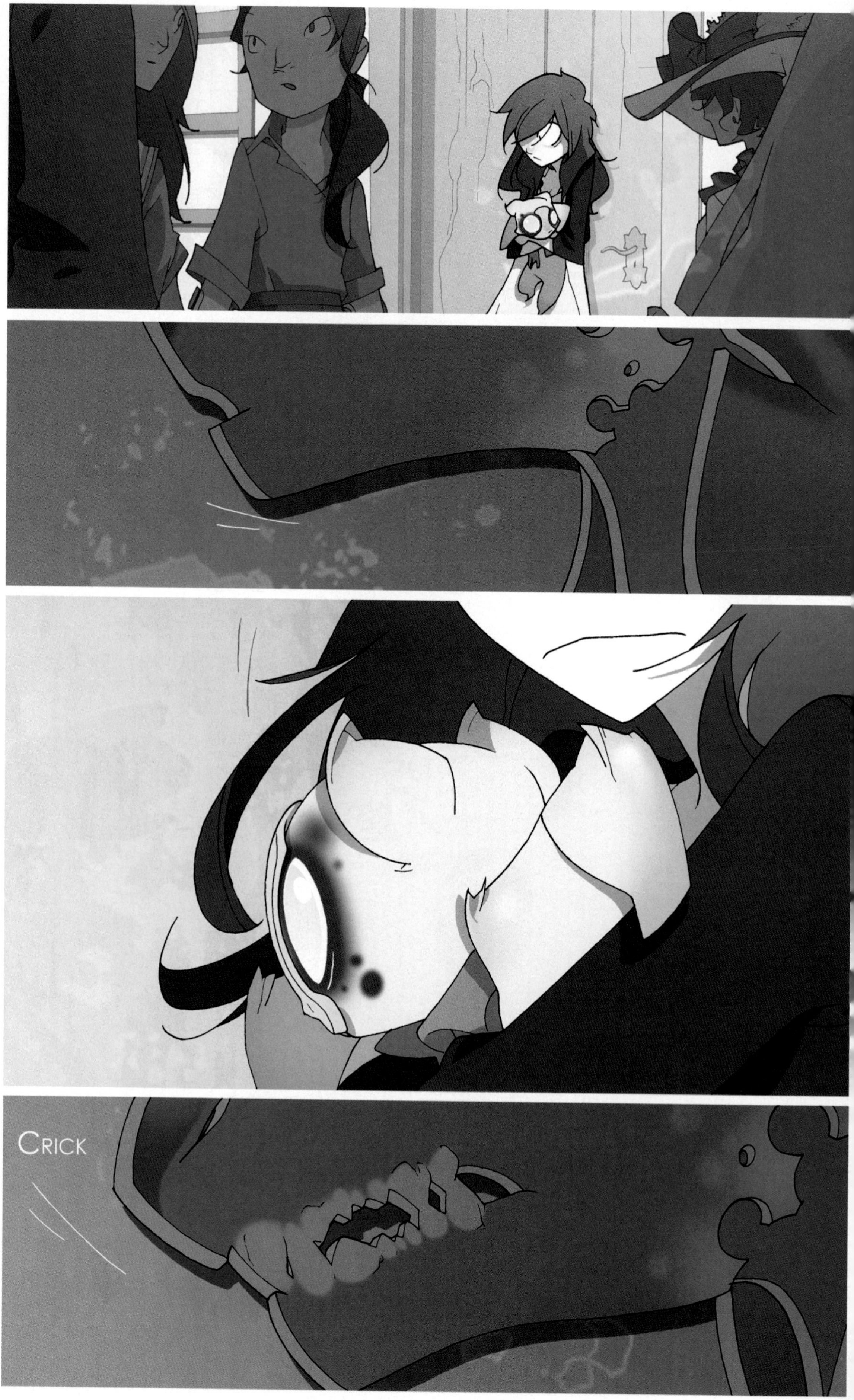
CRICK

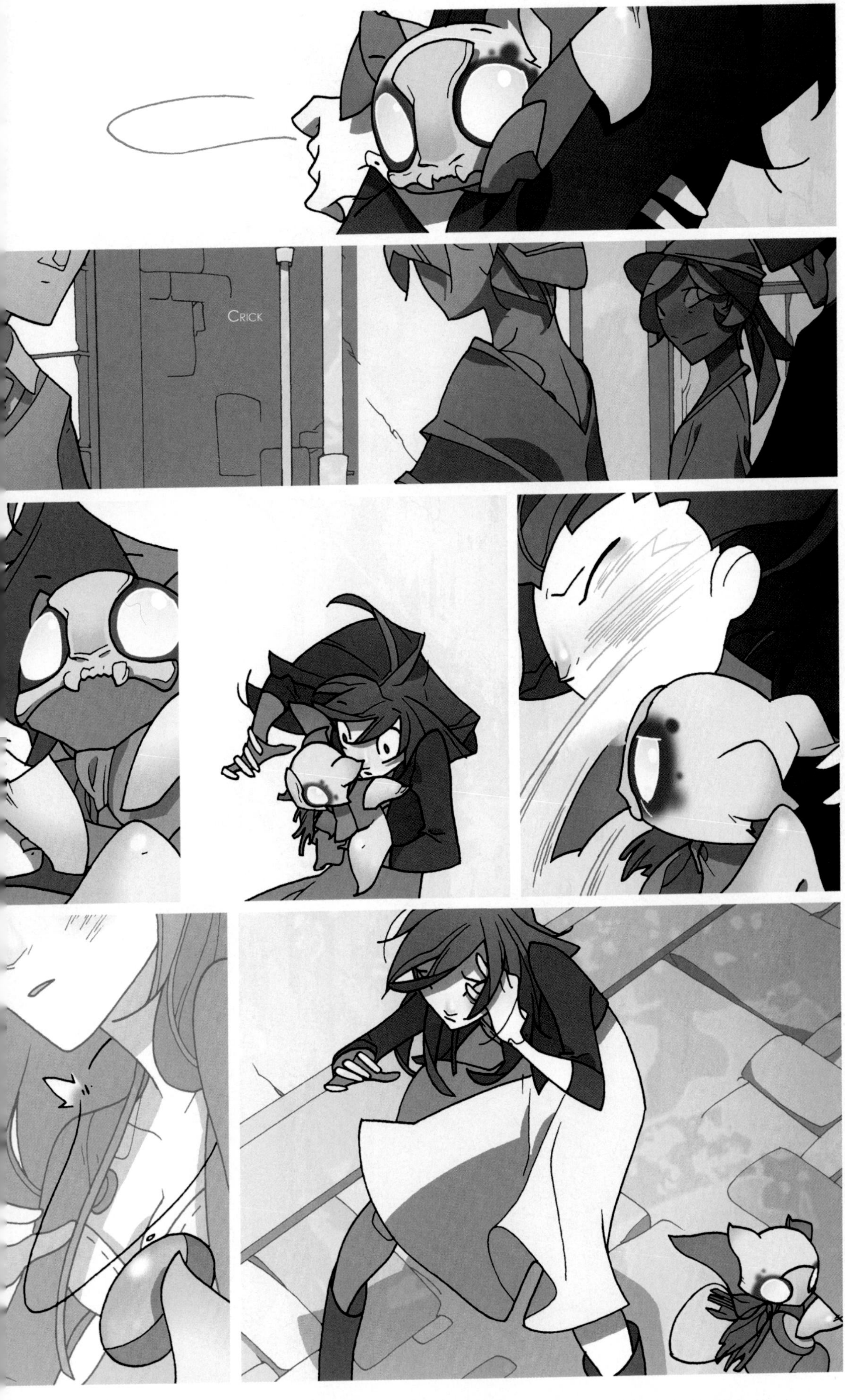
CRICK

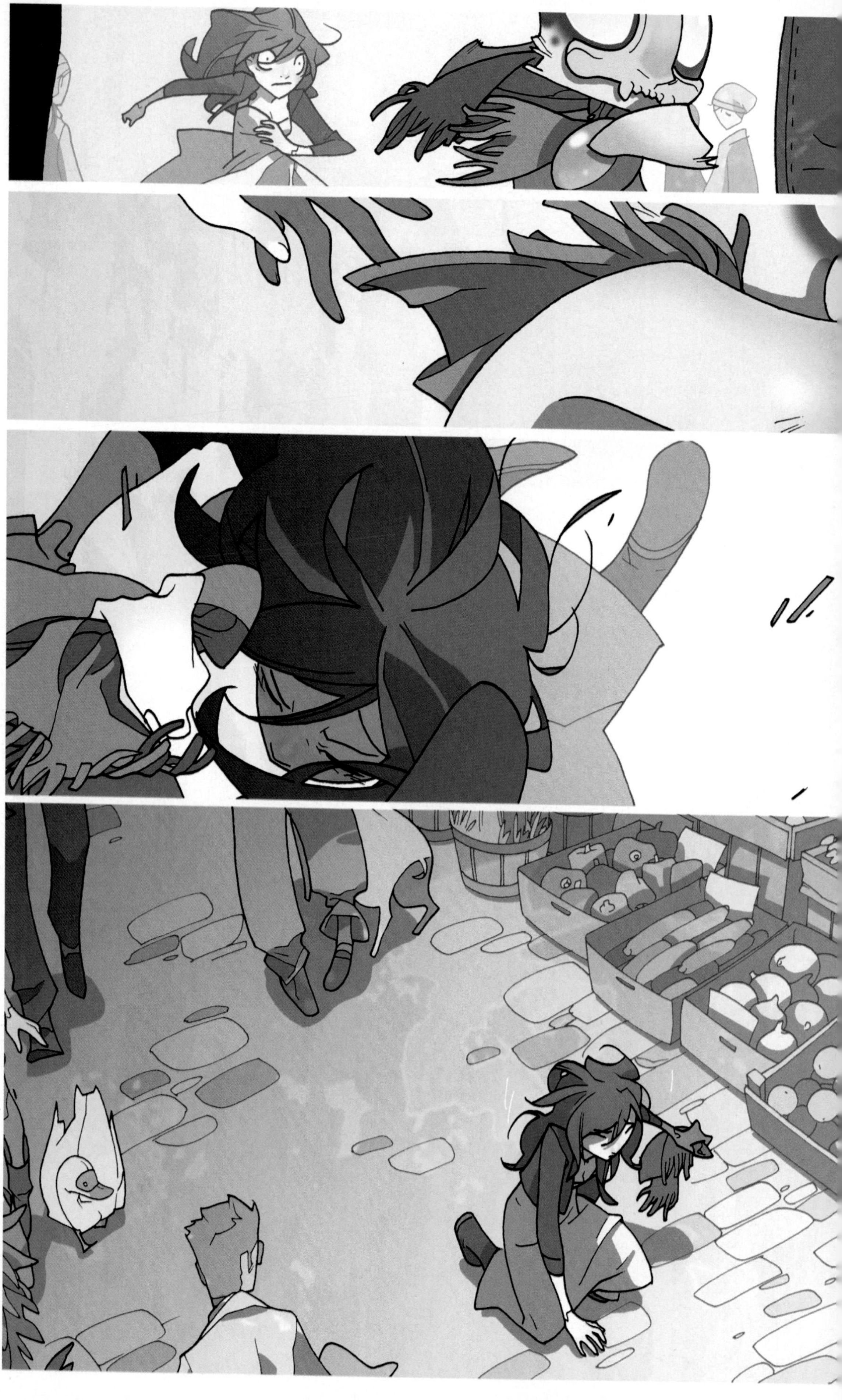

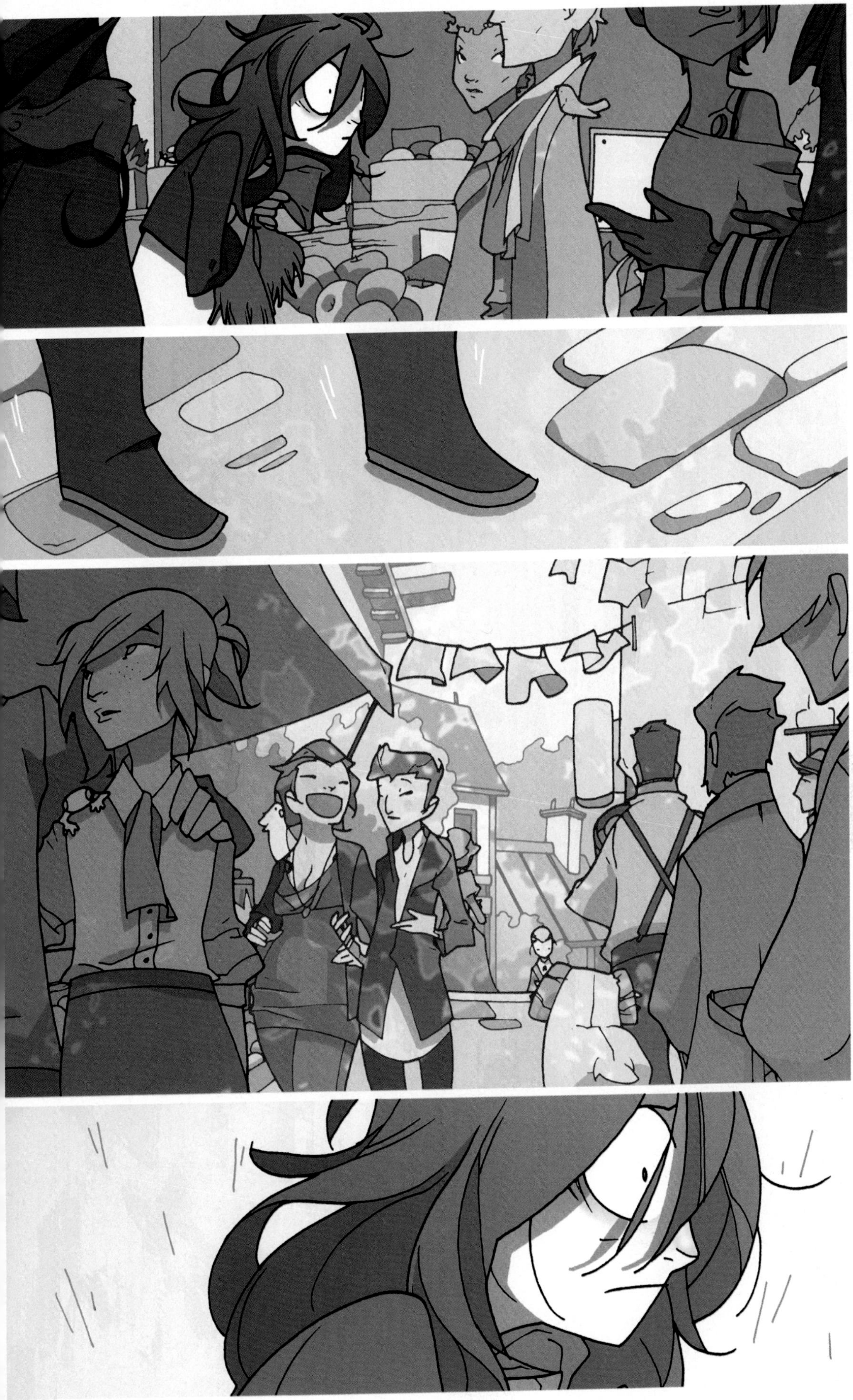

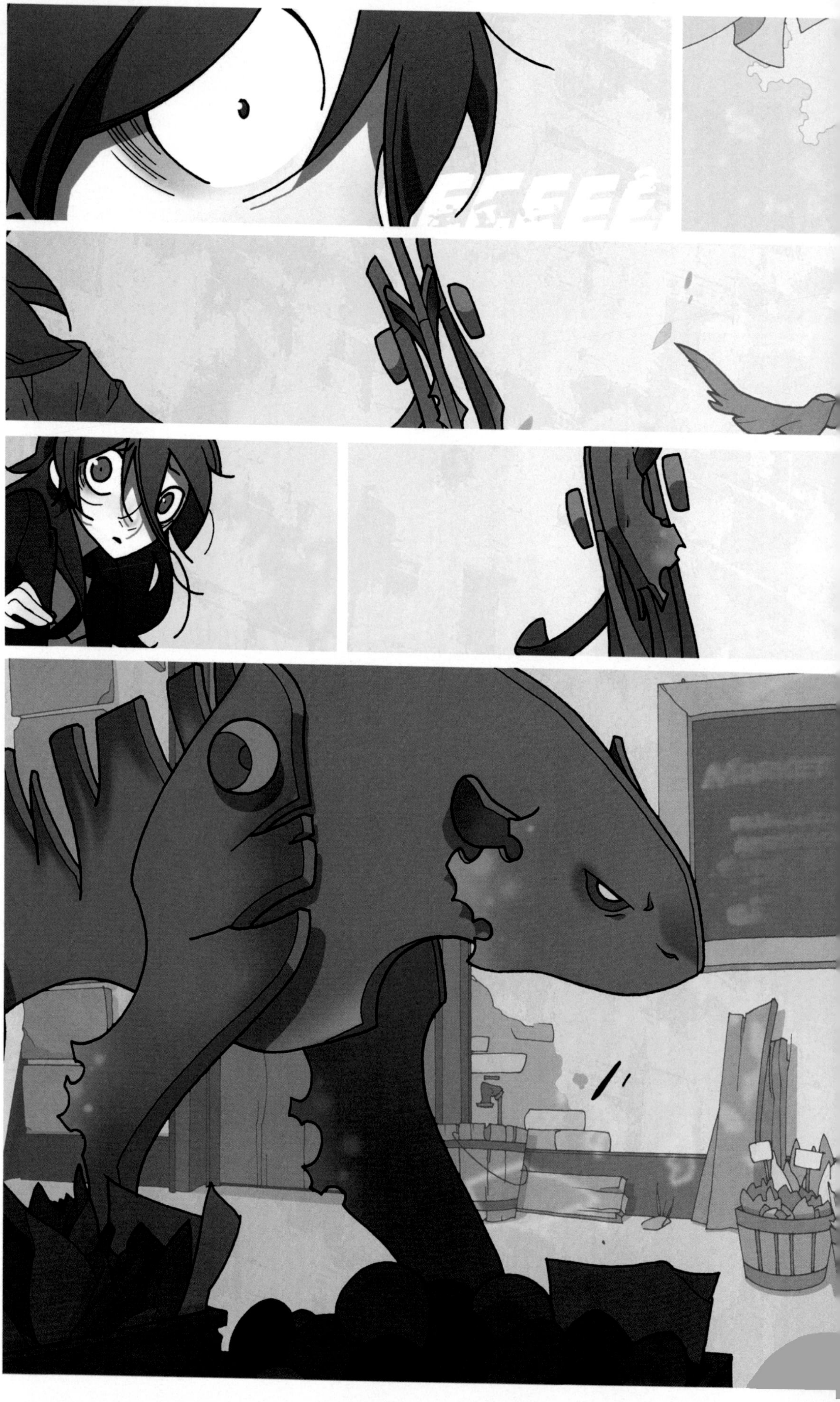

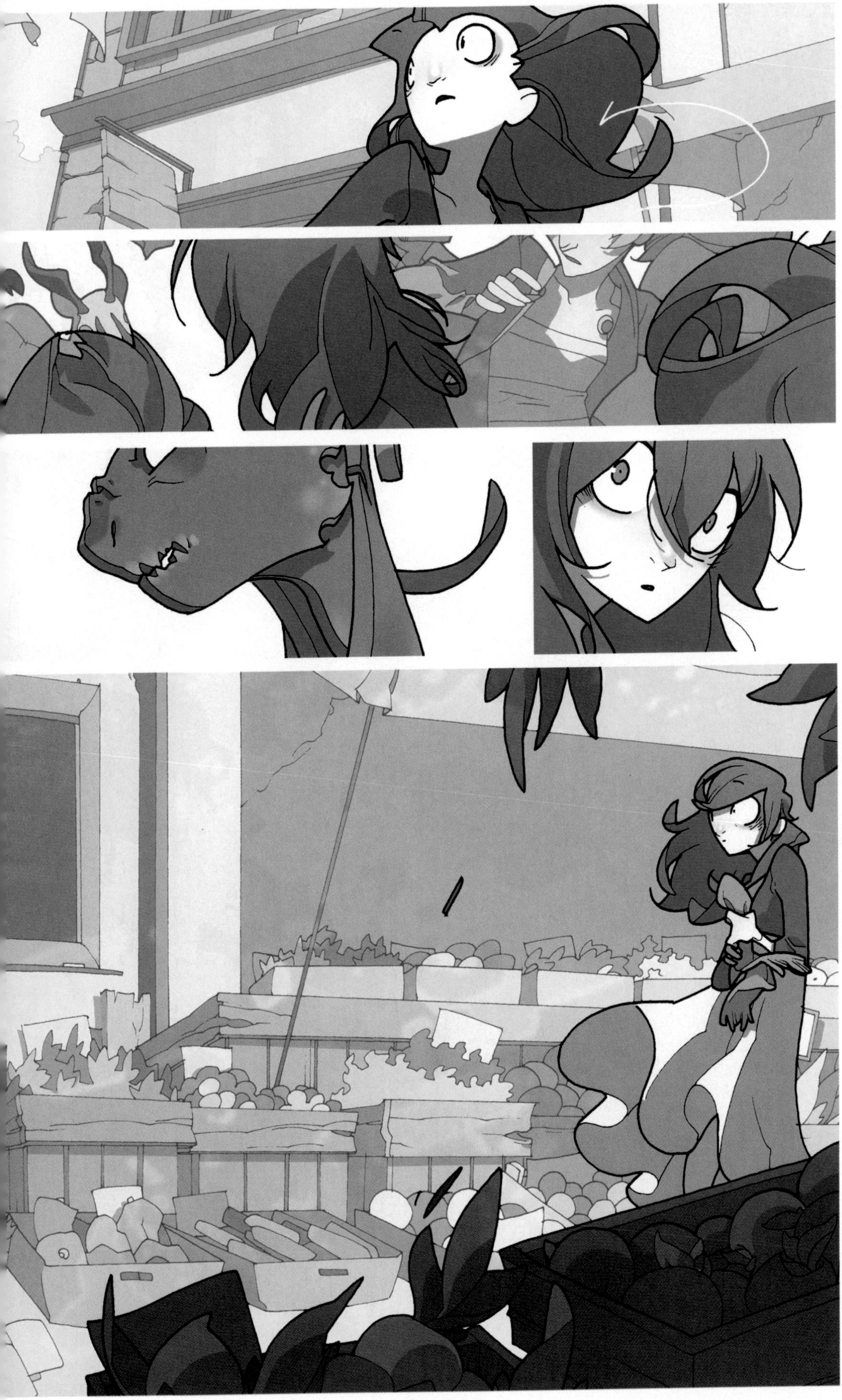

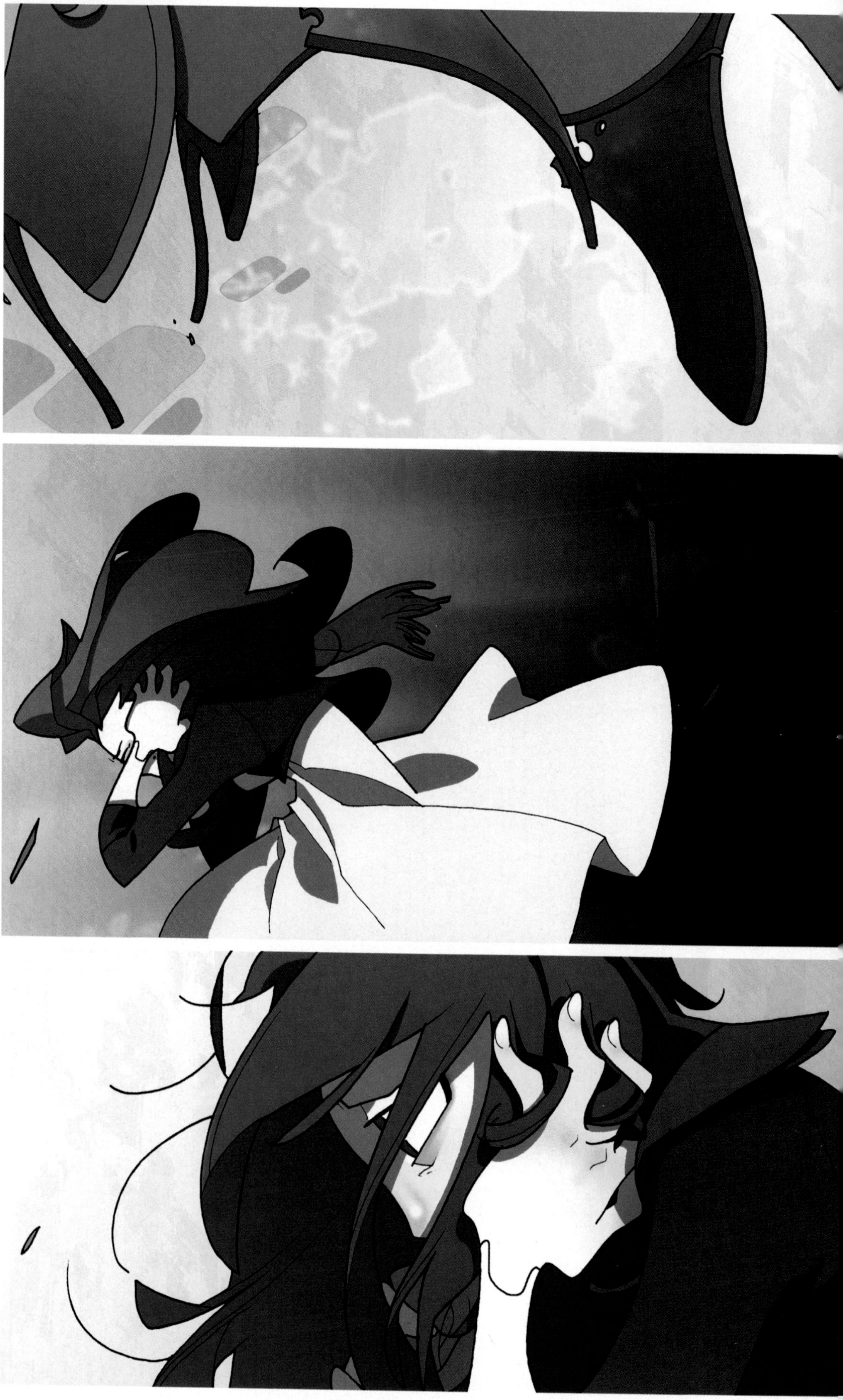

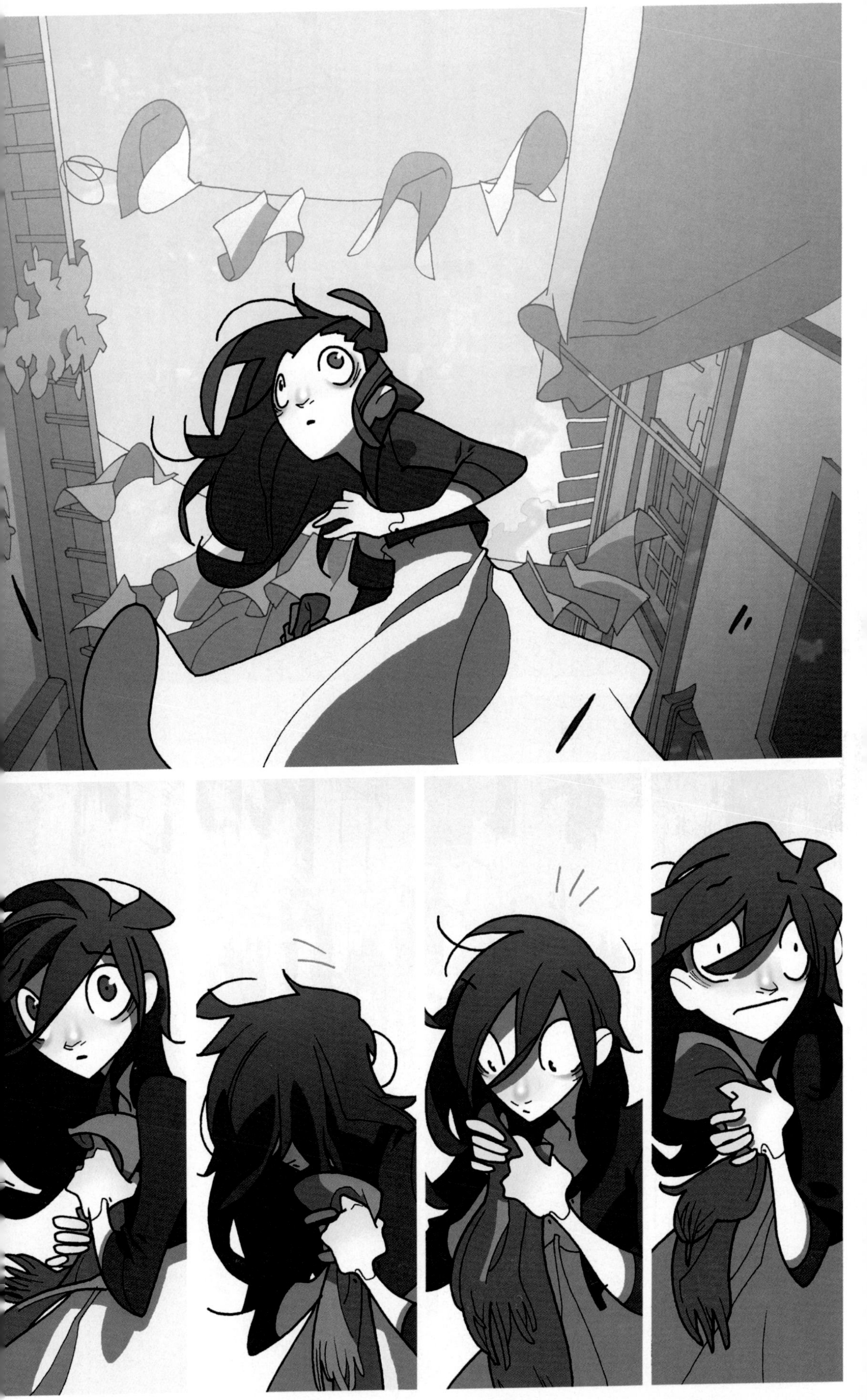

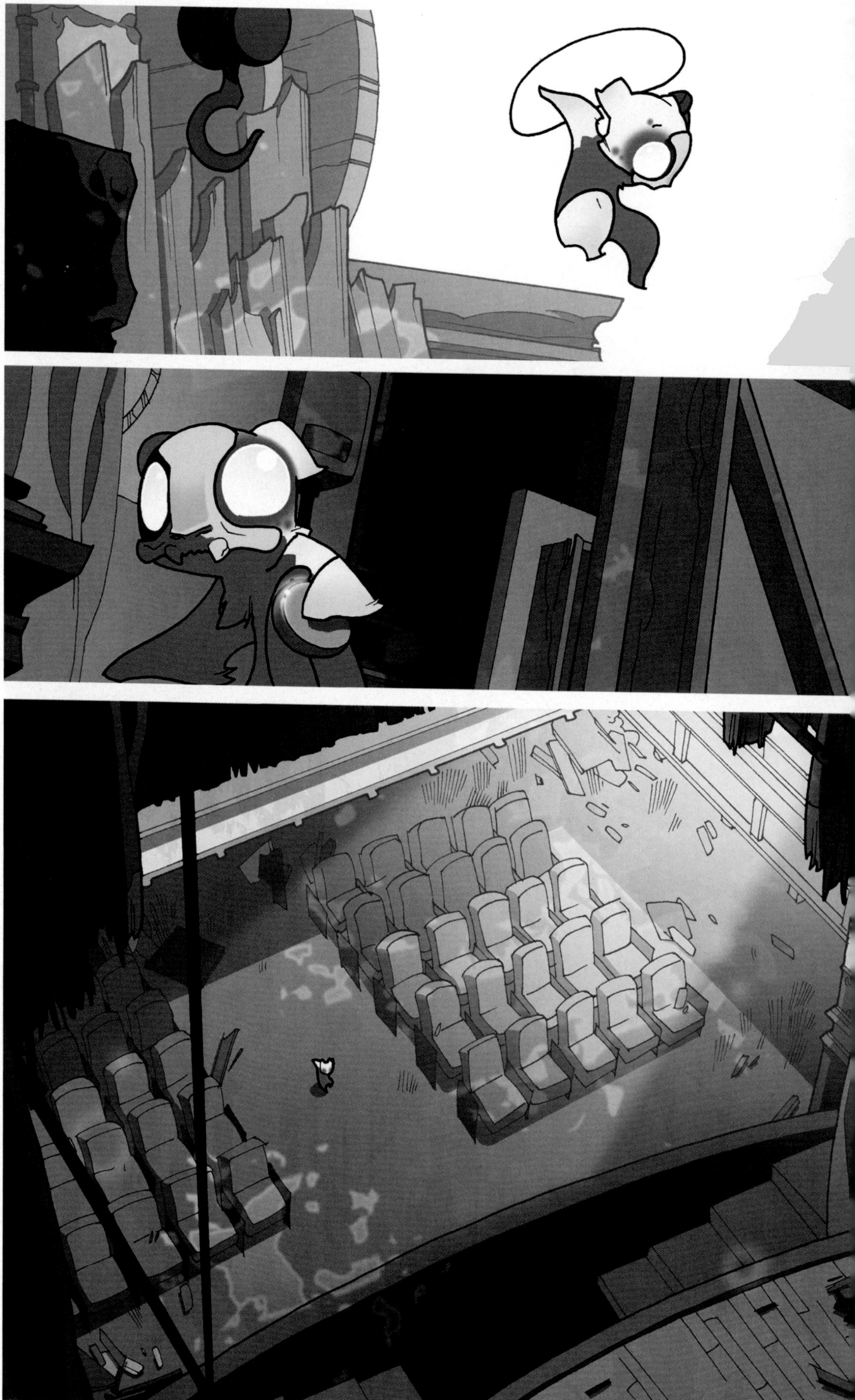

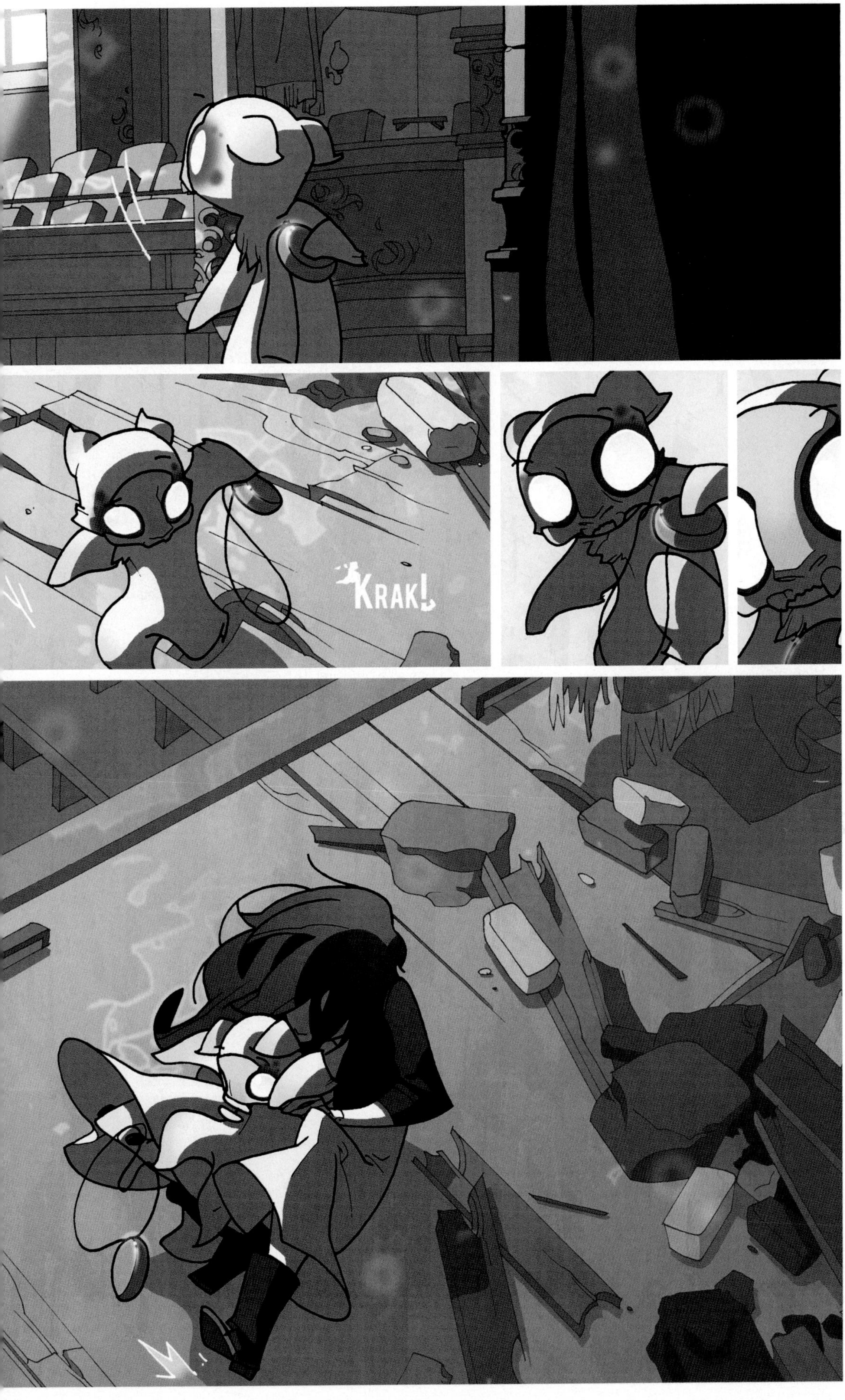
KRAK!

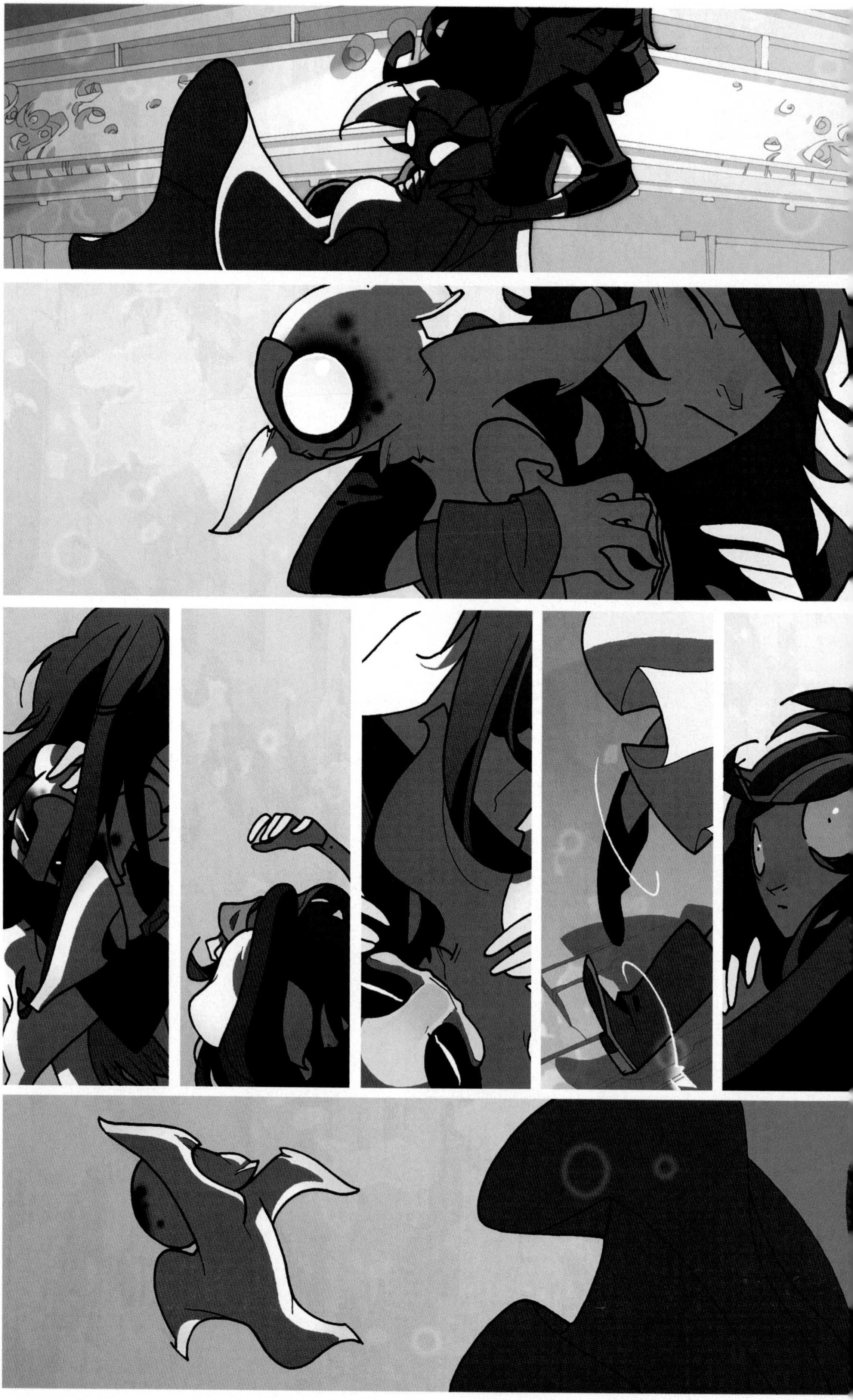

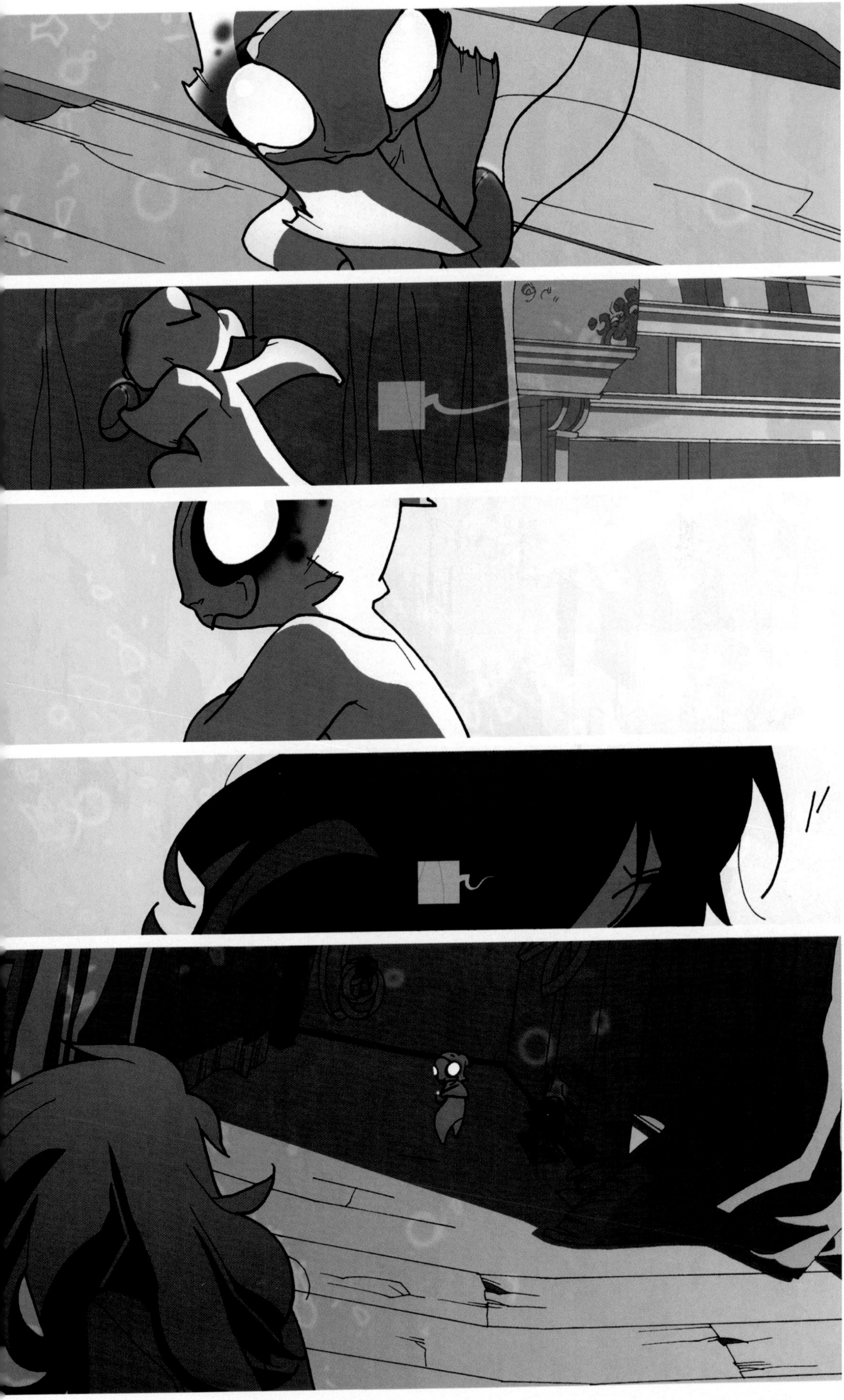

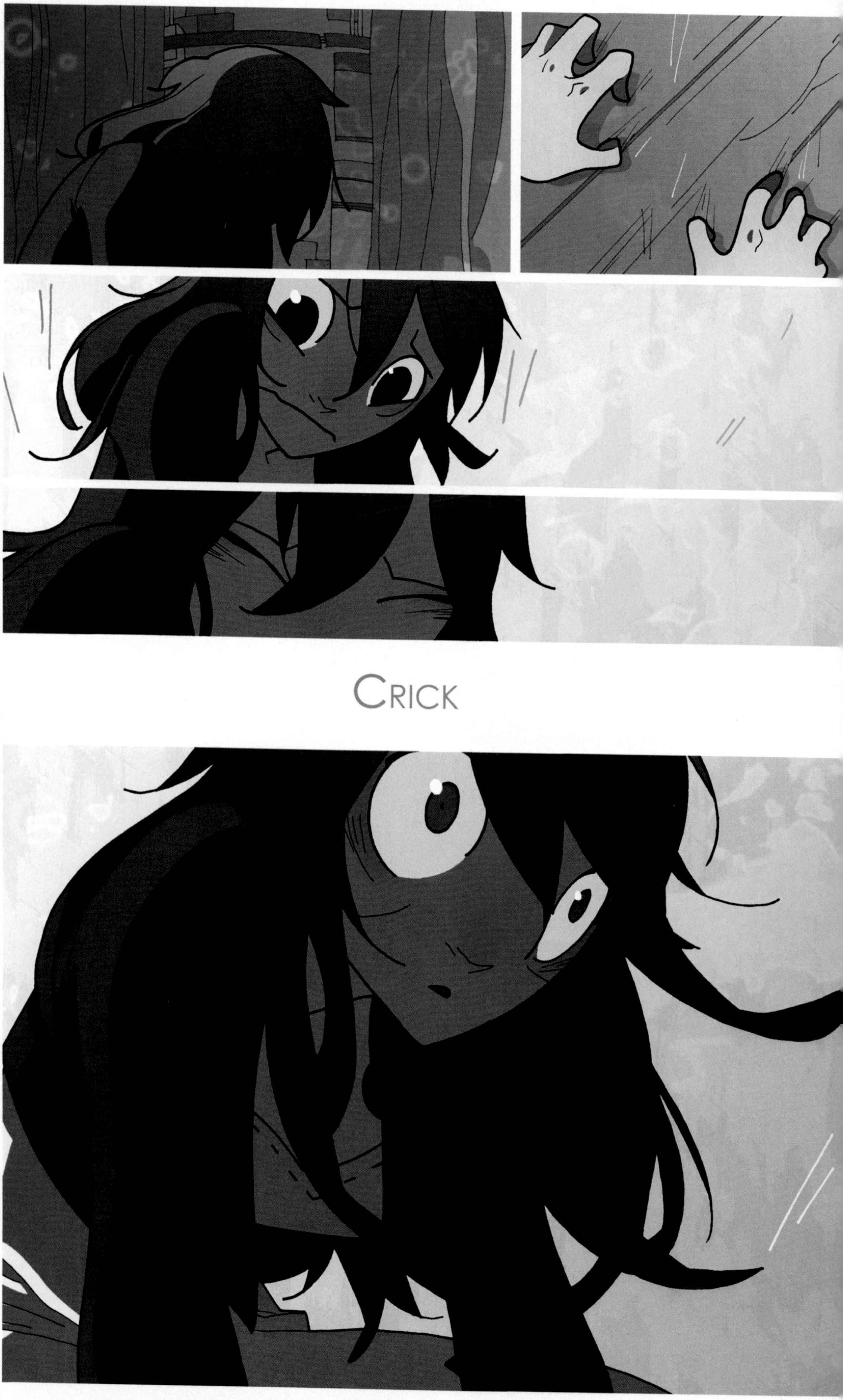
CRICK

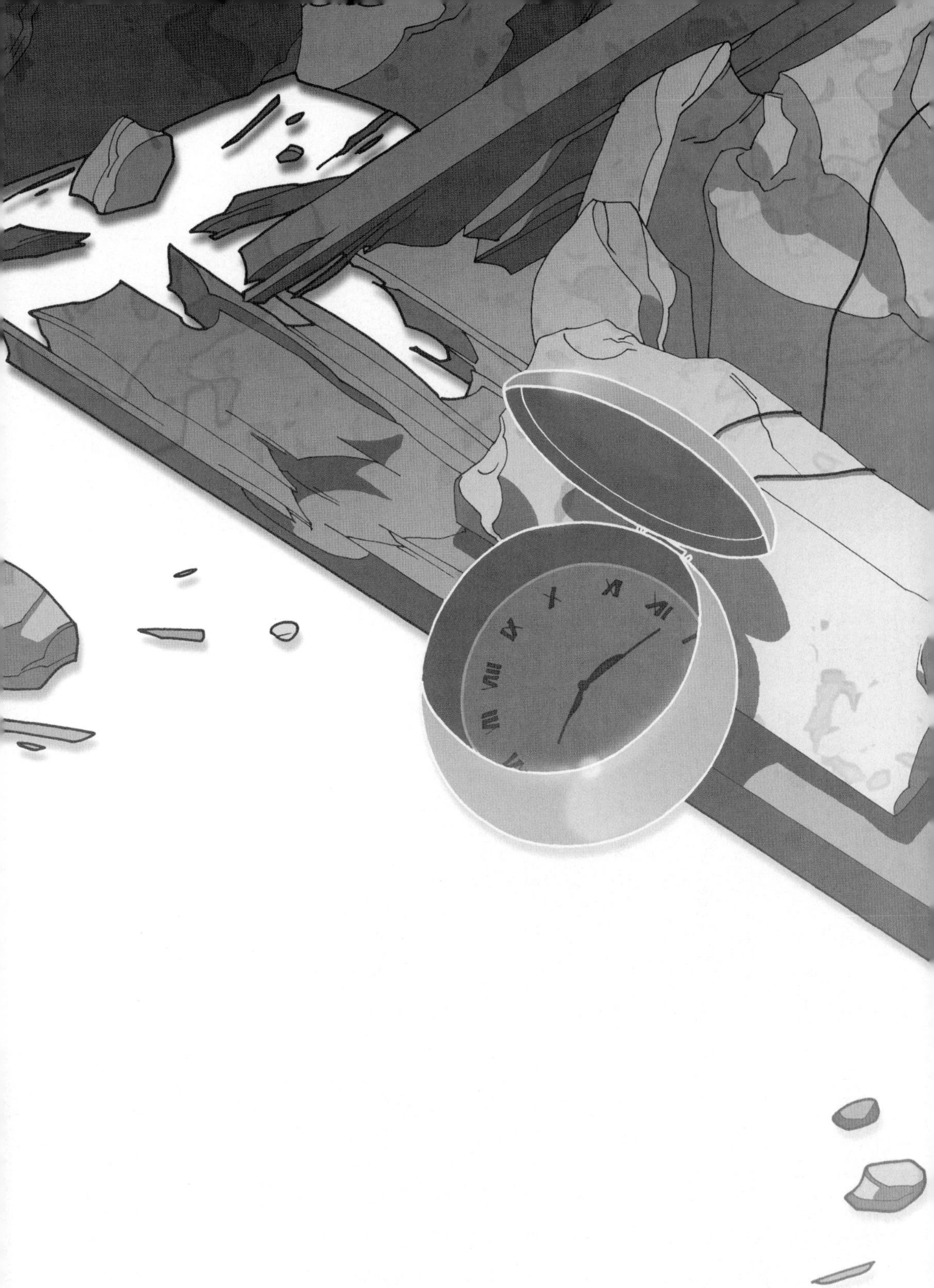

HINGES
CHAPTER 4

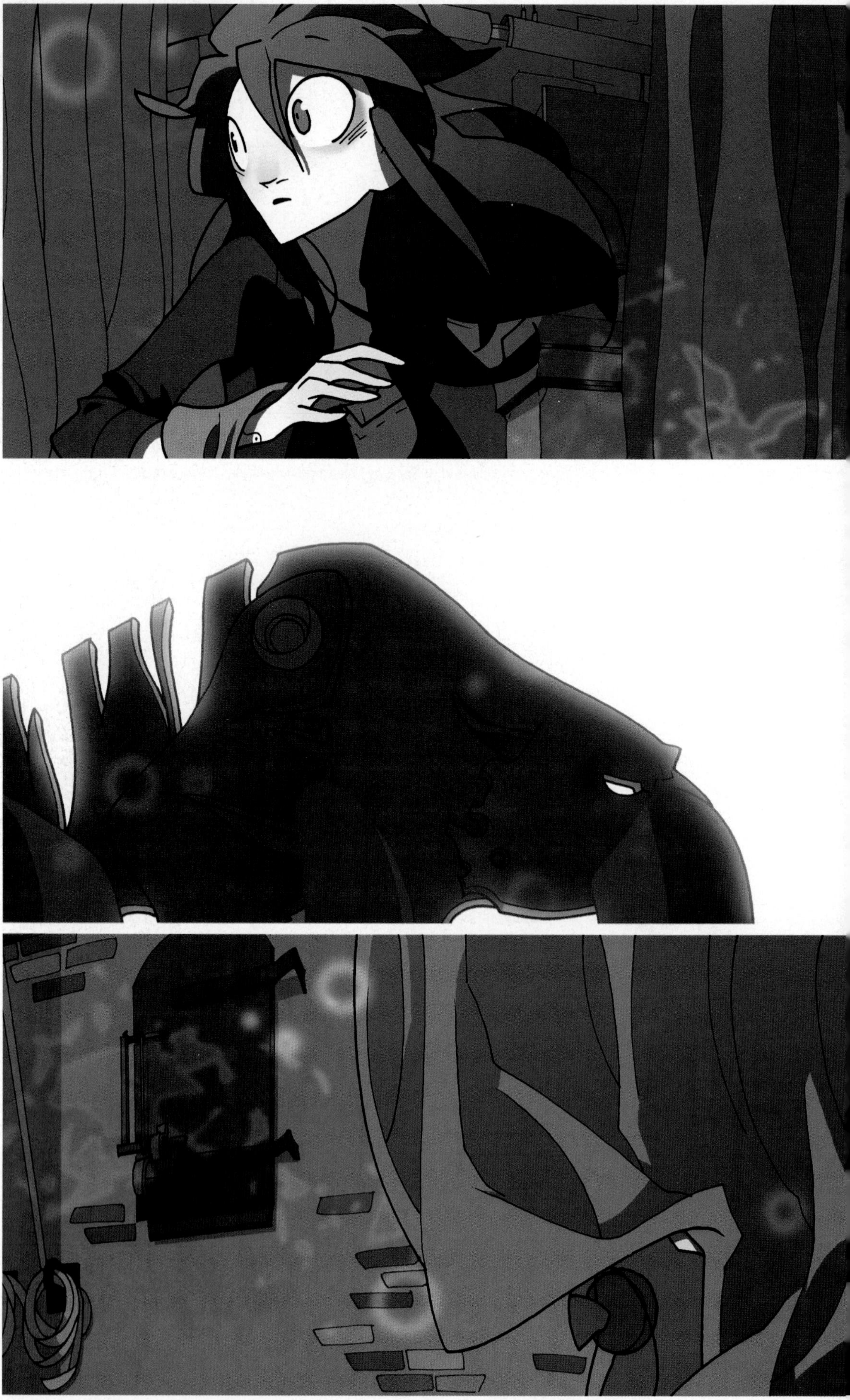

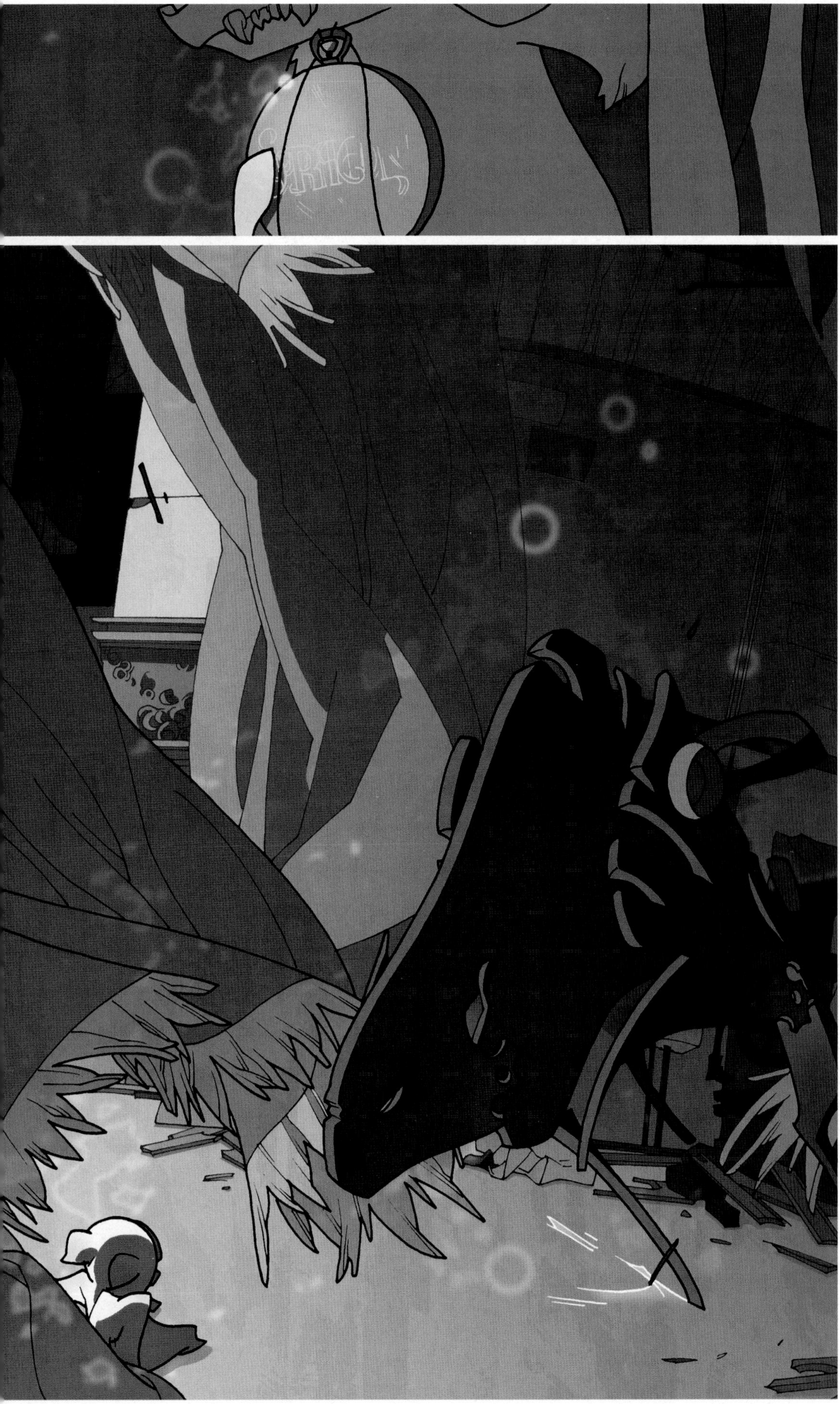

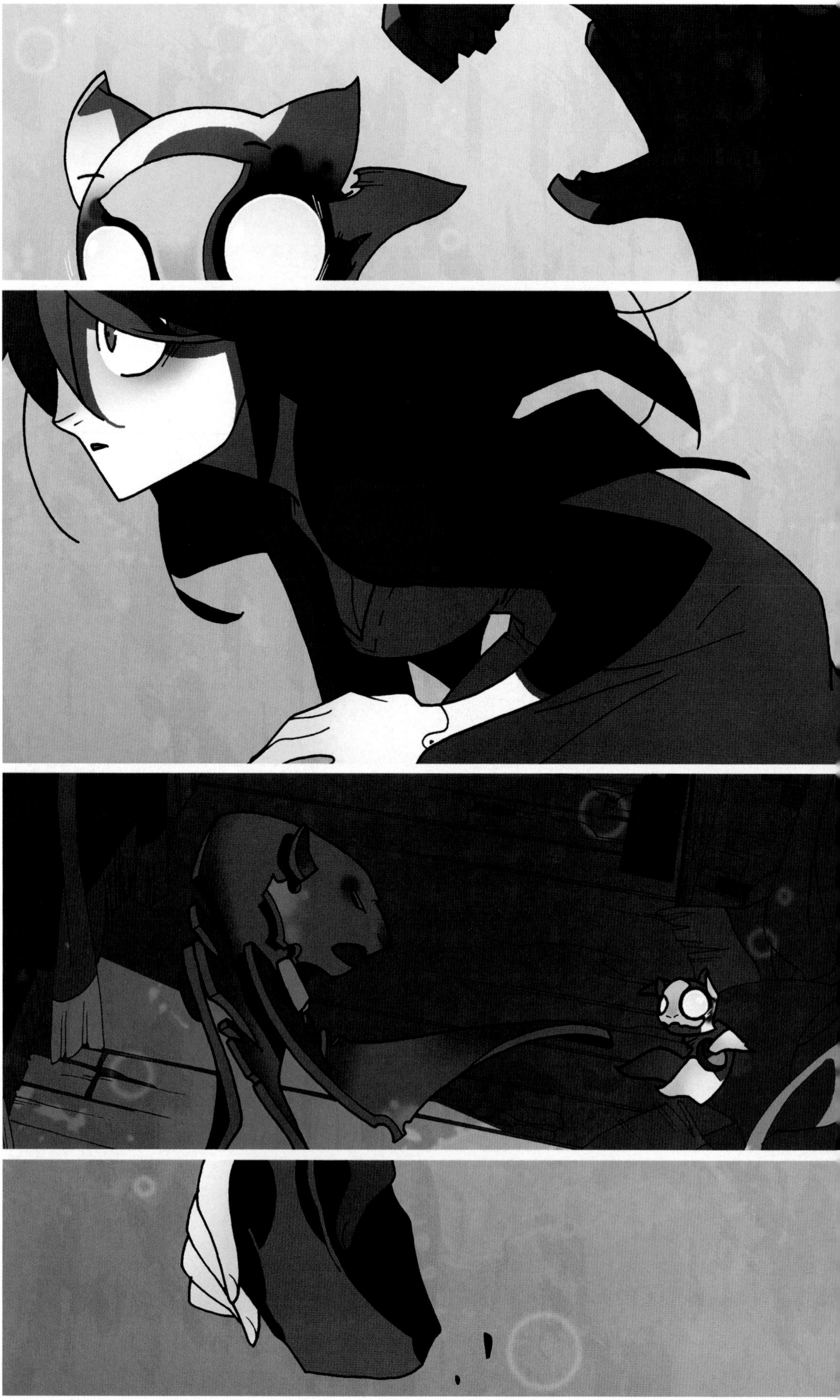

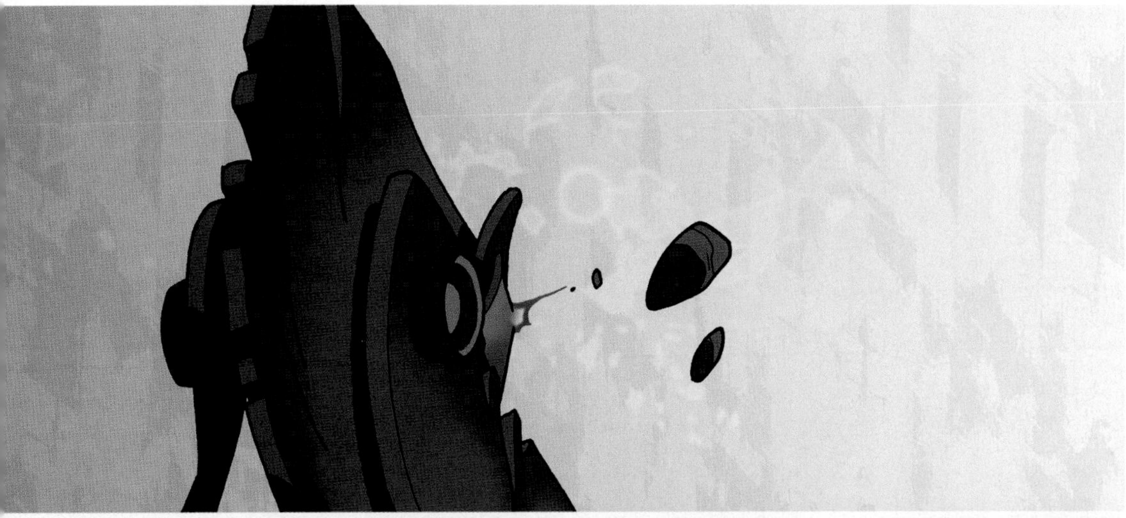

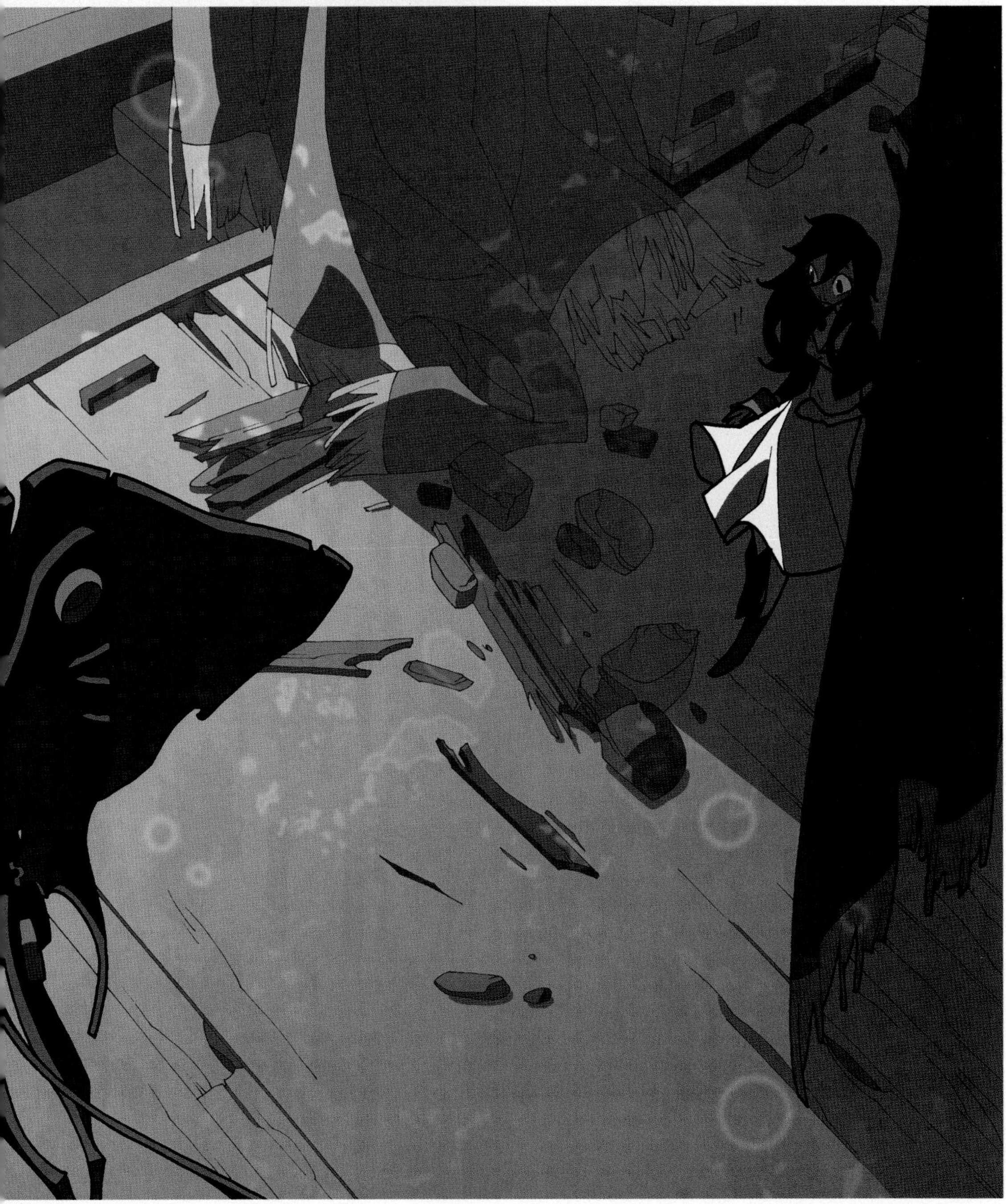

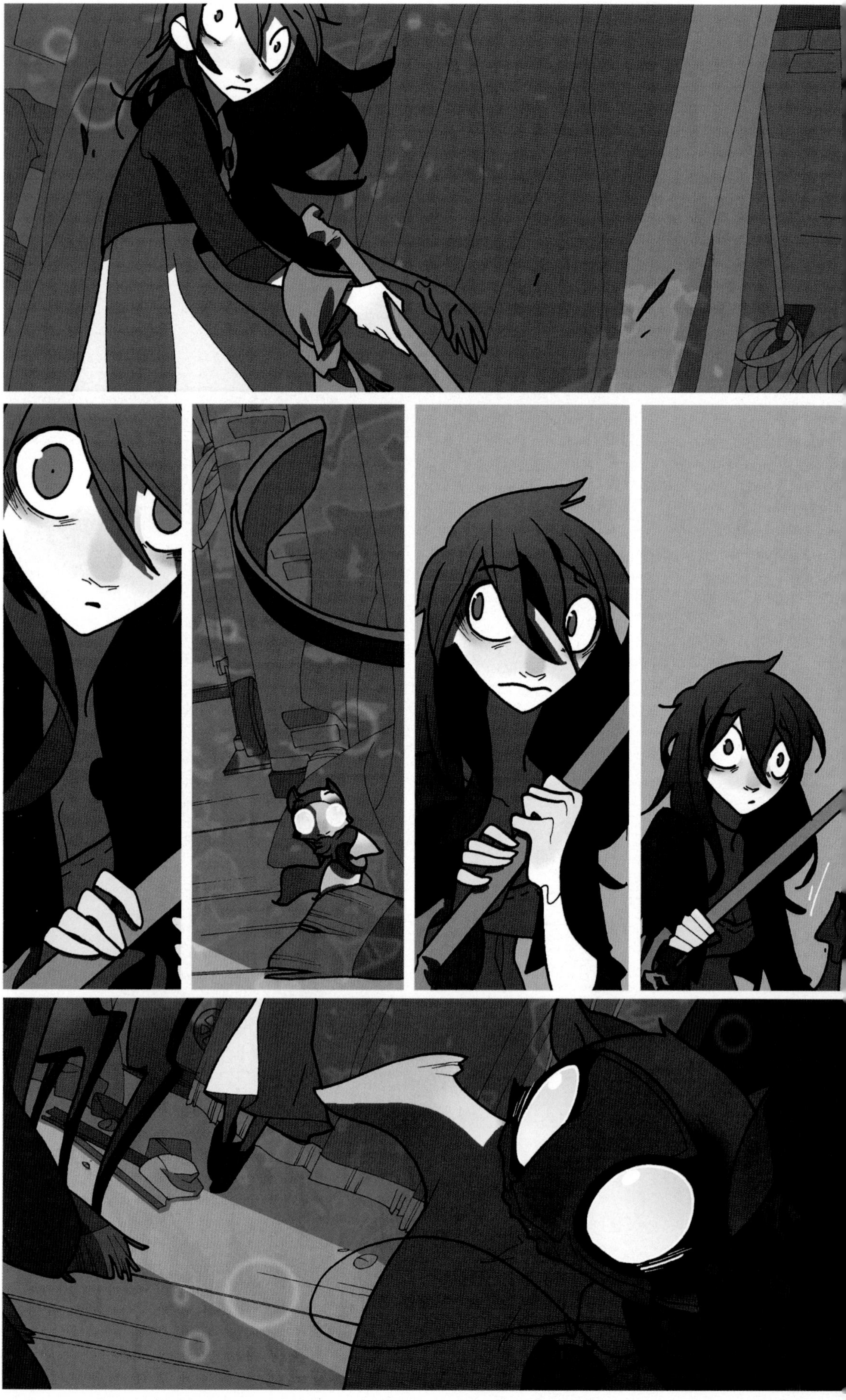

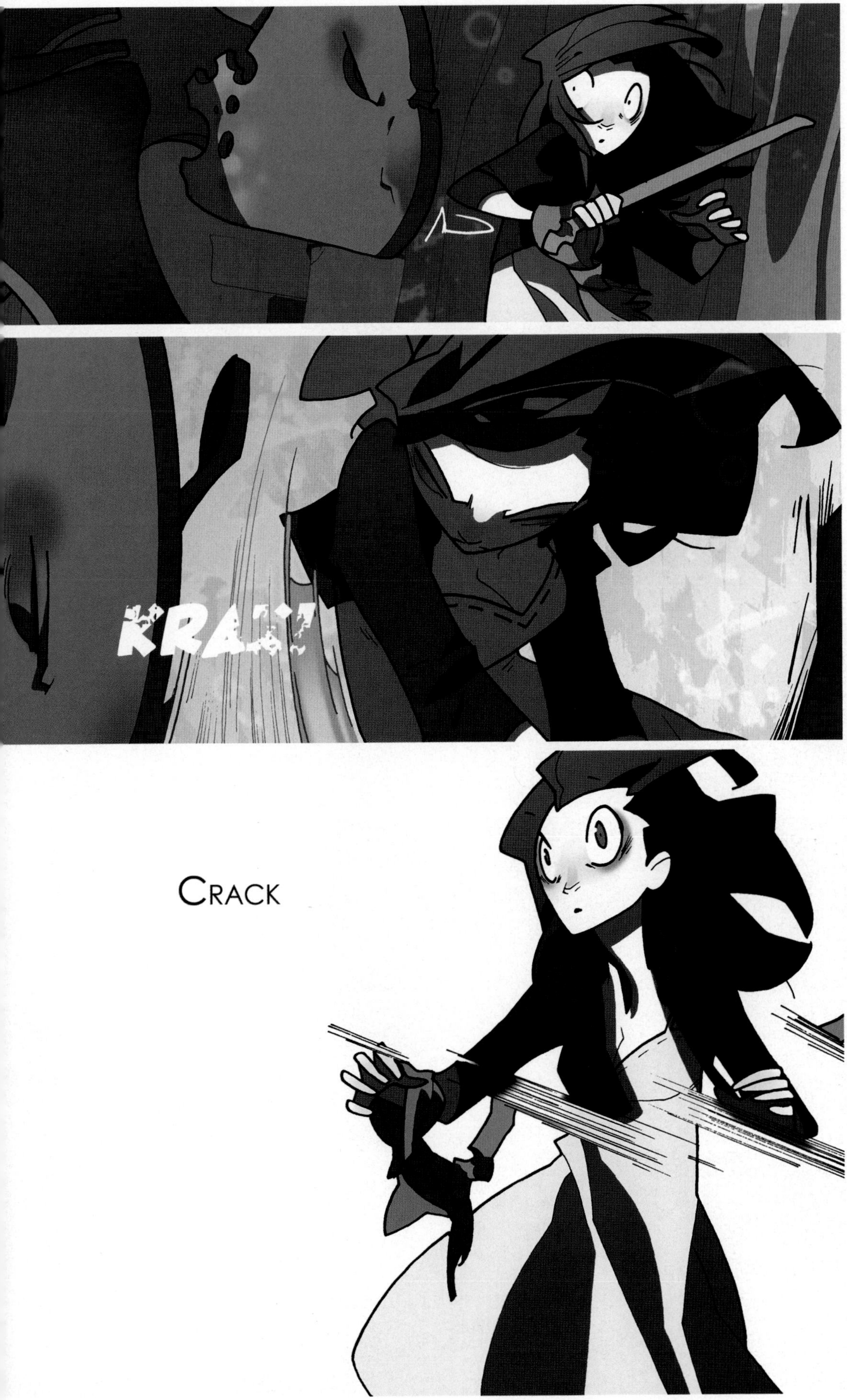
KRAK!
CRACK

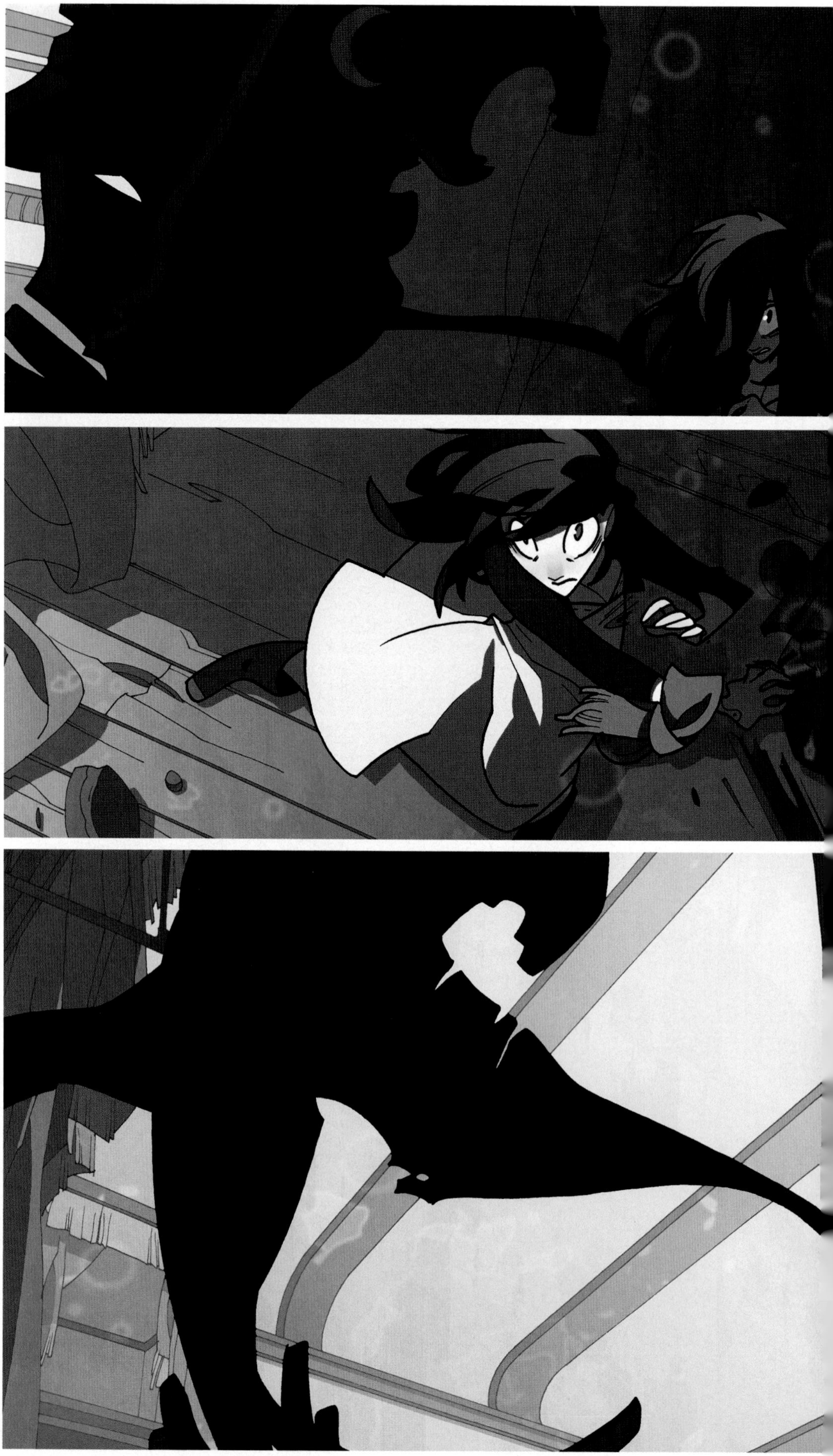

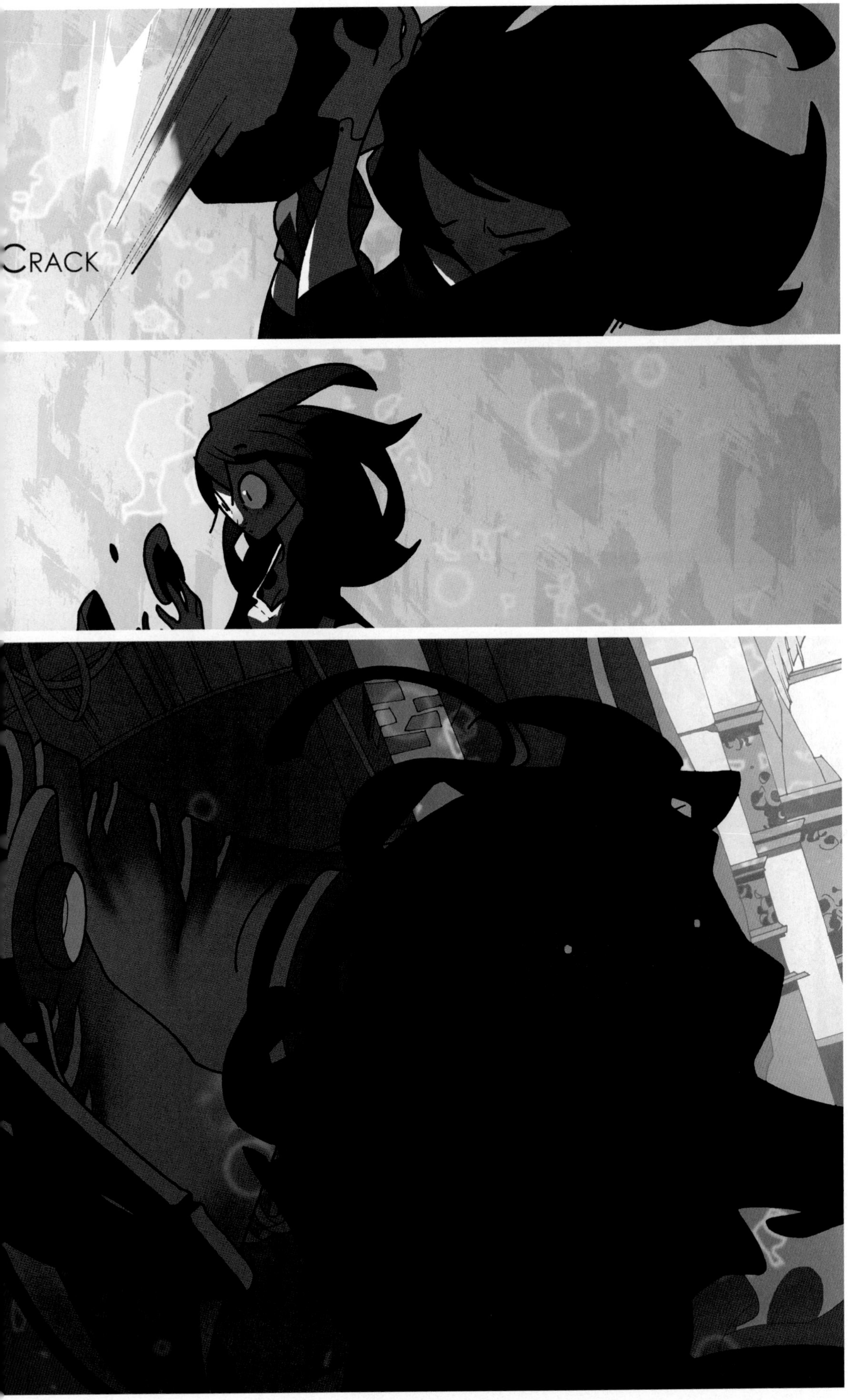
CRACK

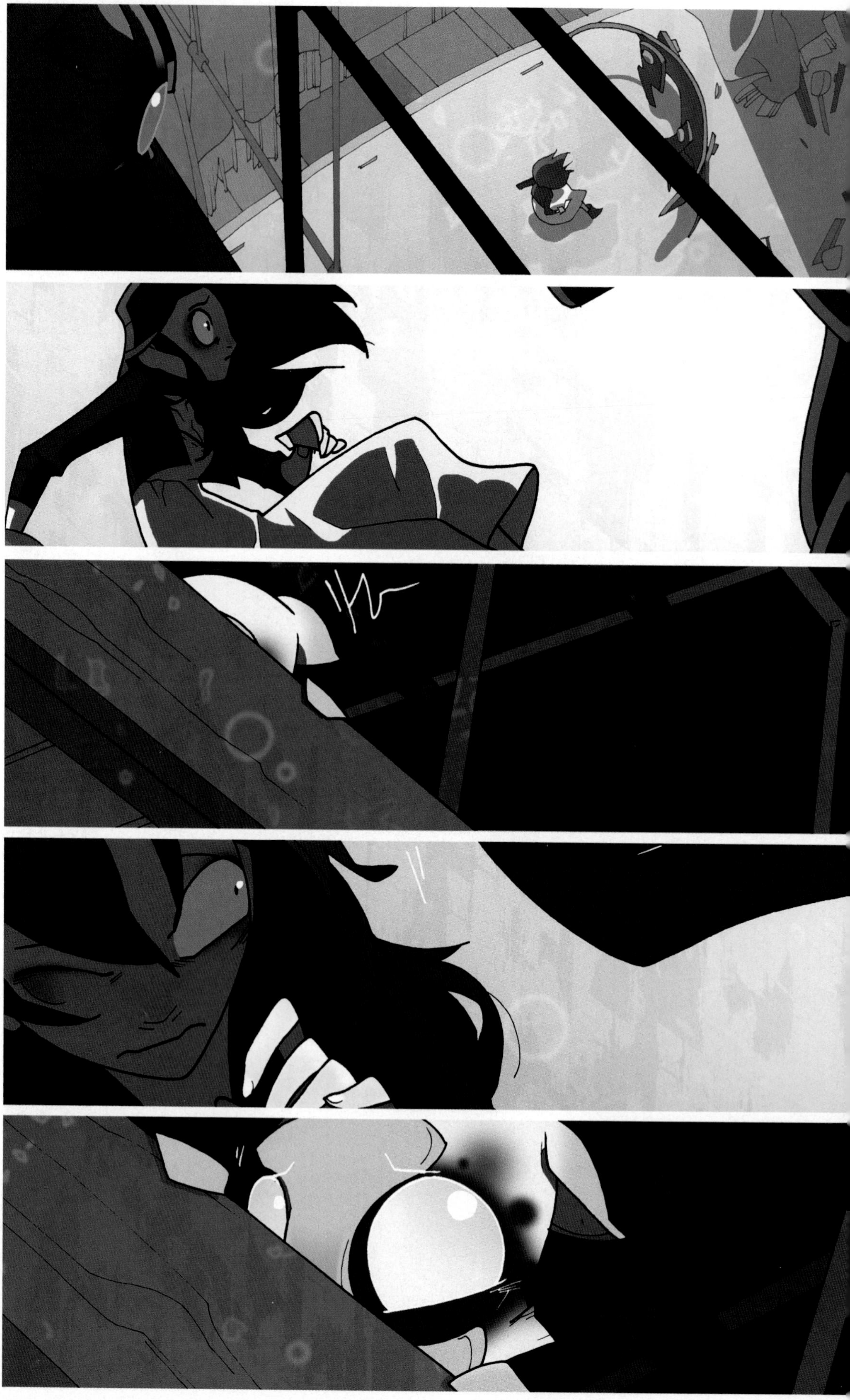

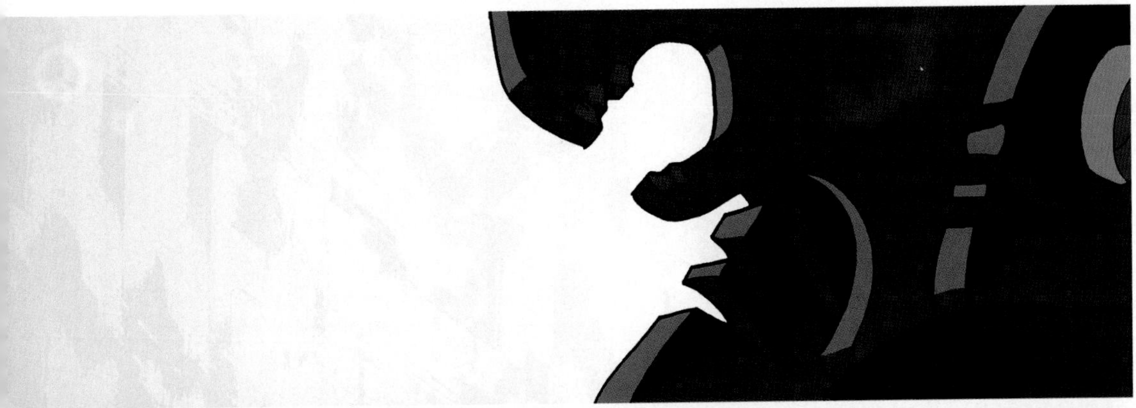

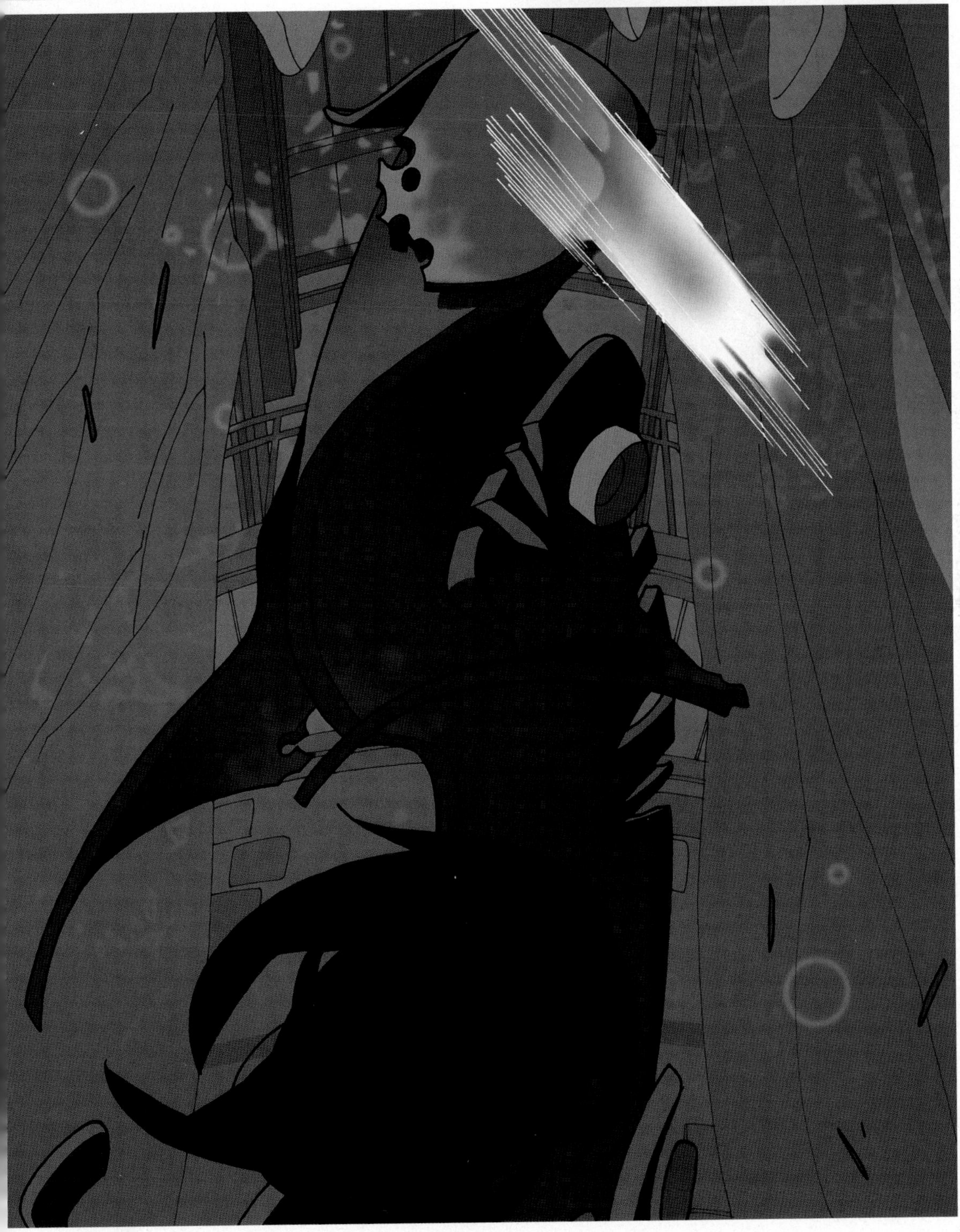

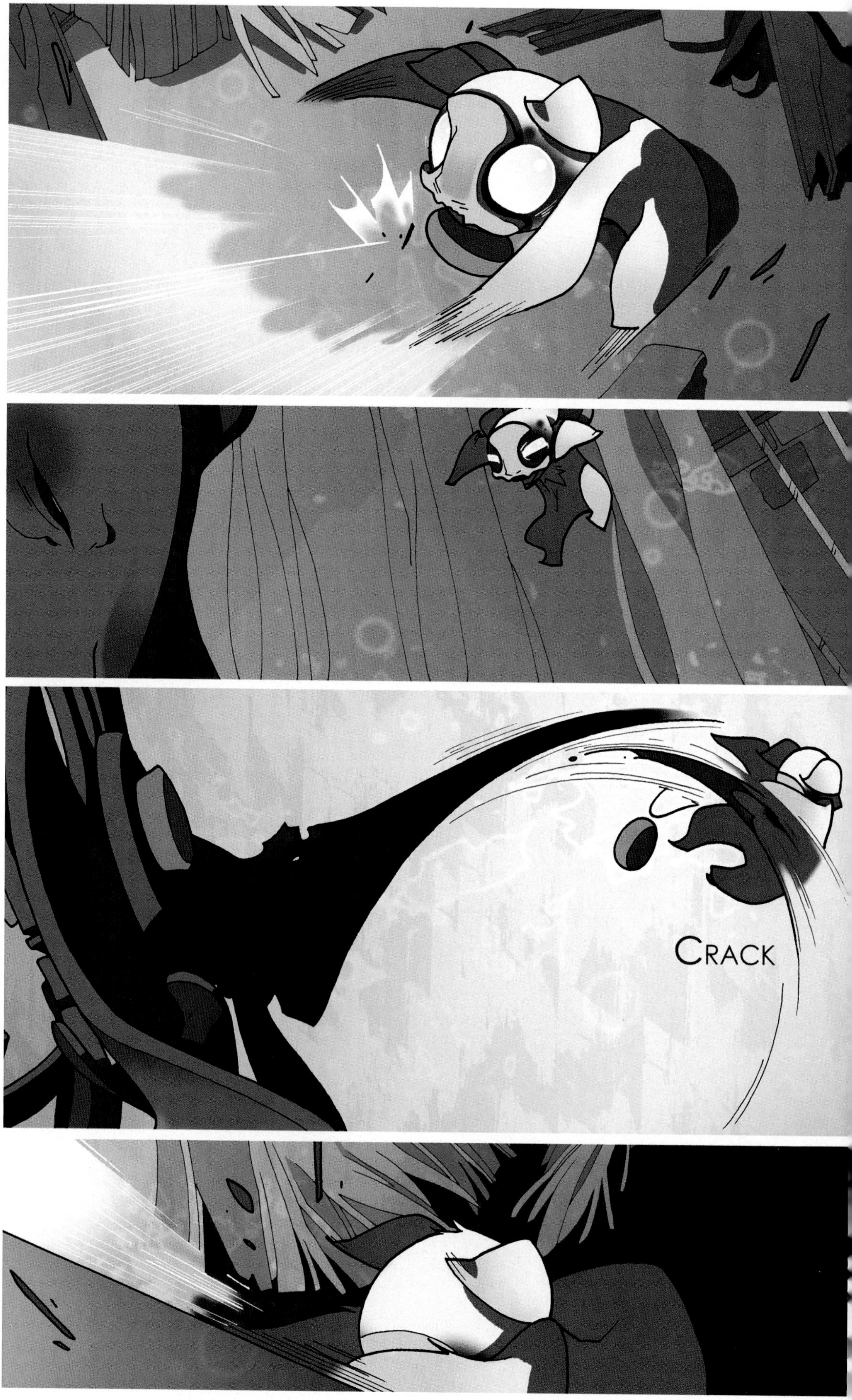
CRACK

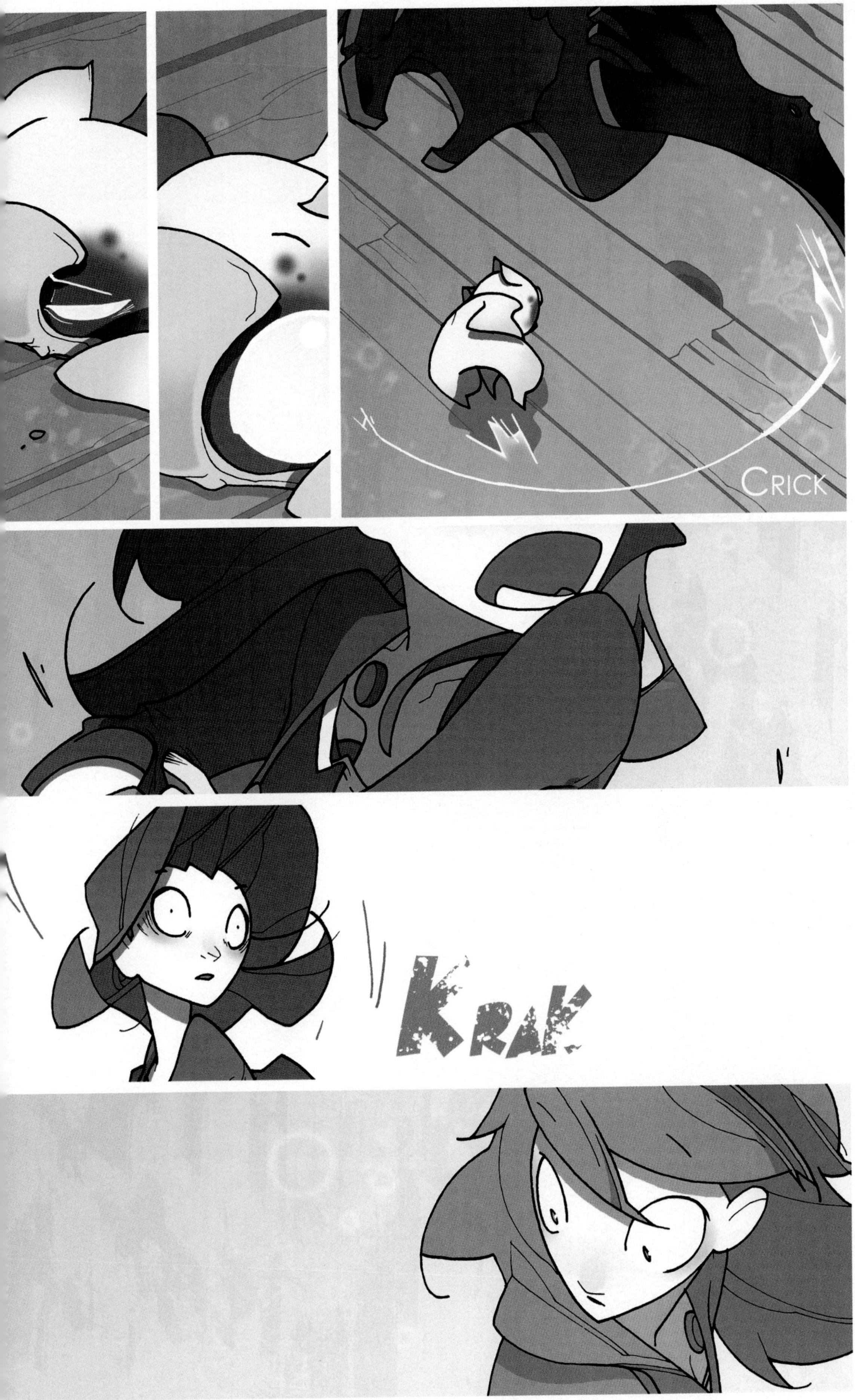
CRICK
KRAK

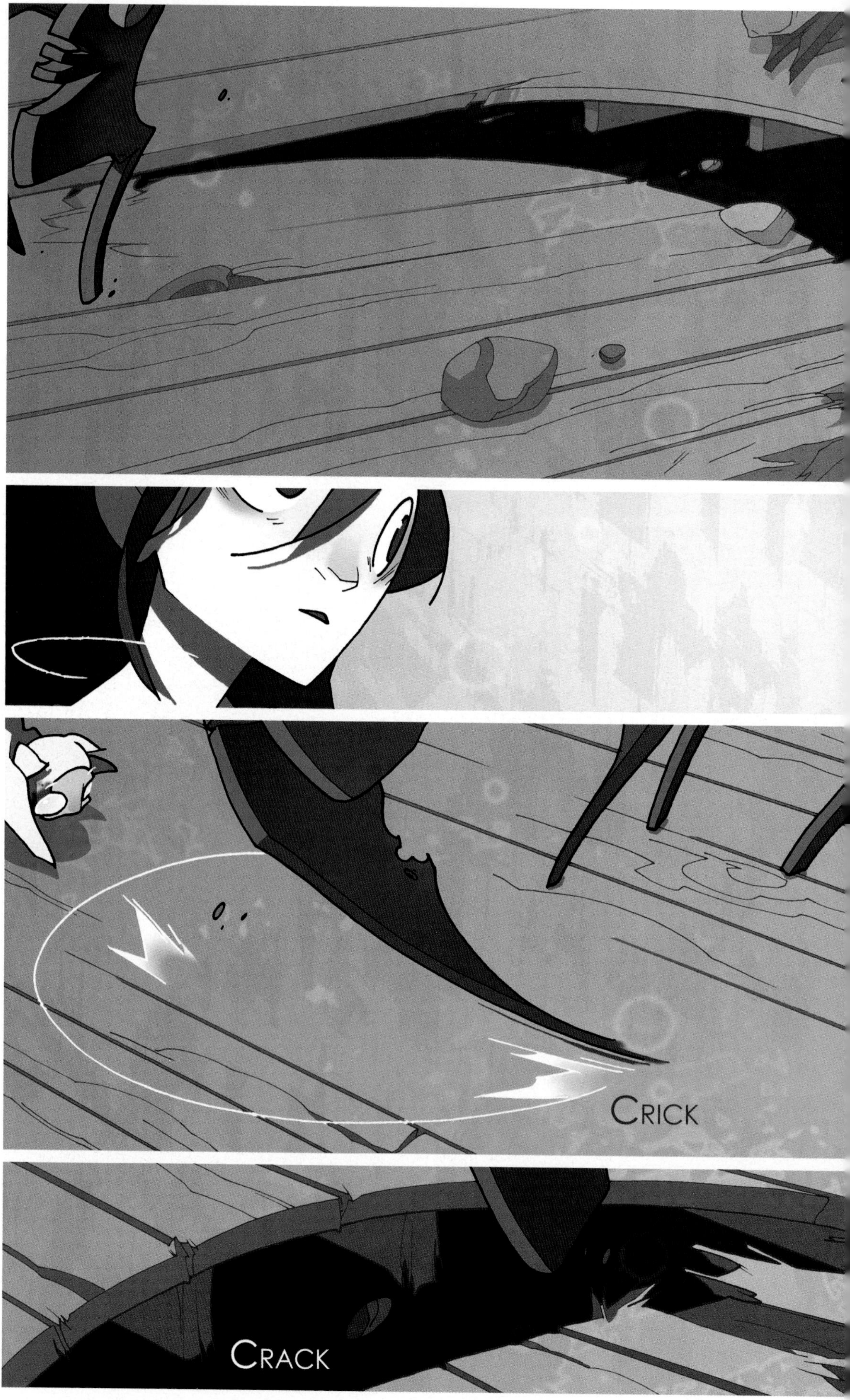
CRICK
CRACK

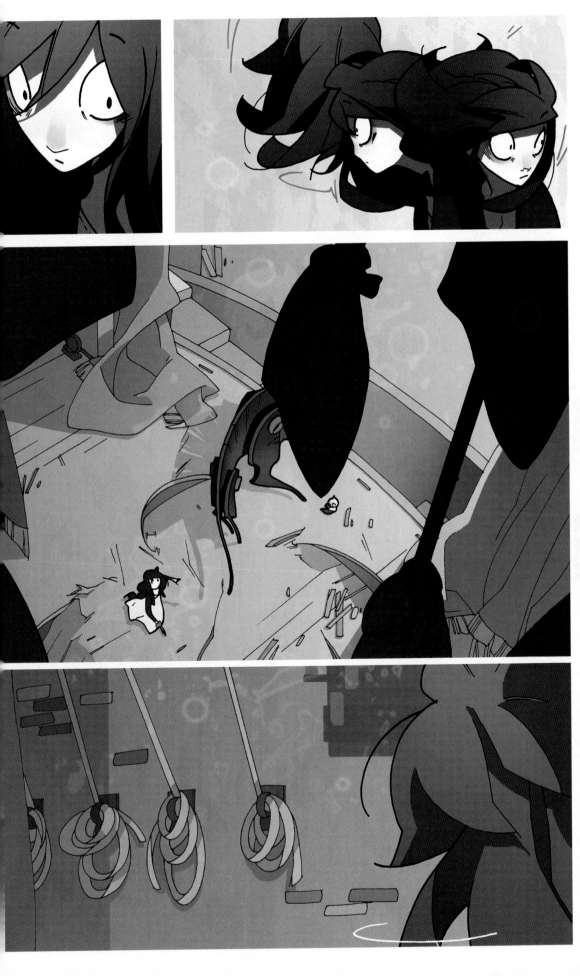

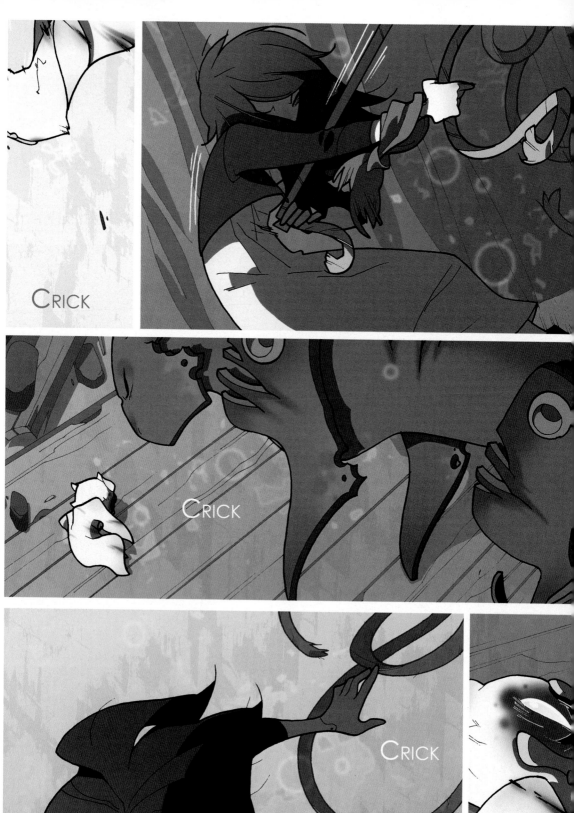

CRICK

CRICK

CRICK

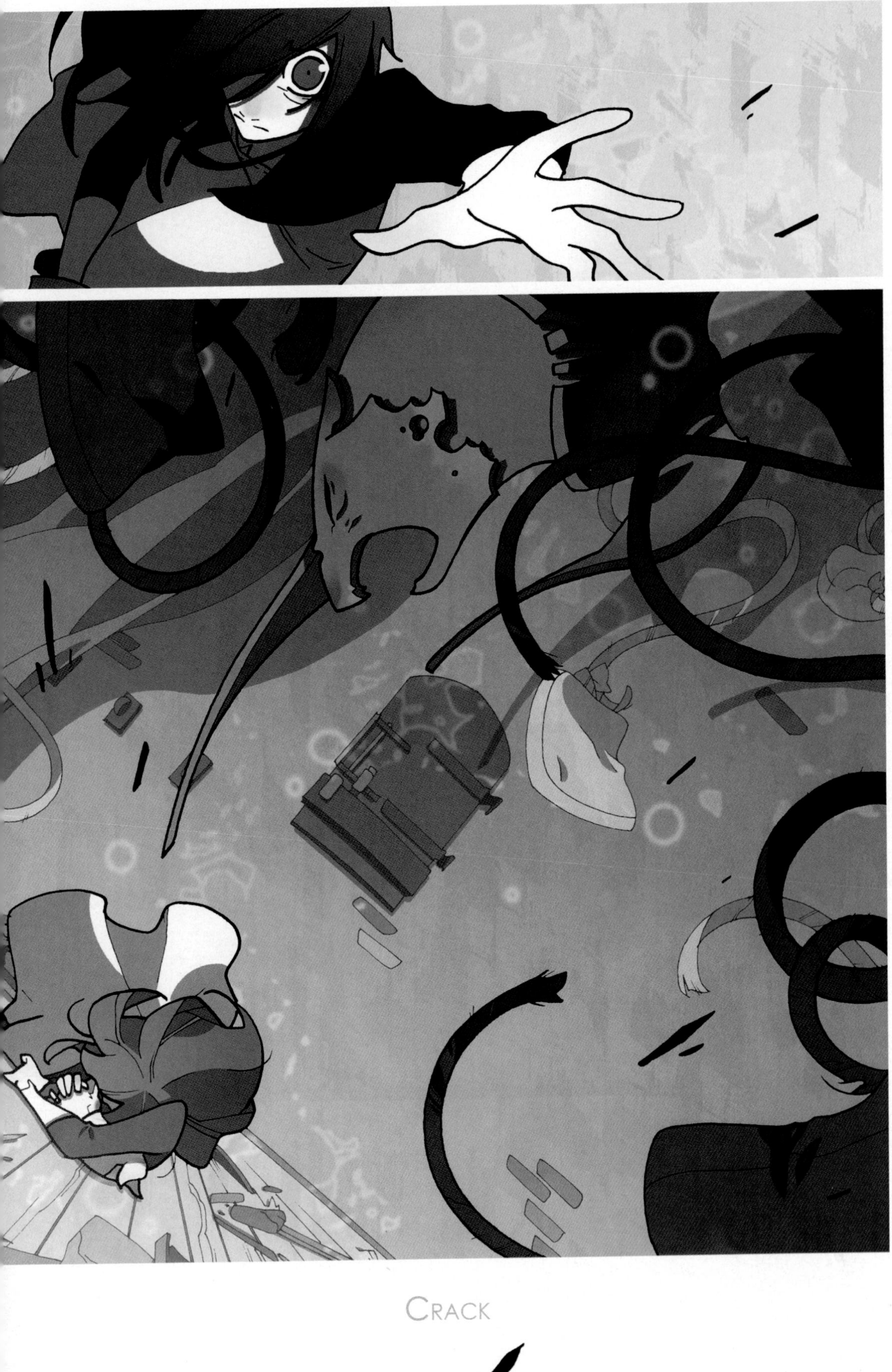
CRACK

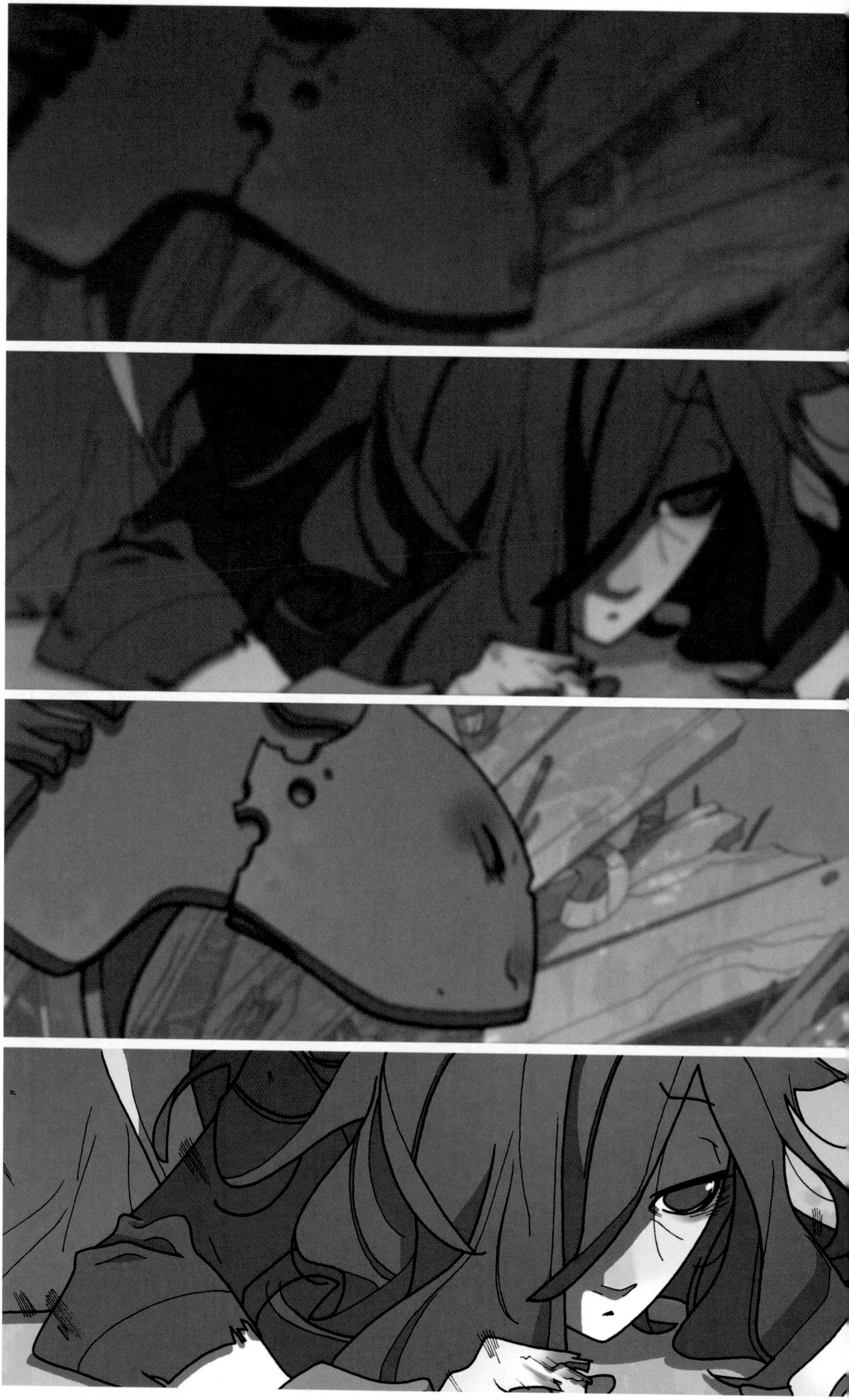

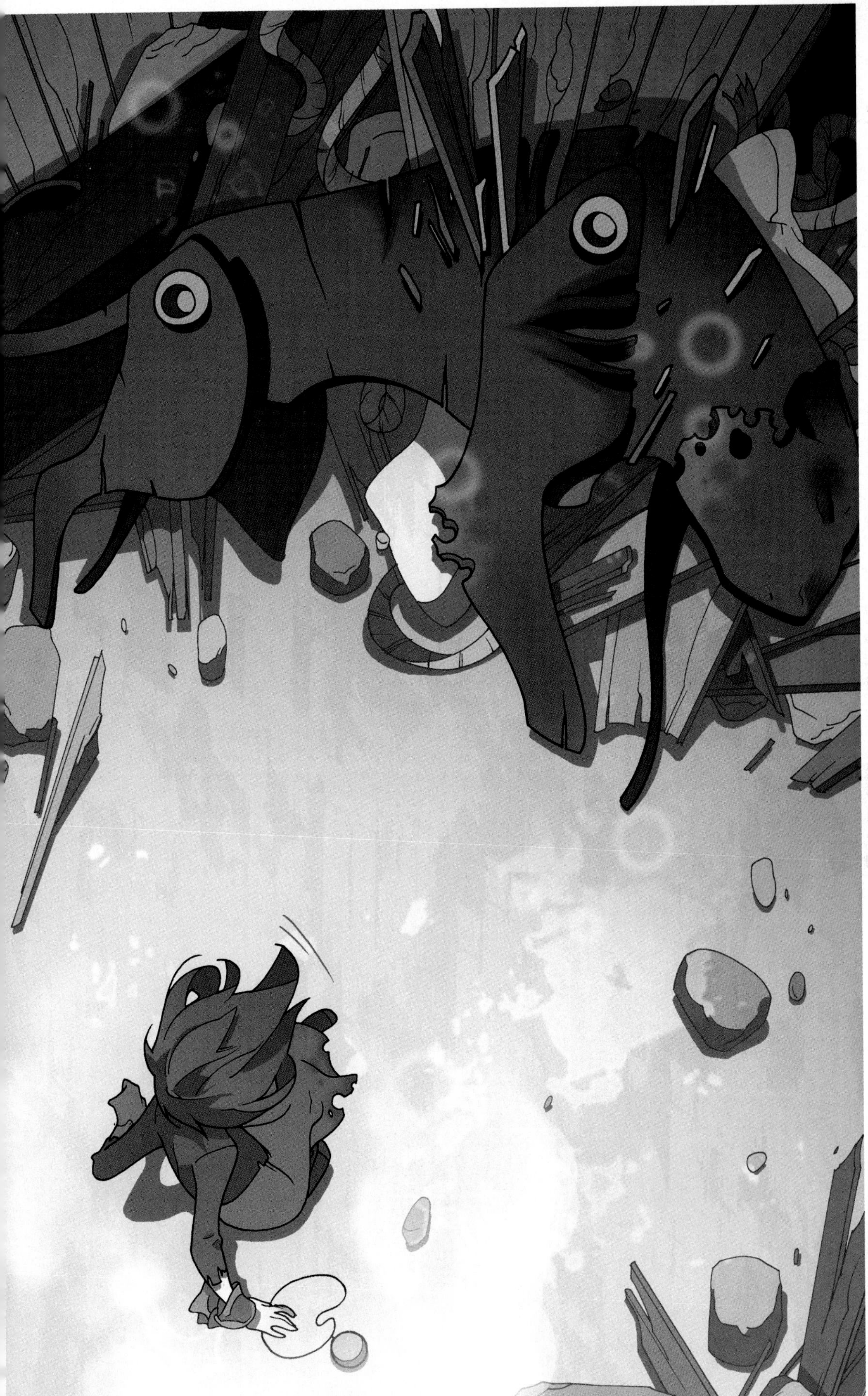

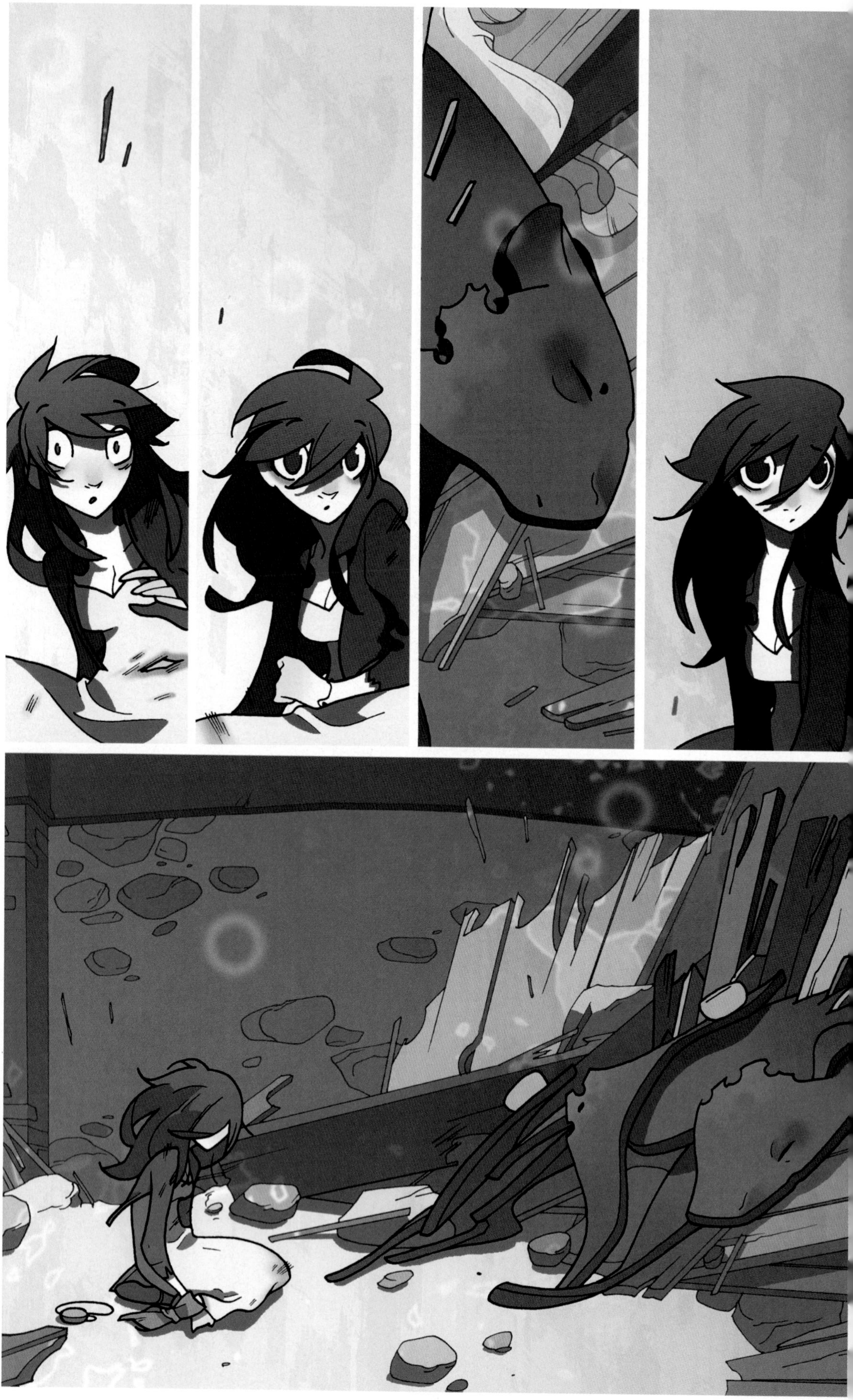

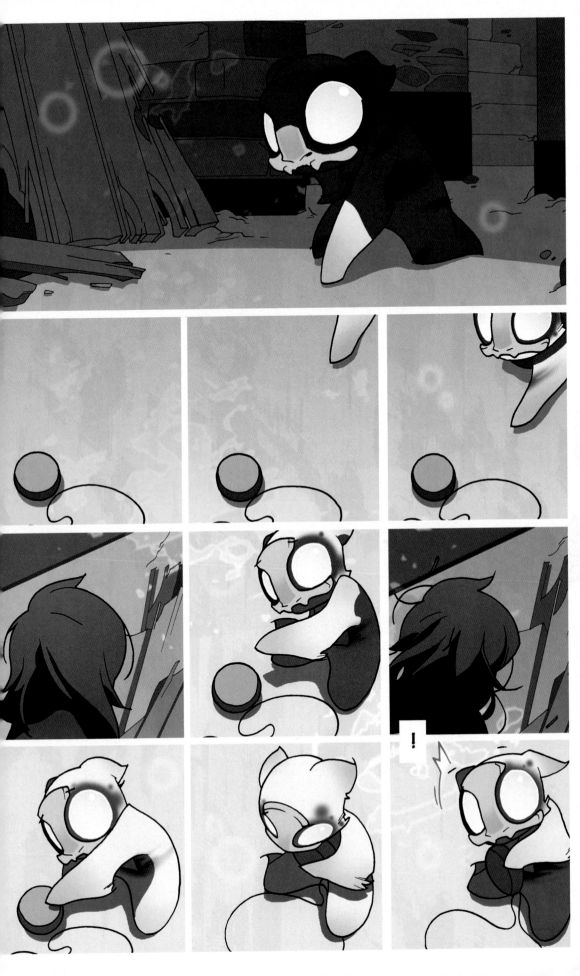

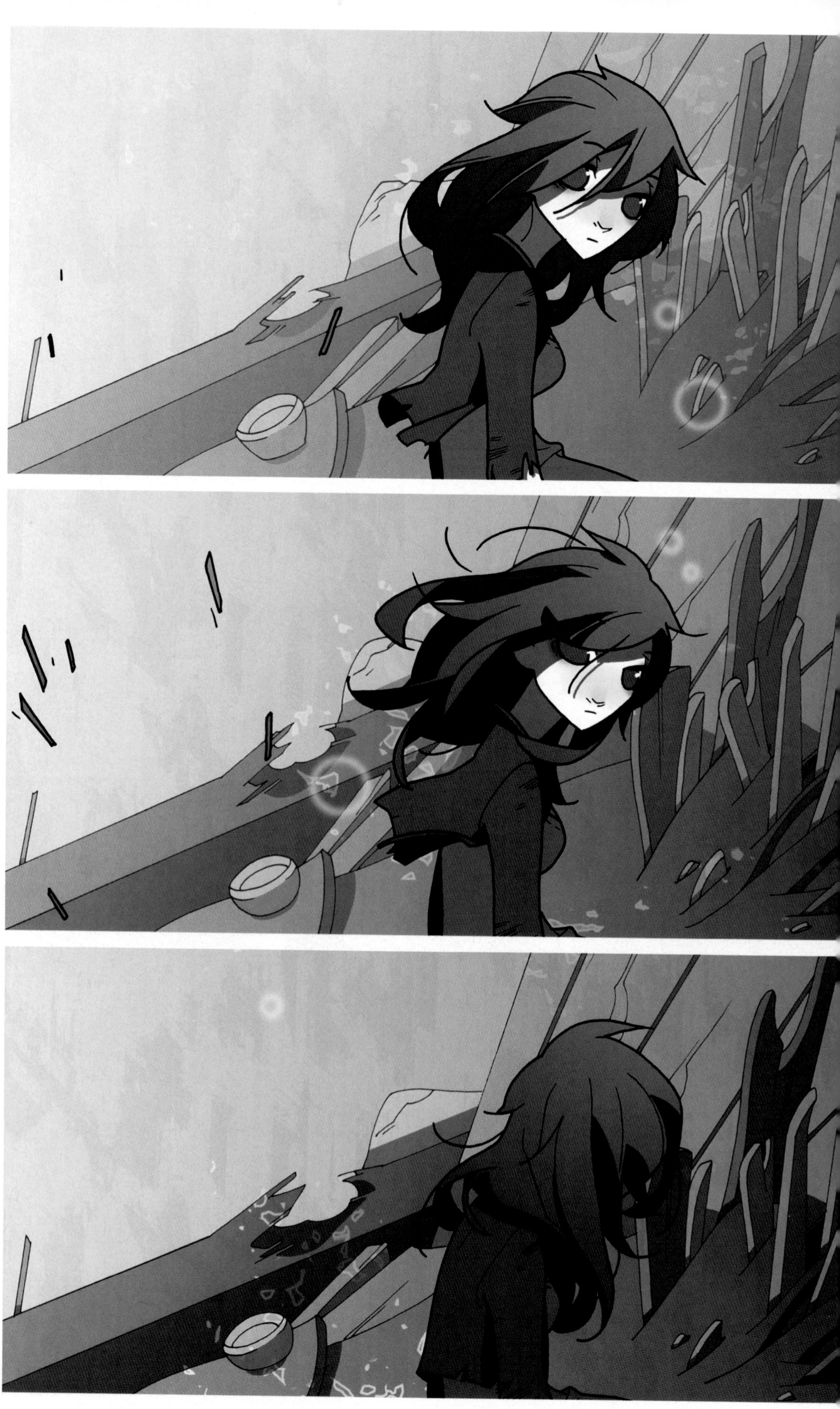

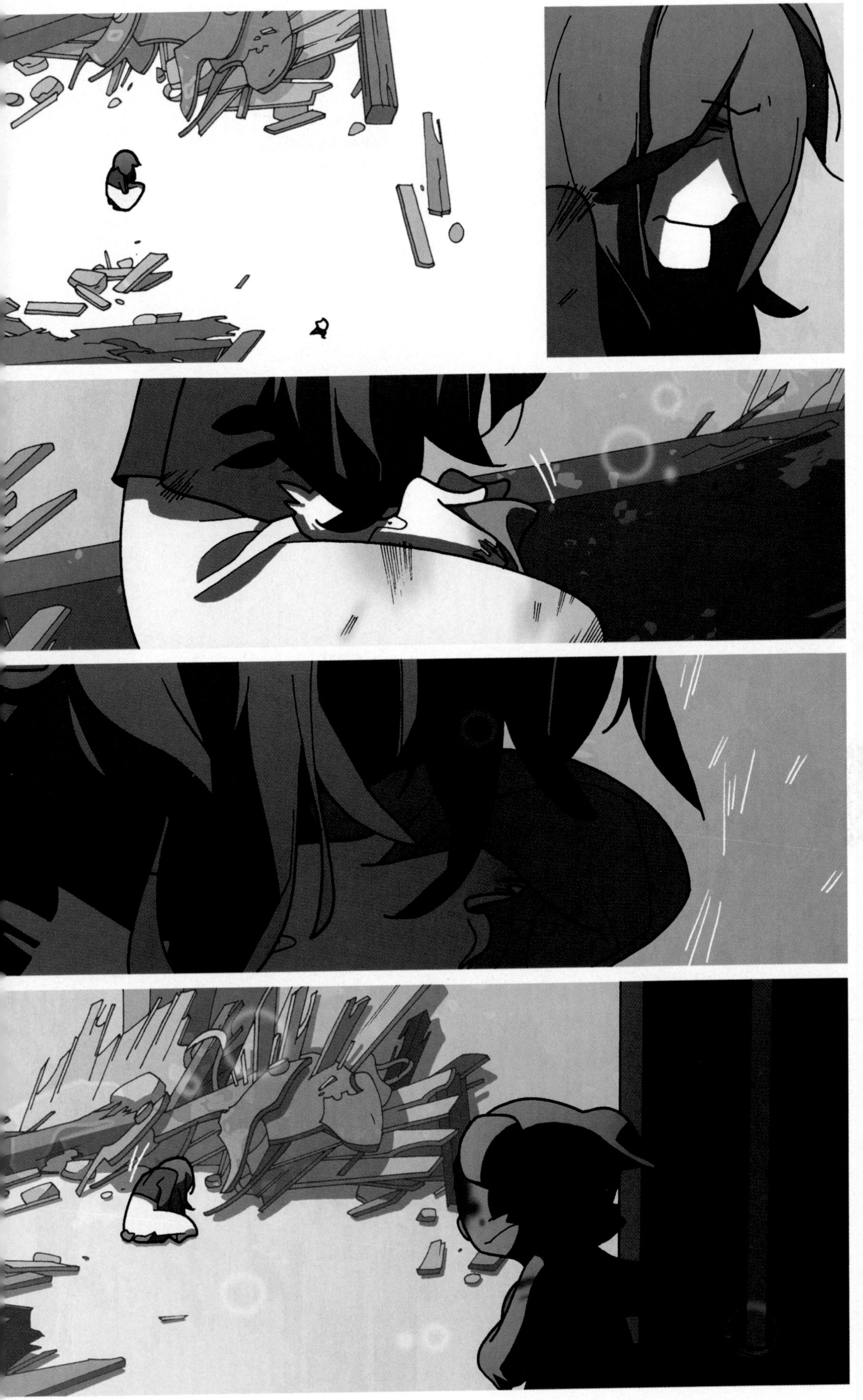

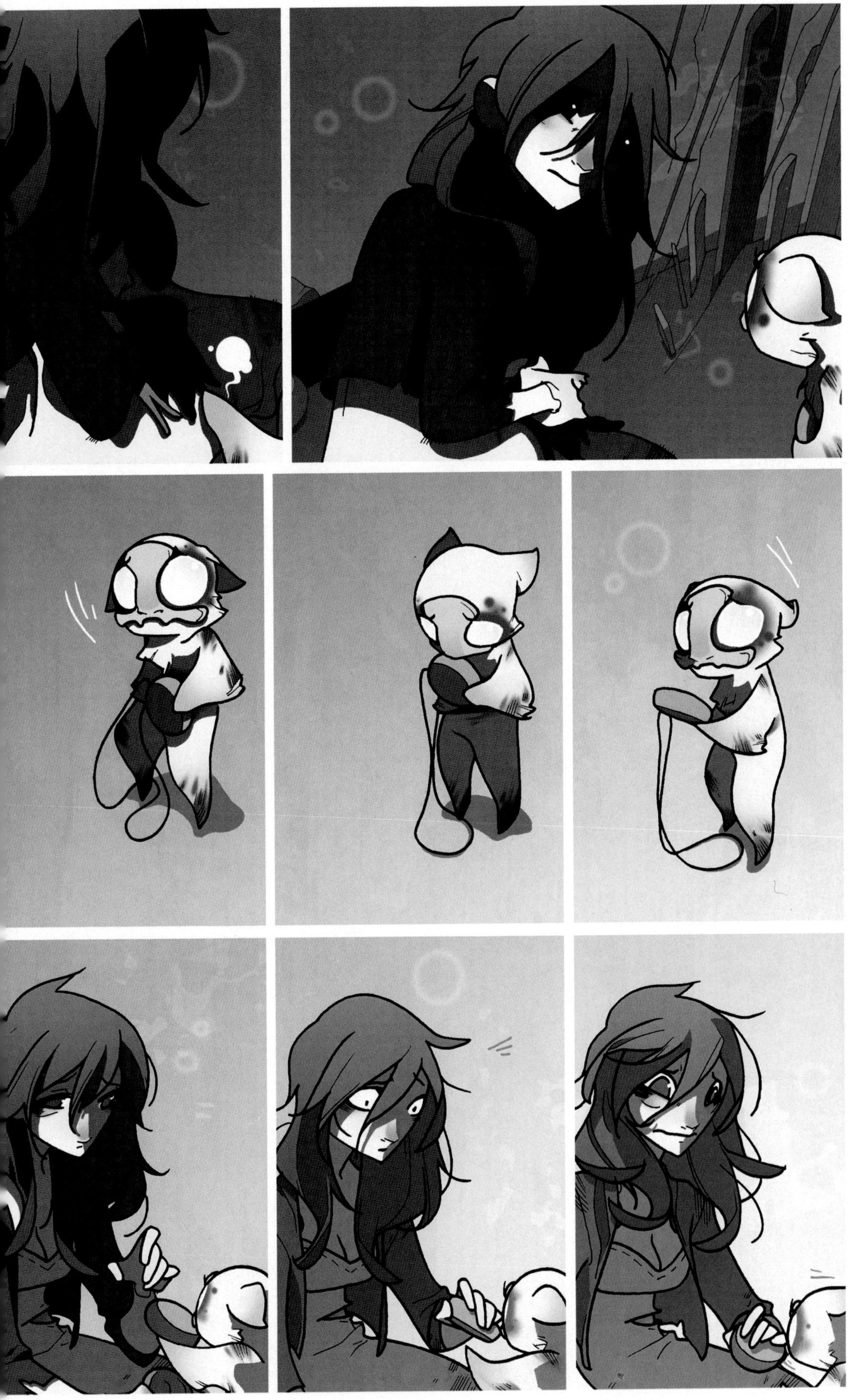

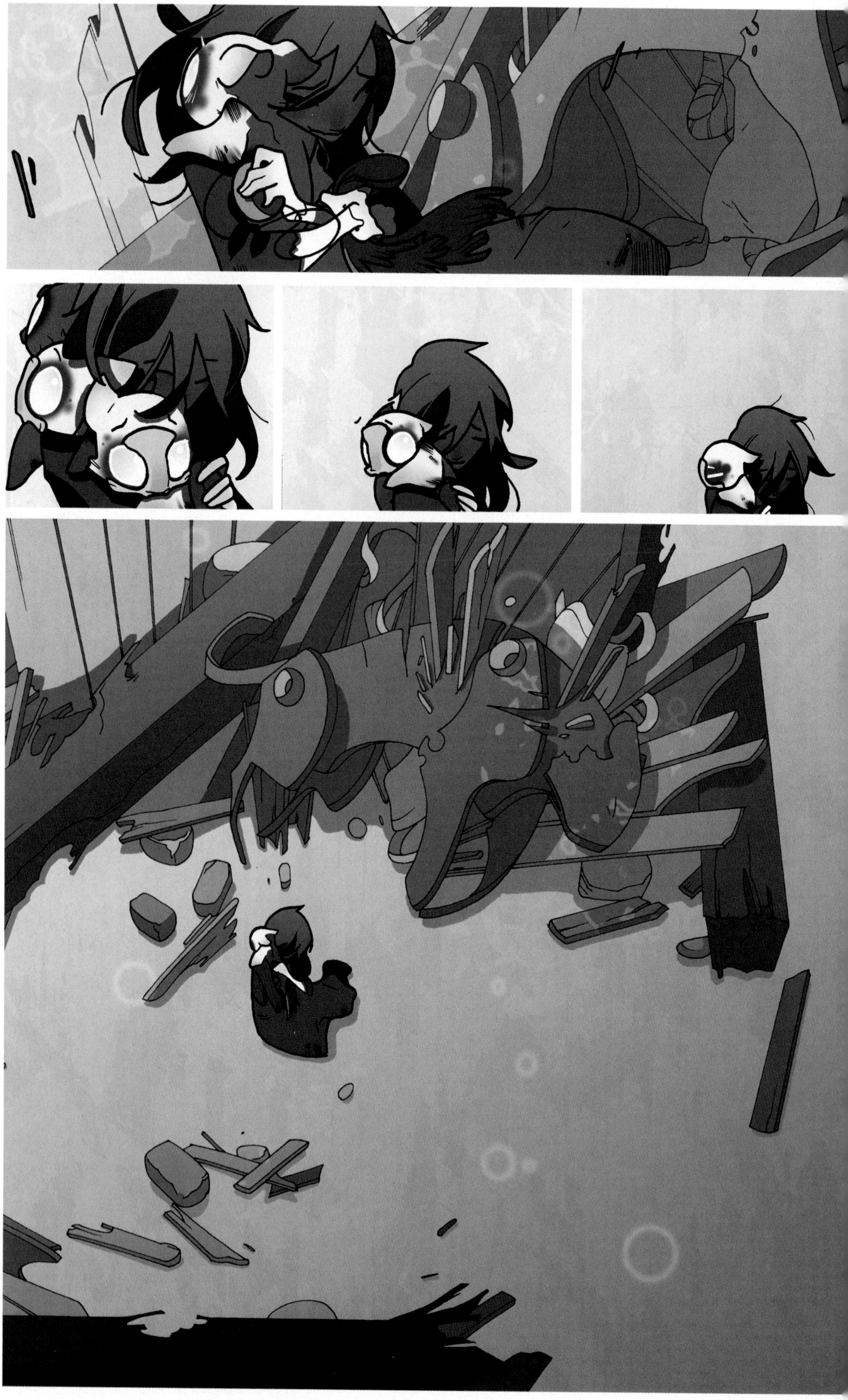

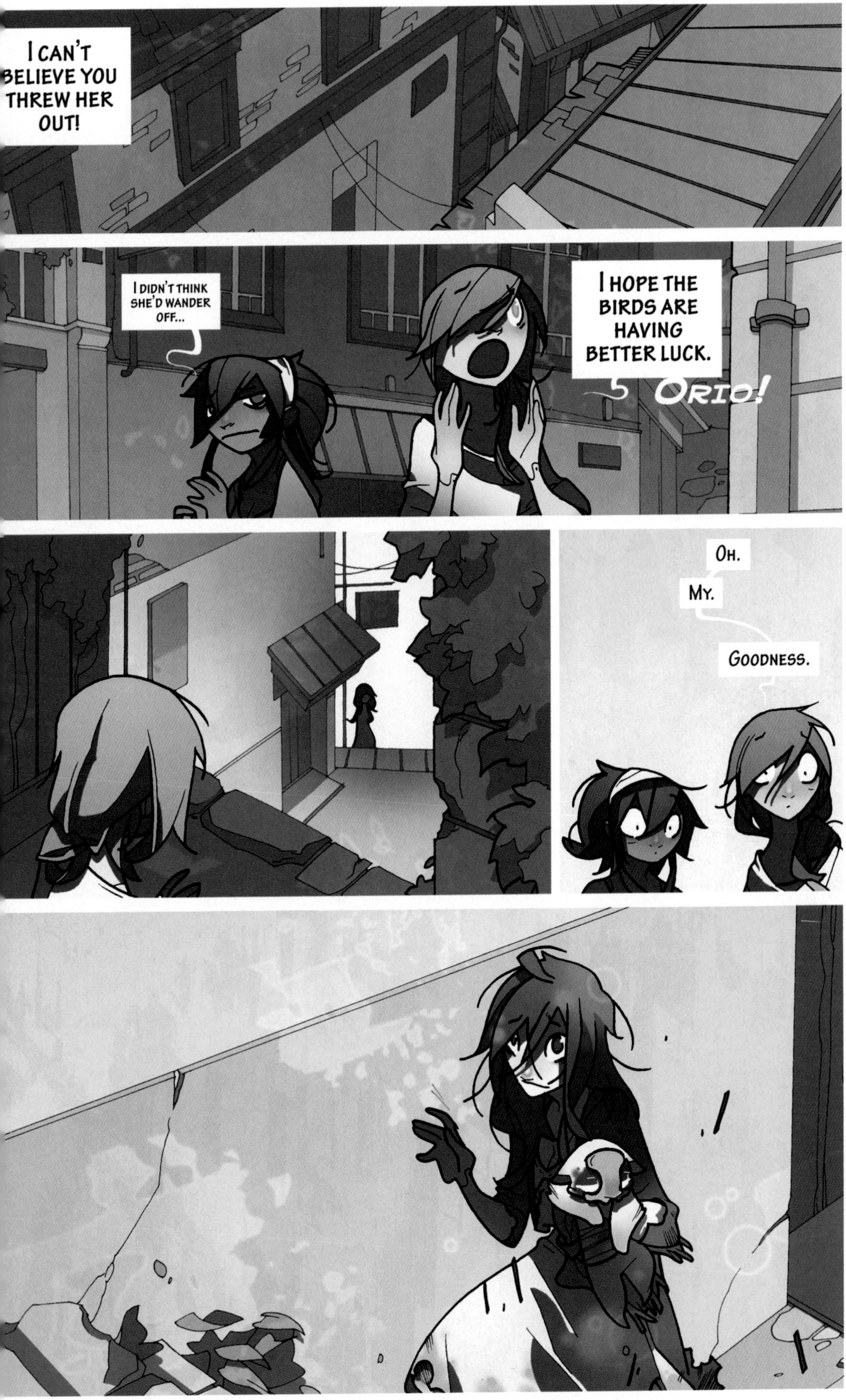
I CAN'T BELIEVE YOU THREW HER OUT!
I DIDN'T THINK SHE'D WANDER OFF...
I HOPE THE BIRDS ARE HAVING BETTER LUCK.
ORIO!
OH.
MY.
GOODNESS.

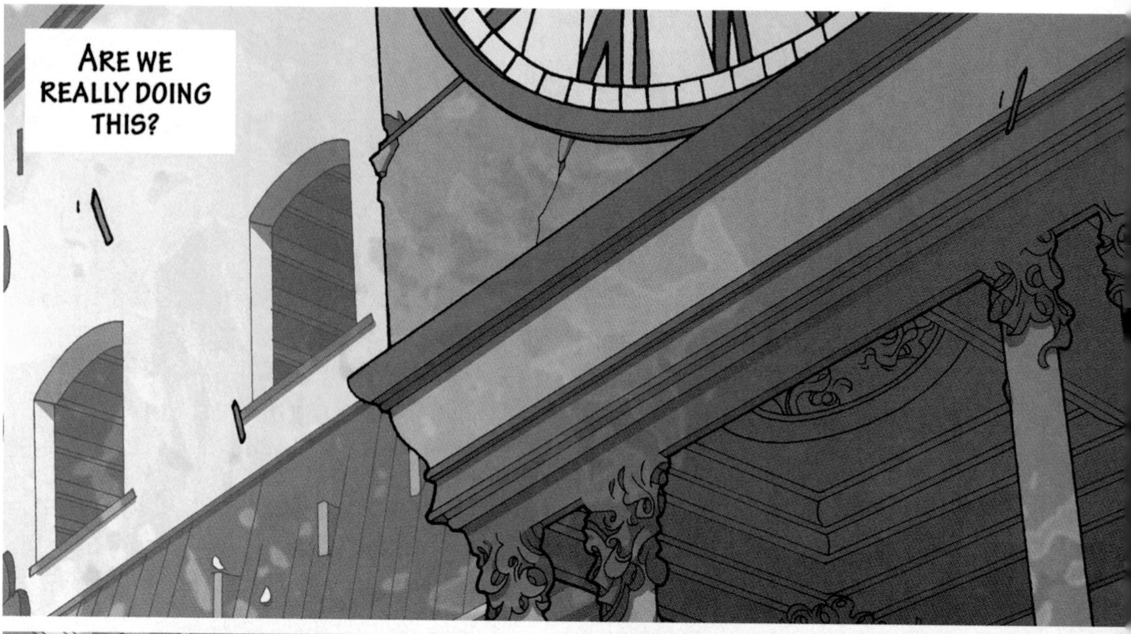
Are we really doing this?

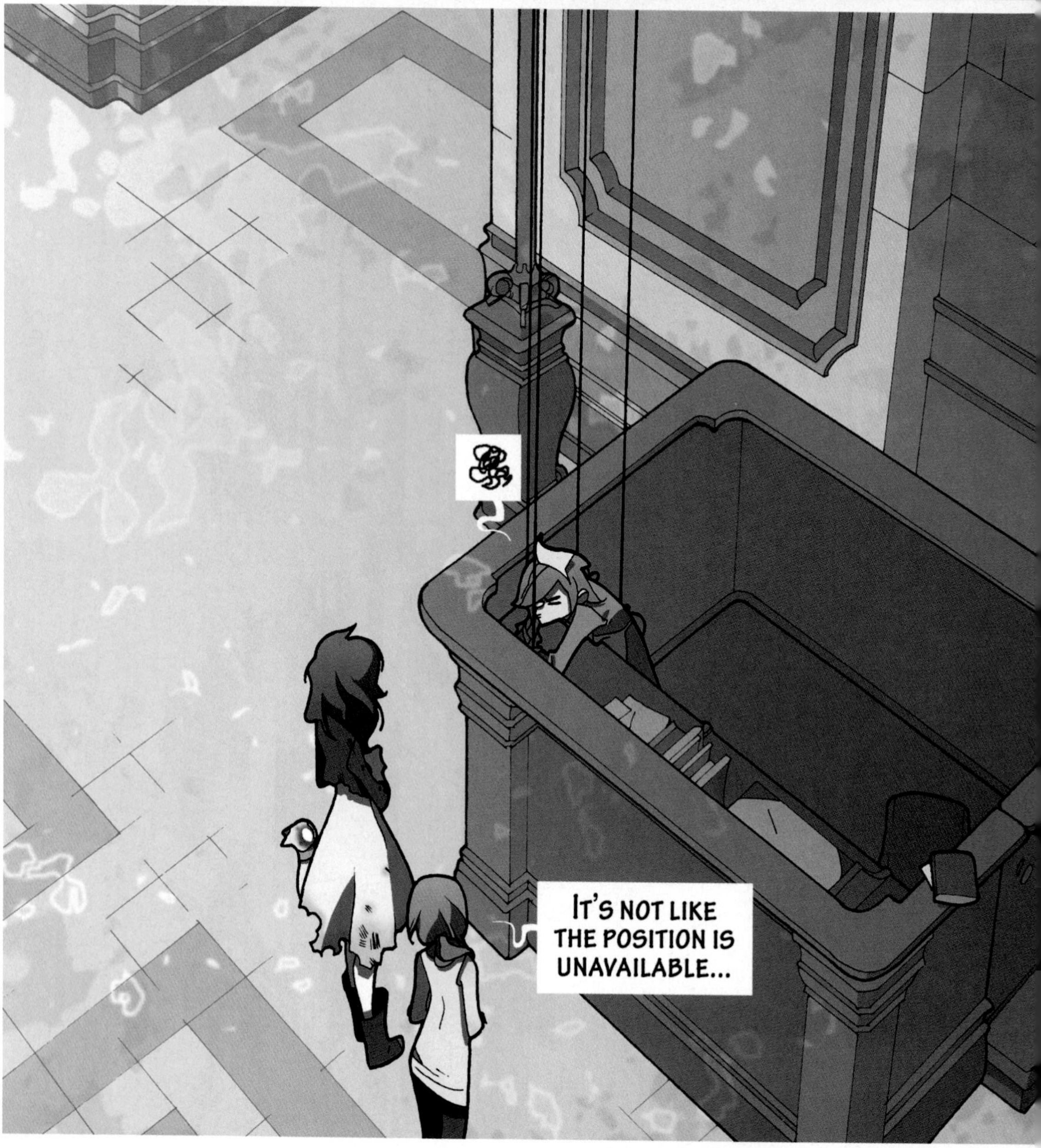
It's not like the position is unavailable...

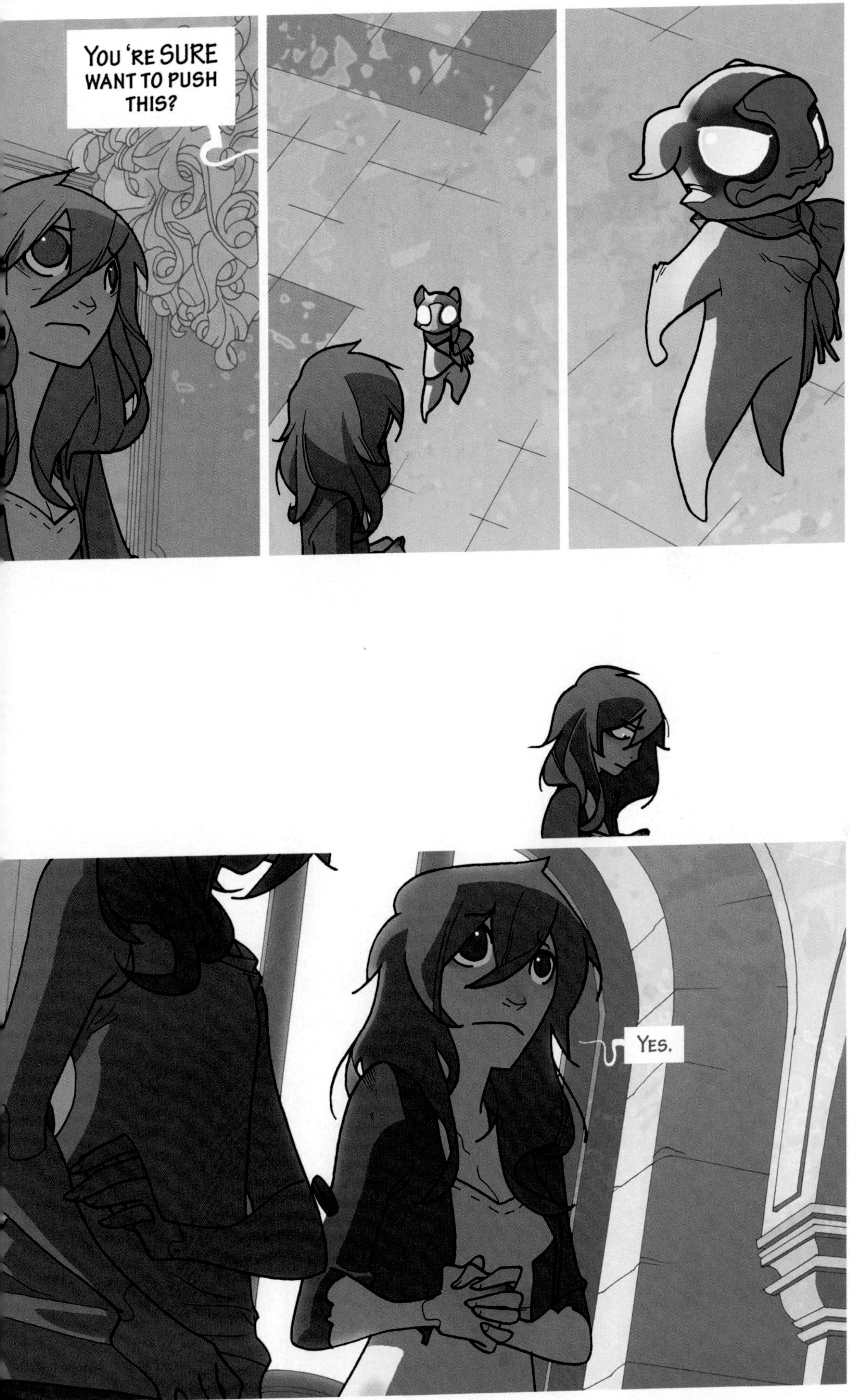
YOU 'RE SURE WANT TO PUSH THIS?
YES.

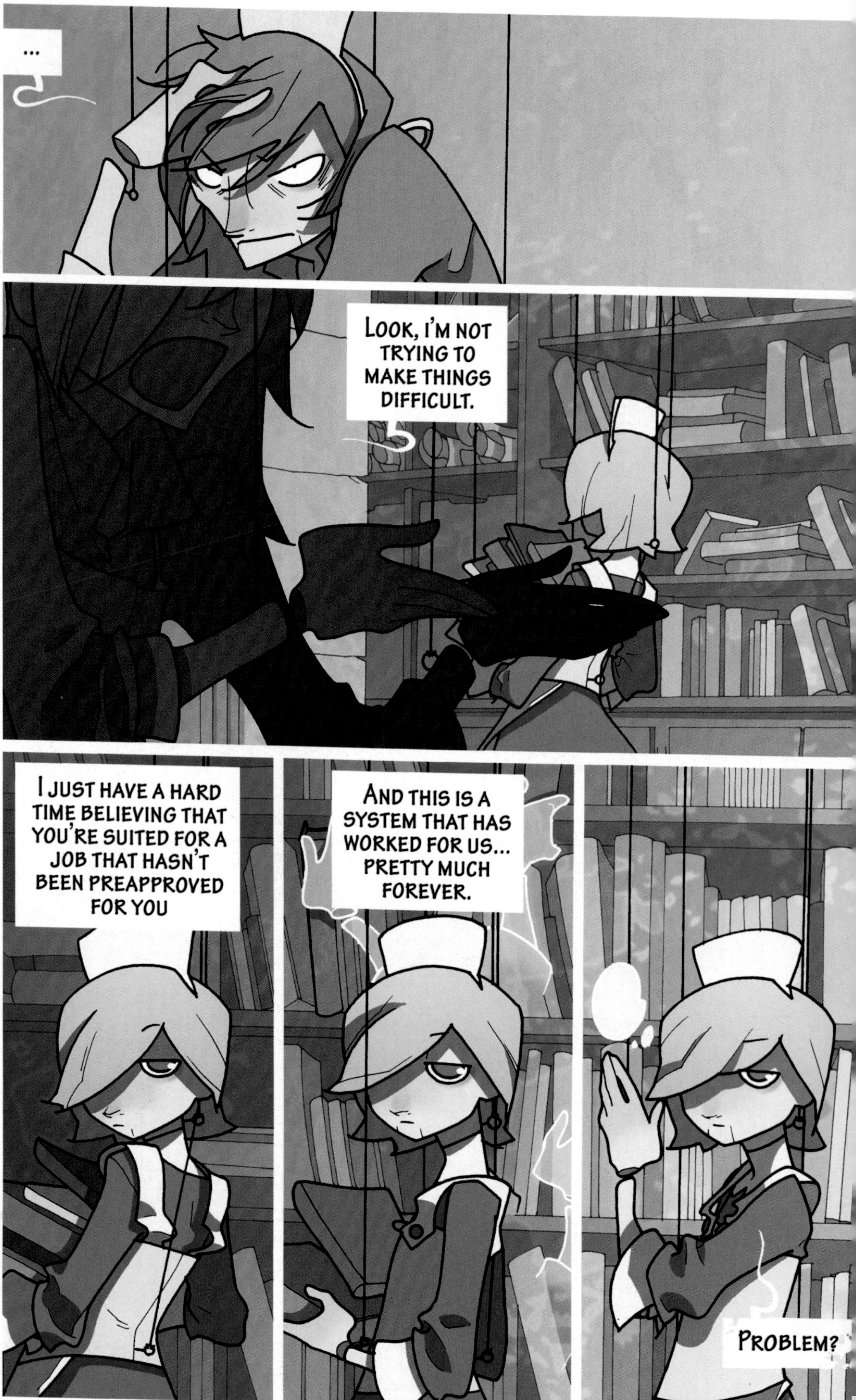
...
LOOK, I'M NOT TRYING TO MAKE THINGS DIFFICULT.
I JUST HAVE A HARD TIME BELIEVING THAT YOU'RE SUITED FOR A JOB THAT HASN'T BEEN PREAPPROVED FOR YOU
AND THIS IS A SYSTEM THAT HAS WORKED FOR US... PRETTY MUCH FOREVER.
PROBLEM?

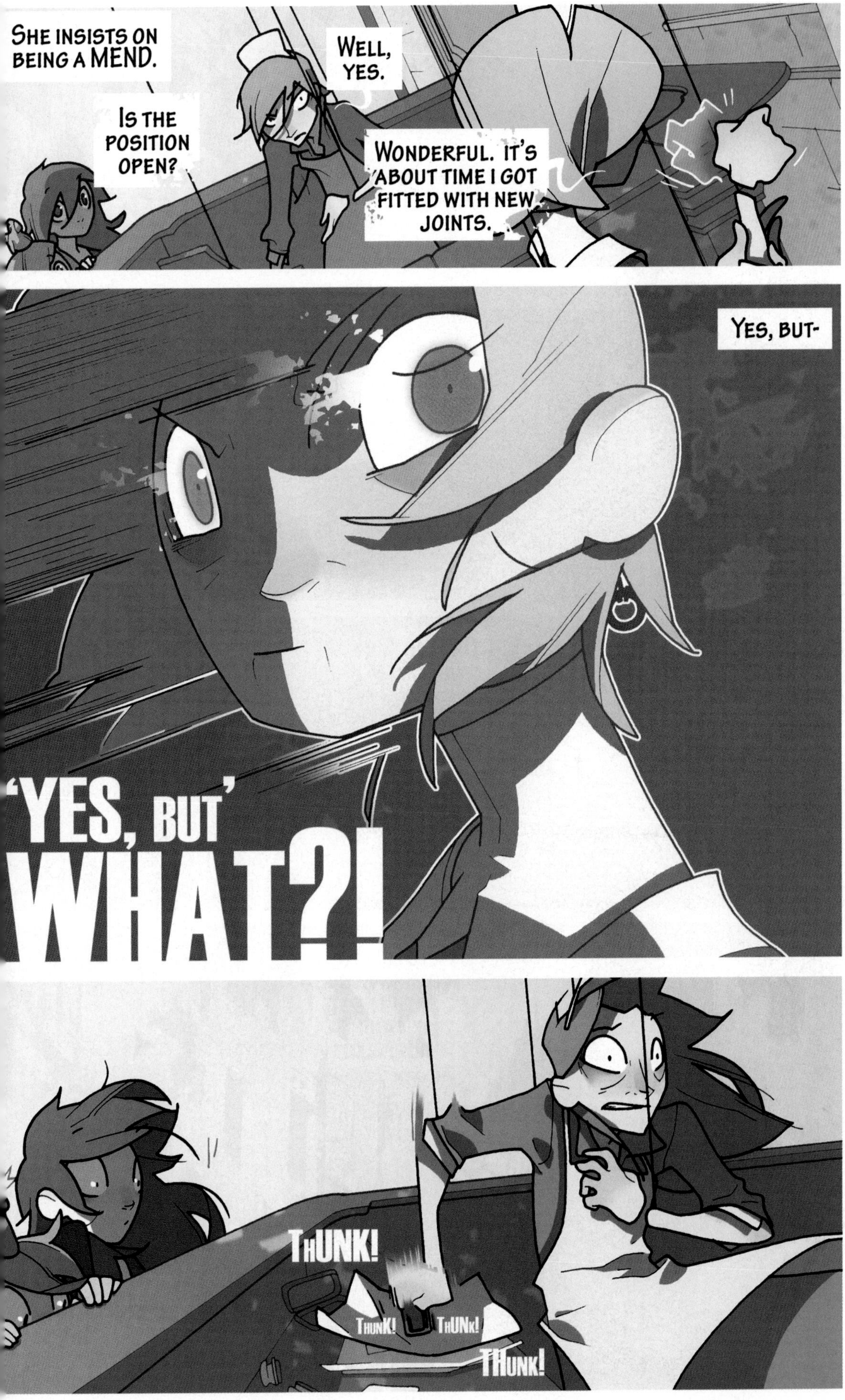
SHE INSISTS ON BEING A MEND.
IS THE POSITION OPEN?
WELL, YES.
WONDERFUL. IT'S ABOUT TIME I GOT FITTED WITH NEW JOINTS.
YES, BUT-
'YES, BUT' WHAT?!
THUNK!
THUNK!
THUNK!
THUNK!

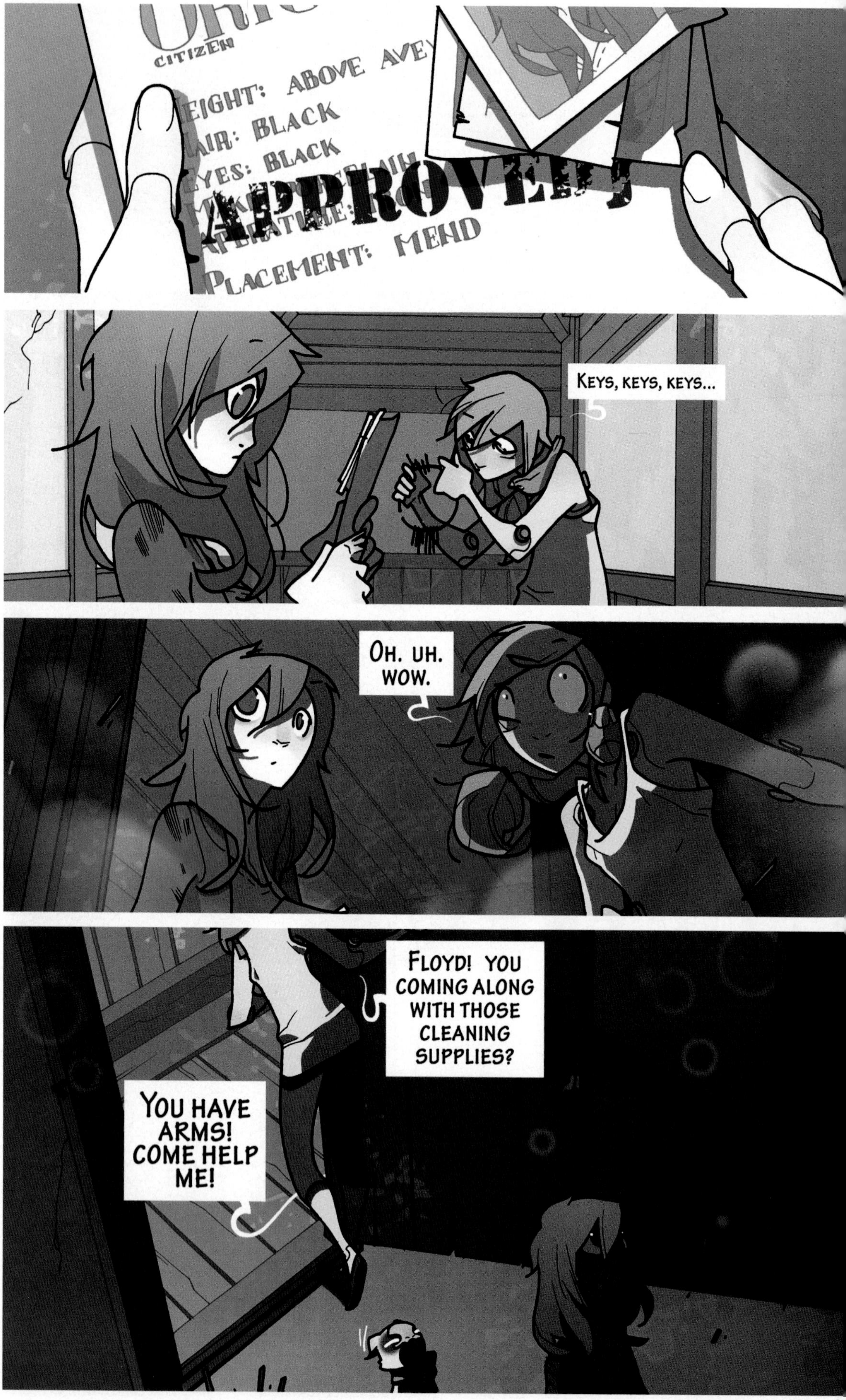
CITIZEN
EIGHT: ABOVE AVE
AIR: BLACK
EYES: BLACK
PLACEMENT: MEND
KEYS, KEYS, KEYS...
OH. UH. WOW.
FLOYD! YOU COMING ALONG WITH THOSE CLEANING SUPPLIES?
YOU HAVE ARMS! COME HELP ME!

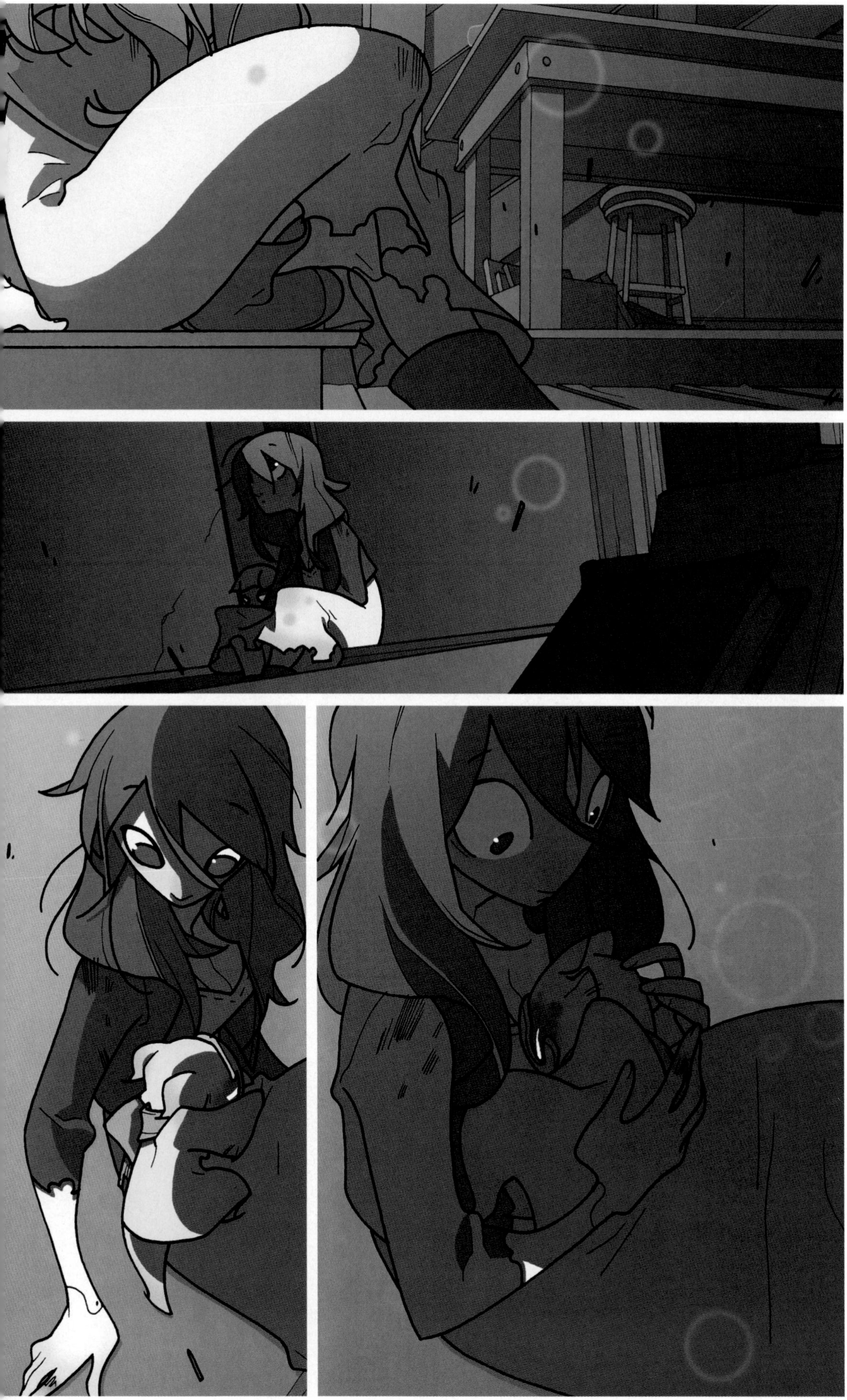

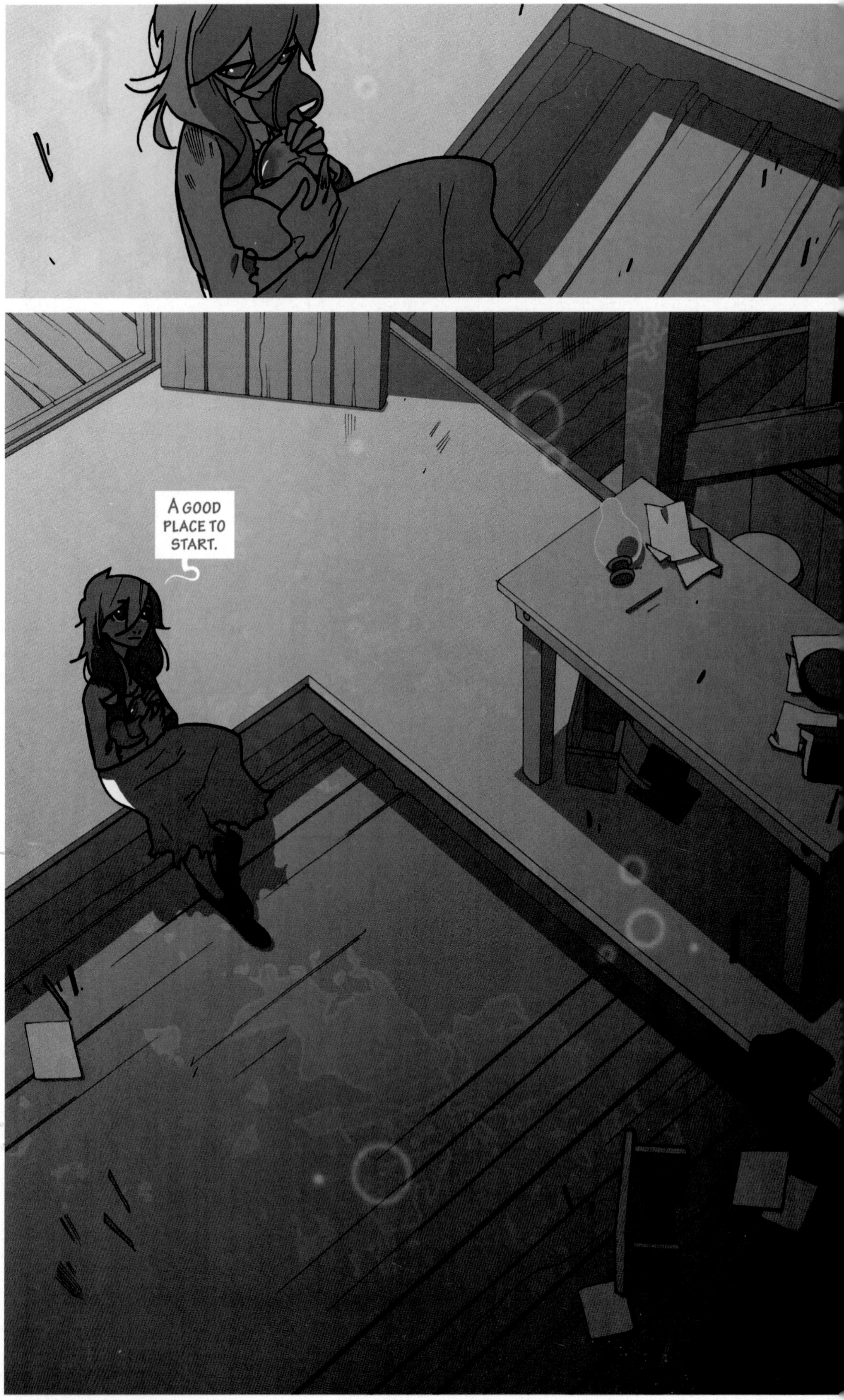
A GOOD PLACE TO START.